P9-DDF-310

THE BOY
FROM
ILYSIES

TOR BOOKS BY PEARL NORTH

Libyrinth
The Boy from Ilysies
Libyrinth 3 (forthcoming)

THE BOY
FROM
ILYSIES

PEARL NORTH

TOR®

A TOM DOHERTY ASSOCIATES BOOK
NEW YORK

This is a work of fiction. All of the characters, organizations, and events portrayed in this novel are either products of the author's imagination or are used fictitiously.

Edited by James Frenkel

A Tor® Teen Book
Published by Tom Doherty Associates, LLC
175 Fifth Avenue
New York, NY 10010

www.tor-forge.com

Tor® is a registered trademark of Tom Doherty Associates, LLC

ISBN 978-0-7653-2097-1

First Edition: November 2010

Printed in the United States of America

0 9 8 7 6 5 4 3 2 1

In loving memory of
my father,
Durelle C. Lane

ACKNOWLEDGMENTS

I would like to thank everyone who supported, aided, and abetted me in the creation of *The Boy from Ilysies*. In particular, my friends and family kept my spirits up and my fingers typing. Thank you, Steve, Kathe, Rick, Betsy, Sharon, Paulette, Jane, Marisa, Michael, Esther, Kris, Laura, and, of course, the whole Seton Hill crew.

THE BOY
FROM
ILYSIES

1

Kip's Tale

P o had offended the Princess of Ilysies. Selene Tadamos, naked and indignant, stood in the copper tub in the center of her chamber in the Libyrinth, every bit as regal as her mother, Queen Thela, at a full state function. Water dripped from her long black hair and ran in tiny streams down her tall, lean form. She glared at him and pointed one elegant finger at the door. "Get out!"

Po dropped the hem of his robe and cringed back against the doorway, forcing his gaze away from her angry splendor. "I'm sorry, I'm sorry," he said, still unsure of what he'd done wrong but certain that he'd gotten something wrong. Again.

Po ducked his head and fled the room. He shut the door behind him, then leaned against it, his labored breath echoing off the stone walls of the small landing at the top of the seventh tower. He was sweating, but not from the steam of the bath. Humiliation and anxiety made his palms damp and his face red.

He didn't understand her anger. She was Ilysian. She'd *told* him that her neck was sore and that she was taking a bath to relax. When an Ilysian woman spoke of relaxing and baths to an unclaimed Ilysian male, there could be no other interpretation: she expected him to come to her, to massage her sore neck and help her relax by offering himself to her.

Only that wasn't what she'd intended at all. What had he been thinking? She was a princess. She could have any male she wanted. Why would she bother with a scrawny young calf like him—just fifteen years old and still untried? But if she didn't want him, why in the Mother's name had she lingered after their workgroup's shift in the fields, helping him put away the farming equipment and telling him about her sore neck and the bath?

Slow realization curdled his stomach. She'd told him for the simple reason that her neck was sore and she wanted a bath. There'd been no "message" in those words, just a statement of fact. And as for "lingering," he had a tendency to wait on her when they were working. He would bring her water and sometimes abandon his own work to try to do hers. More than once she'd told him not to do that. So, by helping him with the equipment, she was probably just trying to impress upon him the notion that they were equals. Goddess, he was so stupid.

And she wasn't Princess Selene, either—not here. This was the Redeemed Community of the Libyrinth and she was Libyrarian Selene and she hadn't lived as an Ilysian for years and she probably had no notion of the effect her words had on him.

The now-familiar feelings of bafflement and shame rose up inside him—and beneath them, loneliness. Since the Redemption, everyone at the Libyrinth was working hard to leave behind their various cultural expectations and forge a new community, but Po was the only Ilysian male here. Nobody else had the same kinds of problems he had, and no one could really help him. He tilted his head back and rubbed at his eyes. His face felt hot. He wanted to cry, but that, too, was something males didn't do around here.

In fact, pretty much everything Po knew about how he was supposed to behave was wrong. And he so wanted to get it right. He'd been so relieved when Selene had invited him up here—when he'd thought she had. It had meant more than just a chance to finally fulfill his function as a consort. It meant having the opportunity to do something right for a change. Instead, he couldn't have been more wrong.

Po fought against the closing of his throat and the burning of his eyes, but it was no use—tears came. He wiped his face on the sleeve of his shapeless brown robe and ran down the stairs before someone could see him.

The stairs of the Seventh Tower opened out onto the large, circular hallway that was the main thoroughfare of the Libyrinth proper. The inner curve of the hallway bordered the Great Hall, with its massive dome, central console, and walls lined with books. Along the other side lay the towers, the dining hall, the kitchen, and the stables.

Po headed left at the base of the stairs, just so he could avoid the main gate. At this time of day—late afternoon—most people were finished with their work and gathered either outside in the open area surrounding the well, or in the Great Hall. The double arches of the main gate led to both. The area would be bustling with people.

Keeping his head down, he ran the long way around to the stables. He unlatched the large wooden door and slipped inside, shutting it again behind him. He turned to face a wide space dimly lit by the late afternoon sun. The air was thick with dust and the earthy aromas of straw and feed and dung. Here, at least, there was one creature he had something in common with.

He walked down the wide central aisle and unlatched the door of a large stall. With practiced ease he clambered up onto the broad back of Zam, the elephant who had borne their Redeemer to the Libyrinth. Like Po, she was here by accident. And like him, she was the only one of her kind.

Zam did not complain as Po sprawled on her back and succumbed to the torrent of feelings inside him. She was accustomed to him, and as Po pressed his face into Zam's thick, hairy hide, the elephant clumsily patted his back with her trunk and gave a low rumble of recognition.

Po soaked in the comfort she offered even as he rebuked himself. Unlike Zam, he could have gone home. When Adept Ykobos returned to Ilysies he could have gone with her, but he had chosen to stay. Why?

All he ever really wanted was to be a good consort and father. Back in Ilysies, when he was Adept Ykobos's assistant in the palace, he'd known how rare it was for a boy to study the art of kinesiology, how much rarer still to be given a post in the palace. And yet, even then, he had longed to be like other boys. So what on earth had possessed him to remain here, where all the rules were different?

He sighed and rubbed his cheek against Zam's scratchy back. It was because of the Redemption. For as long as Po lived, he would never forget what it had been like to be trapped inside the wing, tumbled about and terrified and then, out of nowhere, seized by a feeling unlike any he'd ever known before.

For a space of time—perhaps no more than an afternoon, yet it seemed to hold eternity in its span—he had known he was one with all things, and he had heard the Name of the Ocean and felt its harmonies in his own body and knew that this was the source from which all things arose. And he had known that he was no worse than a woman, that even the wise adept was no more than a variation on himself, and that there could be no difference that did not stem from common ground and therefore be part of the indivisible whole.

It was an experience that, they all learned, was both indelible and transient. When it was over they were no longer in that state, and yet none of them would ever forget that such a thing was possible, was, in fact, the greater reality. Every moment of their lives from that time forward was imbued with that awareness, even if they often fell into fragmentation and dispute.

So when Adept Ykobos chose to return to Ilysies, Po remembered the Redemption and he decided to stay here, where people were trying to live by what they had learned that day. But he'd made a mistake. This was too hard. He couldn't do it.

But oh, how he wished he could. Fresh grief seized him as he remembered what it had been like, who he'd thought he could be. This was worse than never being Redeemed at all. Now, when he failed he knew what he lost.

At last the storm subsided and Po allowed himself a few moments of lying there, empty. He remembered an afternoon when he was small. Somehow, over all the years, it came back to him in every detail—the smell of hot earth and the feel of it in his hands, the buzzing of the bees, the distant voices of his family and the nearer voice of Kip, his mother's old sire.

Though Po's grandmother was dead, the old man had fathered three daughters all in the same landed family. He was well provided for and content, with granddaughters to tease him and dote on him and a vegetable garden to tend now that he was too old to plow the fields.

Po must have been very young, because he was helping Kip weed the tomatoes, and not out with the others doing the hard work of getting the summer grain planted.

"Did you know that a woman's tears come from the ocean, but a man's tears come from the earth?" Kip asked. When Po didn't answer, he continued, "So it is only natural that a man's tears should return to the earth."

Po was crying because his cousin Appolonia had knocked him down and taken his cinnamon cracker at lunch.

Po wiped his face and stared at the old man. He'd always been fascinated by Kip's face, the myriad lines intersecting and curving, always following the immaculate structure of his classic Ilysian features. Kip could be a bit haughty about his rank as a stud but he was a kindly old goat and fond of his grandson.

"It's true," said Kip. "Because long ago, long before Queen Belrea united Ilysies, there were no men."

Po gaped at this. There would never be as many males as women, it was true, but none at all? The old man was lying. "Then how did the women get babies?"

"The women made themselves pregnant, the way the ringtails do. Yes, yes, it's true." Kip could see that Po was skeptical. "At that time, all the women knew the tale of the lizard and they could all reproduce parthenogenetically like the ringtail lizard does. Not just special people. And the land everywhere was green. Not just here east of the Lian Mountains, not just in a few scattered river valleys, but all over the land, yes, the whole land—the plain of Ayor, and even Shenash across the sea. All of it was as green as a low-land barley farm in spring."

"Even up in the hills?"

Kip laughed, and looking back now, Po realized that it was at his naiveté, which could not imagine a world beyond his own dusty mountain town. "Yes, even here in the hills. And the reason that the land was green everywhere was that a certain flower grew that was called the Lion's Bloom. The Lion's Bloom put out a pollen that was a powerful fertilizer and everywhere it fell, it made things grow.

"Life was good in those days, and everyone danced and sang all day long. But one day, the blooms forgot that they were plants and fell in love with the women. Indeed, the beauty of a woman living in contented abundance is so powerful that it caused the blooms to grow arms and legs, and they dug themselves out of the ground and turned into men, and when they stood before the women, the beauty which had formed them made them continue to grow, their bodies taking the form that will please women most.

"The women were delighted with their new companions and life continued quite happily for all until the next harvest. With no more blooms, the plants did not grow in the same abundance as before. In fact, they were in danger of dying off entirely.

"When the women saw this they were most dismayed, and this made their men unhappy. Everyone cried. The women's salty tears only made the land more barren. But where the men's tears fell, things began to grow again. One man loved his consort so much that he begged her to sacrifice him, to cut him down like a stalk of grain, and his blood flowed across the land and became the Lian River, where the land is most fertile of all.

"And that is why a man must give his tears and sometimes his life to the soil, so that some of that fertilizing property he still possesses is returned to the earth for the generation of plant life, and that is why other parts of the world that do not practice this are more barren than ours.

"So when you cry, hang your head, so that your tears drip down onto the earth."

Po sat up on Zam's back and wiped his eyes. For a moment he chided himself for wasting his tears, when he could have let them fertilize the land. But that was childish. Men's tears did not make things grow. It was an old goat's beard—a tale spun by old men to comfort little boys, nothing more.

Finally, Po patted Zam's neck and slid down her flank to the ground. It would be dinnertime soon and he wanted to wash his face before going into the dining hall. The last thing he wanted was to attract more attention. He was already in enough trouble. Would Pri—*Libyrarian* Selene tell others what he'd done? Would she tell the Redeemer?

He latched Zam's stall door behind him and paused to brush straw from his robe. How he hated this garment. A boy his age should be going about in a short tunic and hose, both cut to display his masculine features to their best advantage. In these robes, everybody looked the same, which he supposed was the point, but how on earth could he be expected to attract a consort dressed like this?

Suddenly he heard the door to the stables opening and voices talking. He considered ducking back into the stall, but it was too late.

"She wants me but I'm holding out for something better," said Baris as he and another Singer boy, Rossiter, entered the stable. They paused in the doorway, staring at Po. Baris smiled. It wasn't a friendly smile.

Po hated Singer boys in general and Baris in particular. For one thing, Baris was fat. It was disgusting. And he fancied himself attractive to women, which was a travesty, given the way he let himself go. He had short blond hair, a snub nose, pale blue eyes, and two chins. But what was most infuriating of all was his attitude, difficult for Po to put into words. He acted as if his sexual attentions were somehow both a gift and a debasement to any woman who might receive them. Po could not understand this, and yet it enraged him. Baris made males look very, very bad. Furthermore, he'd bet anything that Baris was still a virgin, and therefore a liar on top of everything else.

Po walked toward Baris and Rossiter, his bearing straight and tall, his gaze fixed on Baris, staring him in the eyes, openly provoking him. It felt good. Po's blood sang in his ears as his adrenaline spiked. A fight—that's what he needed.

He was about to ask Baris who he was talking about. Clearly he was disrespecting a woman, and Po was not about to let him shame males that way, but before he could speak, Baris said, "Crying again?"

Oh, right. Po had forgotten about his tears. Or rather, forgotten that he was supposed to hide them. Singer boys thought tears were a sign of weakness. The Libyrarians less so, but still, everyone thought he was too emotional for a male. But he was a male! It was his nature to be emotional. He couldn't help it. His hormones made him irrational, impulsive, aggressive, and desperately dependent on female approval and gratification.

"Still a virgin?" said Po, because he knew Baris was, and hated it enough to lie about it, despite the fact that he took no measure either with his appearance or his personality to make himself alluring to women.

"I get enough," said Baris.

It took Po a second to figure out what he was talking about. He meant sex. As if it were barley to be gathered in bales and stored. "You lie. What woman would have a fatso like you?"

"Hey, both of you, what are you doing?" said Rossiter, who had hung back as Po and Baris approached each other. His gaze flicked from Po to Baris and back again.

Rossiter was tall and thin, with dark, shoulder-length hair and blue eyes. He could almost pass for Ilysian, except for his olive skin tone and his small nose. Rossiter wasn't bad for a Singer. He'd been the very first to accept the written word. It had happened while he was being tortured by Libyrarians, prior to the Redemption, but oddly he didn't use that fact to lord his status over other males. He was a healer and Po worked with him in the infirmary tent sometimes. As long as Rossiter didn't blatantly challenge him with questions or suggestions, Po could tolerate him.

But Baris was another matter and as far as Po was concerned, there was no need for more words. With less than four feet left between them, Po ended the preamble to their fight by stepping in and faking a punch with his right. Baris fell for it and Po was ready with a left punch to Baris's jaw. The sting in his knuckles was as satisfying as the smacking sound his fist made as it connected with the hard bone beneath Baris's pudgy flesh.

Baris let out a grunt and grabbed Po by the hair. "You fucking he-girl," he said. One of his insults, though it never made any sense to Po.

"Hey, both of you, stop it!" yelled Rossiter. "This isn't how we're supposed to act."

Baris swung Po by the hair and released him and Po staggered back a few steps before regaining his balance. When he did, he wasted no time. He rushed Baris, tackling him around the waist, hurling them both down onto the straw-covered ground.

Baris wheezed at the impact, and before he could move Po straddled his chest, pinning Baris's arms beneath his knees.

"Stop it," said Rossiter. "It's yourself you're hitting. Remember? We're all one!"

Yeah. Po did remember that. But only with his mind. It was not in his heart at the moment. One of the things he'd learned since coming here was how easy it was to lose big truths amid little ones. There was a difference between understanding something with your mind, and feeling it inside. At the moment, his anger crowded out the profound interconnectedness he'd felt at the Redemption. Peace and compassion were concepts. If they had a home in his heart, it was hidden by Baris's provocation. Po punched him in the nose.

Blood poured from Baris's nose, bright red and gratifying. "Augh! Get off me!" he yelled. The coward.

Po stood. "Limp dick," he said, loading the words with

all the disdain they could hold. He started to walk away. Rossiter watched him warily, a crease between his brows. Only then did Po realize that there would be repercussions from this. Rossiter was going to tell. Unless he could stop him.

He stopped in front of Rossiter, looming close. They were of a height, but Po was stronger. "Don't tell anybody about this," he said. It wasn't a request.

Rossiter gave him a strange look. Pity? Why would Rossiter pity him? He glanced to where Baris was getting up, holding a hand to his bleeding nose. A clear-cut victory—why—

"And what if I do, Po, will you beat me up, too?"

Well, yeah, that was the idea. But still Rossiter gave him that sad look and Po had the feeling he was missing something, again. The Redemption. Oh yeah . . . Sudden shame came upon him and that just made him more angry.

"What are you going to do when you run out of people to hit?" Rossiter asked him.

Po tried to formulate an answer but he couldn't. He really did want to hit Rossiter now, and that was completely wrong. And it had been wrong to hit Baris, even though it felt so utterly right. But why? How could it be okay *not* to punish Baris for his insufferable attitude? This was impossible. He couldn't do this. He was just about to give up and shove Rossiter and see where that went when a terrific wind blew through the stables, stirring up hay and dust and making them all blink.

Through the wide archway that led into the stableyard came the Wing of Tarsus. Twelve feet from wing tip to wing tip, its graceful form gleaming gold, the Ancient flying machine eased through the doorway and settled in the triple-wide stall nearest the door. They'd had to knock down two walls to make room for it, but everyone agreed that the stable was the proper place for the wing, which like most Ancient technology was not quite just a machine.

All the same, the wing looked incongruous in the rustic setting. Its surface was engraved with waving, spiraling lines—songlines, the Singers called them, but Po knew them as the Name of the Ocean, so called because they were a reminder of the source of all life. On the underside of the flying machine was a face—a large, golden face in the center—where the vessel widened out between the two backward-curving wings.

And of course they all knew who flew it. Clauda of Ayor, the second Redeemer, the hero of the Libyrinth.

Po looked at Baris wiping the blood from his nose and trying to brush the straw off his robes. It was hard for Po to think of himself as one and the same with someone like Baris, but they did have one thing in common: neither of them wanted Clauda to know they'd been fighting. Even though Baris could say with all truthfulness that Po had started it, and Rossiter would back him up, Baris still wouldn't want the kind of attention the incident would bring him. He'd be counseled about the "assault." And he wouldn't want that because the more people like Clauda or Haly talked to him, the more likely they'd discover just how little of the Singer attitude of male-superiority he had set aside. Not to mention, it would be a lot of fuss over a fistfight. "I won't tell if you don't," Po told Baris.

Baris started. "Okay."

"But what about him?" asked Po, nodding toward Rossiter.

Baris turned to Rossiter. "Look—keep this to yourself

and I'll tell Jaen you saved Monat's life in the infirmary. She'll be impressed."

Rossiter frowned, weighing it. "I shouldn't . . ." He turned to Po. "You fight too much."

"You let him get away with talking about women as if they were . . ." Men. Po didn't finish.

Rossiter swallowed. He looked uncomfortable now. "Okay, I won't say anything. This time. But don't compound things by lying about me, Baris. Just—"

A portal in the gleaming hide of the wing opened and Clauda stepped out onto the wing of the wing. The simplicity of her robe suited her broad, tan face and copper brown hair. Her blue eyes stood out like beacons.

Clauda was brave and kind and crafty, and Po had been fascinated with her since she'd first come to the Ilysian Palace. He had taken every chance he could to be around Adept Ykobos's workshop when it was time to visit the Ayorite. He thought it was exotic how she had no last name. People in the palace called her Clauda of Ayor. But it wasn't just that she was an Ayorite. It was her matter-of-fact regard for him, as if she had no doubt that he could contribute something of use. He'd never really gotten over it.

All quarrels forgotten, the three boys ran to the stall, but he was there before either of the other two, and he knelt in the straw and offered his back to her as a step. He heard Baris snicker, and then there was a whoosh of air beside him and he saw Clauda's sandal-shod feet hit the ground. His face burning, Po stood. Clauda was already walking away, fast. Of course, how stupid of him. She was embarrassed by his gesture. She didn't want to be his superior. She was an Ayorite. She wanted him to be an equal.

Baris stared at him with barely suppressed glee and Rossiter looked quietly horrified. But neither of them pursued Clauda. Po hurried after her. "How was your flight, Clauda?" he asked her, being sure to use her name in the familiar way everyone did around here.

She paused in the doorway to the Libyrinth and turned. Not for the first time, Po wished that instead of returning to the Libyrinth, Clauda had flown the wing to some deserted island somewhere far away where no one would ever find them. Of course that was wrong and of course Adept Ykobos was always conveniently written out of these fantasies of his, but when her gaze fell upon him he could not help but long for it just the same. "Hey guys," she said, by way of greeting, and Po became aware of Baris and Rossiter behind him. "Po, look, I can't chat right now. I'm sorry. I have to give my report to Haly."

For the first time he noticed the scroll in her hands. It had a red seal on it. Was that the bull of Ilysies?

As Clauda trotted away down the hallway, Po heard Baris snicker behind him and then Rossiter's urgent "Shhh!"

He thought about starting another fight with Baris, or Rossiter, or both, but it was nearly suppertime. He took a deep breath and left the stables.

2

After the Miracle

When Haly had been imprisoned by the Singers, she'd persuaded her principle jailer, Censor Siblea, to accept her version of the Redemption. Teaching everyone to read, she'd argued, was as much a miracle as the Singer's original goal of destroying the Libyrinth. What she hadn't known then, however, was that one miracle demands another.

Now, they could make good on the blessing of the Redemption, but only if the farming worked out, if they could all get along, if they could avoid becoming a protectorate of Ilysies . . . If. If. If.

Haly sat behind her large desk in her small office and regarded the chaos of papers and books scattered across it. How could she bring order and prosperity to her community when she couldn't even keep her desk clean? There was so much to do, and she had no idea how to accomplish most of it.

The food situation, for instance. They'd been researching agriculture since the day after the Redemption and fertilizer and irrigation had at least made growing crops possible, but there was no way around the simple fact that this was a desert land. The rocky soil and the low water table made it difficult to keep crops nourished. In short, no amount of goat manure was going to turn it into the Ilysian Valley, where food grew in abundance all year round. The Libyrinth's mammoth store of grain had held out admirably so far, but was finally starting to run low. They would have just enough to make it to their first harvest, but if that failed, everything failed, and they must hope to get help from the villages of the plain, who had precious little food to spare. Or they could accept the queen of Ilysies's generous offer of aid, and her leadership. It would be the end of their dream, but it might be their only alternative to starvation.

And that was just one aspect of this tricky situation. Every day Haly had her hands full, maintaining the rickety coalition they dared to call a community. Everyone at the Libyrinth was supposed to love one another like themselves, but the day-to-day reality was that the Singer men and the Ilysian women were at odds and the Ayorites still resented the Libyrarians who still looked down on them as peasants. And everyone looked to her to sort everything out. Not for the first time did she curse Head Libyrarian Griome for dying so soon after the Redemption, and leaving her, by popular demand, in charge of this mess.

And she was only sixteen. Panic threatened to overwhelm her. She forced herself to focus on her breath
and tap into the Song inside her.

From birth Haly had been gifted with the capacity to
hear text as if the words read themselves aloud to her.
But at the Redemption, when the Libyrinth had powered
up after centuries of slumber, it had a profound impact
on Haly's ability to hear the books. At first she'd been
overwhelmed by a multitude of voices as every book in
the Libyrinth spoke to her at once, but then the voices
had combined into one voice, lifted in song. But not just
any song—the Song, as the Singers called it, a harmony
that united all things. The Ilysians called it the Name of
the Ocean and the Ayorites called it the Last Wind of the
World, but the basic idea was the same in all cultures. It
was the force of life, and she and everyone else present at
the Redemption had become, for a brief span of time, one
with it.

Only for Haly that span was not so brief. The Song still
hummed inside her. This she had in advantage of all others
here: she could experience the Song at will now. It made a
big difference. Even now, her panic receded as the sacred
melody flowed through her and she became calm in the
realization that all was one and that the answers, whatever
they were, would be there for her when she really needed
them.

She sighed and directed her attention to the first thing
on the stack: a report on the sewer project from Peliac,
who had taught Haly and every other Libyrinth-born child
the alphabet. Now her relentless, detail-oriented mind was
focused on this most imperative of tasks. Everyone's roles
were changing. Peliac's report stated that they were fin-

ished with the trenches and ready to start the composting pits. Good.

Next was an update on the windmills from Vinnais, who as a traveling Singer soldier-priest had worked with many villagers on similar projects. He and his team could begin construction of the scaffolds as soon as they could find the lumber to build them with. As with all of their building projects, the scarcity of wood was a problem.

A knock on the door interrupted her. "Come in," she said, setting aside the report.

It was Selene and by the looks of things, she was upset. Jaw set and shoulders rigid, she shut the door behind her and strode to Haly's desk, bracing her arms against it.

Haly had served as Selene's clerk prior to the Redemption. The daughter of the queen of Ilysies, Selene had rejected her mother's life of court politics and come to the Libyrinth to study. It was she who had discovered the location of *The Book of the Night* and instigated their quest to rescue it. And that had led to Haly's capture by the Singers, and ultimately the Redemption. So in a way, everything that had or would happen was Selene's fault.

Haly suppressed a smile. Selene would not find the idea amusing. In fact, she would take it seriously. Selene had been a kind master and she was a good friend now, but she always took things seriously. "What's wrong?" Haly asked her. "What's happened?"

"Po came into my chamber uninvited while I was taking a bath."

"What?" Haly couldn't believe it. Not Po, of all people.

Selene paced. "Just because I mention that my neck hurts and I'm going to take a bath does *not* mean I'm inviting male companionship."

Haly shook her head. She was missing something. "Of course not. Why would it?"

"Exactly!" Selene stabbed a finger at her. "We're at the Libyrinth. This isn't Ilysies. And he keeps acting like . . . like such a *male*."

There was no missing the derision in that word. Despite a window and several glow warmers, the light in here wasn't the best; still, Haly could make out the blush on Selene's cheeks. She was embarrassed. Interesting. "Selene, sit down. I'll make some tea."

Tea and listening were turning out to be her two most helpful administrative tools next to the Song. Making the tea gave her time to think over Selene's words and gave Selene time to settle down.

"So what did he do, exactly?" asked Haly once they both had a steaming cup of silverleaf twig tea. She leaned on the edge of her desk, letting the cup warm her hands as she watched her friend and former master closely. It still felt a little odd to be the one offering counsel, after so many years of working under Selene's direction.

Selene pursed her lips and stared into her teacup. "In the traditional Ilysian manner, he displayed his desire for me."

Song or no, Haly was far from perfect. She couldn't repress an amused grin. "His desire? You mean he hiked up his robe and—"

Selene stood abruptly and pretended to find great interest in a book on the shelves to the side of Haly's desk. "He clearly misinterpreted my words."

"The remark about the bath?" asked Haly.

Selene nodded reluctantly. "In Ilysies, that would have been an invitation," she admitted.

"Then perhaps it wasn't really his fault." Haly tried to make the suggestion gentle.

Selene swung around and glared at her. "I did *not* invite him! You think I wanted him to debase himself before me in that way? It's disgusting. I never liked that. I was so relieved when I came here and discovered that things aren't done that way at the Libyrinth."

Ah. Now Haly understood. "Po's behavior is an unwelcome reminder of an aspect of your heritage that's always been odious to you. No wonder you're so upset. You don't want anyone expecting you to act on Ilysian female privilege."

Selene turned away again, but Haly caught the flash in her eyes and knew she'd struck a chord. "Or to think I did. But it's not just that. I think he should go back to Ilysies."

"Because he embarrasses you?"

Selene turned to face her. She'd had time to put up her icy defenses, and her tone now was detached, calm. "For his own sake, and for the good of the community. He's clearly unhappy here, and disruptive. Always getting into fights, having temper tantrums over the littlest thing."

"He's still adjusting."

"I don't think he can. He's a liability."

Anger colored Haly's own cheeks, and she breathed with it. She listened to the Song inside her. "If we send Po away because he is too difficult to deal with, we start down a road where sooner or later, we solve another problem by getting rid of somebody else, and before you know it, it's you, me, Clauda, a million books, and a vegetable patch. That's not going to do anyone any good. We must begin the way we plan to go on."

Selene sighed. Haly could see her trying to come up with an argument in favor of banishing Po. But before she could muster one, someone else knocked on the door. It was Clauda, with a scroll in her hand. "Po and Baris have had another fight," she said as she entered.

"See?" said Selene.

Haly smiled and put a hand to her forehead. "We were just discussing Po. Want some tea?"

The way Clauda brightened at the sight of Selene made Haly wonder for the umpteenth time why she didn't make her feelings known. For that matter, Selene's expression as she greeted Clauda was far from the dour chagrin she'd displayed a moment ago.

The two had barely known each other before they set off to find *The Book of the Night*. Clauda had been a servant at that time and Selene a Libyrarian. But something had happened between them in Ilysies. Haly still didn't know what, really. Selene seldom shared personal information and was not the sort of person one asked about such things. Haly and Clauda, however, had been friends all their lives and had always told each other everything. Except in this case.

All Clauda told her was that she and Selene had argued at first, and then they learned to respect each other. Haly knew there was more to it than that. She'd known Clauda all her life. She could tell by the way her friend looked at Selene that she liked her. The fact that she didn't discuss it with Haly only meant it must be pretty serious.

But it was none of her business. They all had responsibilities now and little time to spend together as friends. "How was your patrol?"

Clauda lifted the scroll in her hand. "I spotted an Ilysian envoy."

Haly focused on the scroll. "Dear Exalted One," it began in a rather snotty tone of voice.

"I landed to find out what she was up to," continued Clauda, breaking Haly's concentration. She had to focus, these days, to hear the voices of text. It took some getting used to but it was nice not being interrupted all the time.

Clauda said, "She was on her way here with this message from Queen Thela. She seemed pleased enough to hand it over to me and return home. I hovered in the area for a long time, to make sure she was really leaving. I'll scout again for her first thing in the morning, to be sure she's not hanging around." She handed the scroll to Haly.

The red wax seal on the document bore the imprint of the bull of Ilysies. Haly broke it and handed it to Selene. By now, Clauda had taken a seat next to her. "You two read it. I'll just listen."

Dear Exalted One, or whatever it is your people call you,

Since you have seen fit to refuse my generous offer of aid, and since you persist in keeping my flying machine despite the fact that you also retain what is left of my army, I must reconsider my offer of friendship to you and your community.

Though it pains me as it would any mother whose children remain obstinate in their errors, I must accept that the Ilysians among you have chosen their course. I send this merely to inform them that they are Ilysians no longer. Should they attempt to repatriate to the fertile land of their birth, they shall be declared traitors and dealt with accordingly.

I rely upon your honest nature to share this information freely with those affected by it.

Yours,
Queen Thela Tadamos of Ilysies

They all stared at one another for a moment. Then Selene said, "If we had any doubt whether she was angry that we refused her offer of aid, this settles it."

"I'm sorry, Selene," said Haly.

Selene gave a little shake of her head, her brow knit in puzzlement.

"This means you can't go home again," Haly explained.

Selene's jaw was firm. "I am home."

Clauda frowned. "Why is she making it necessary for Ilysians to stay? I mean, this actually helps us, doesn't it?"

Haly nodded. "Not as much as it would have if Ymin Ykobos were still among us, but yes, I think it does."

"There's a reason," said Selene. "She always has a reason."

"Making it impossible for you to go back and challenge her assigned heir, Jolaz, would be reason enough," said Clauda.

Selene inclined her head to one side. "She needn't go to such trouble. I never intended to do any such thing."

Haly exchanged a look with Selene. "It also means there will be no banishment for Po, no matter how problematic he may be."

"Maybe that's her reason," said Selene.

"Oh, come now," said Haly. "You don't believe he can single-handedly destroy the community, do you?"

"Wait, what? Who's talking about banishing Po?" said Clauda.

"I don't think either of you understand how disruptive an unattached Ilysian male can be," said Selene. "We're supposed to be nonviolent, and he's going around attacking other males right and left. He's out of control, and he's just fifteen. He's only going to get worse."

"But we don't banish people," said Clauda. She looked at Haly. "Do we?"

Haly shook her head.

"You said yourself he's been in another fight with Baris," Selene told Clauda.

"And Selene and Po had a misunderstanding this afternoon," said Haly.

Clauda leaned forward. "What happened?"

Selene told her the story.

"So, what did he say when you explained it to him?" asked Clauda.

"What?" said Selene.

"When you told him it was a misunderstanding. What did he say?"

Haly knew there was a reason she'd wanted Selene to talk to Clauda about this.

"He didn't—I didn't—I told him to leave!"

Clauda raised her eyebrows. "And then what did he do?"

"He left!"

Clauda nodded. "That must have been humiliating."

"It was!"

"No, I meant for Po."

Selene was taken aback for a moment, but soon rallied with, "Well, what would you have me do? Take advantage of him?"

Clauda drew her brows together. "No, of course not. But, I mean, you could have tried to explain about the misunderstanding."

Selene stared at her, openmouthed and mute.

"You yelled at him, didn't you?"

Selene sighed and stared at a corner of the room.

Clauda nodded. "And then he ran into Baris and they fought."

"So that makes it all right, then."

"I didn't say that. It just puts things in context, is all. I know the fighting is a problem but Baris fought, too, and he's not exactly adapting seamlessly to life around here, either. I notice we're not talking about banishing him."

Selene sighed. "True."

Clauda nodded. She was on a roll, now. "And don't forget how helpful Po was to me when I was ill and under guard in Ilysies. He could have prevented me from stealing the wing and escaping, but he didn't. He helped me and that's why he's here now. He never asked for any of this."

"True, but he could have left when Ymin did," said Selene.

"But have you considered what he'd be going back to?" said Haly.

Selene stared at her.

"If you deplore the Ilysian standards and expectations for males, how can you send him back to a place where he must conform to them?"

Selene's eyes seemed even darker than usual. "I do deplore them, but he . . . I think he wants to be treated that way. He's always trailing after me, calling me princess and trying to wait on me hand and foot. Maybe he can't understand anything else."

"Are you saying he's unfit for equality?" said Clauda.

Selene stood. "What difference does it make what I think? He's here. He's not going anywhere." She turned toward the door but stopped and looked back at Clauda. "And you're right. He helped you and I should be grateful for that. I just wish he'd remember that he's more than a breeding stud."

"Well, maybe his work in the infirmary will help with that," said Haly.

"Let's hope," said Clauda. "If his kinesthetic sense manifests, that could make a big difference. In the meantime, try to be more patient with him, Selene."

Selene nodded. "I'll try." She looked like she wanted to say more, but all she added was, "I have to go now."

"So do I," said Haly, standing. "My exalted self is on kitchen duty tonight. I have to go or I'll be late."

3

Hilloa

The dining hall in the Libyrinth was crowded and noisy. Po stood in line, watching all the different people milling about the long rows of tables, talking, eating, laughing. The noise echoed off the large room's low, arched ceiling and stone floors. The line moved and Po reached the serving counter. Jan, an Ayorite boy who had the cot next to him in the boys' dorm, was on kitchen duty that night, and next to him, the Redeemer herself ladled out portions of barley porridge. This had happened before. Everybody took shifts. Still, he couldn't get used to it. The queen of Ilysies would never lower herself so. What did Halcyon the Redeemer think it gained her to do this? As he stepped forward and took a bowl from the stack on the counter, she smiled at him.

She was part Thesian, with dark eyes and dusky skin and long wavy hair. A white scar ran from her temple to just below her eye in a single, graceful curve. She had a smile that was like the Song itself. It went right into him. For a moment, Po looked right back at her, directly into her eyes. What did she see? Could she tell about his mistake with Pri—Libyrarian Selene, or his fight with Baris? Quickly he lowered his gaze. Embarrassment at being served by a woman, and not just any woman but their beloved leader, forced him to bend his head as she ladled porridge into his bowl.

Po took a seat at one of the less crowded tables and looked with sadness at the contents of his bowl. It was the same thing every night: barley porridge, pickled eggs, and preserved greens. The blandness of their diet and its monotony boggled Po's mind. Three dishes. At home, even a simple meal would have four or five different things—fresh vegetables and fruit, not to mention fish, and everything spiced and flavorful. How he missed fish. That salted, dried stuff they sometimes tried to revive by soaking in milk did not count.

It would be better when the harvest came in. Still, Po didn't understand why the Redeemer had refused Queen Thela's generous offer of aid. Cartloads of luscious vegetables and fruits could have been theirs for the asking, but the refusal had been firm, and most everyone supported it. The one time Po had ventured to question the decision, that old Singer, Siblea, told him that their independence was more important than the kind of food they ate. Po's jaw tightened at the memory of the old man's sharp tone. He hadn't hit Siblea. He knew he was supposed to be glad about that.

A group of three young women sat down near Po. As he dutifully consumed his porridge, he cast covert glances in their direction. Their names were Hilloa, Jaen, and Bethe. They were all Libyrarians, all his own age, all without consorts. Bethe was Thesian, dark-skinned, with a halo of tightly curled brown hair and luminous sable eyes. Jaen was obviously of Ilysian extraction, willowy and tall, with pale skin and long, wavy black hair. Hilloa was olive-skinned and green-eyed, with honey brown hair and an intoxicatingly curvy build. At home, his hungry looks would be considered a tribute, but not here. Po pretended to find the contents of his bowl fascinating and contented himself with listening in on their conversation.

"Of course, I told him it was only for fun, you know," said Hilloa, "but Leck is so sentimental, I'm afraid he's fallen for me after all."

"Never mind that," said Bethe. "Help me figure out how I'm going to get Neith to notice me. He's all wrapped up in his unrequited feelings for Arche."

"I don't know why you waste your time with him," said Hilloa. "If a boy treated me like that I'd stay away from him. The next thing you know, you're going to be dating Singers."

"Ewwwww," said the other two.

Hilloa shushed them. "They'll hear you."

"So what? They're a bunch of jerks," said Jaen.

"They think they're making progress," said Hilloa.

"They think they are," countered Jaen, "but they still treat us like we're second best. Yesterday I had kitchen duty with Rossiter and we had to light the fire. He goes and gets the flint and tinder, leaving me to fetch the fuel. Without a word. He just assumed I'd be the one to do the dirty job. And he's one of the good ones. He switched with me right away when I pointed out what he'd done, but still."

Po snuck a glance in time to see Bethe grinning. "You like Rossiter, right?"

Jaen glared at her. "He's okay, but it's not like that."

Bethe and Hilloa shared a look and Jaen caught it. "What?" she said. "Sure, he's cute, but it's not like I'm daydreaming about him and awaiting the day we get married so I can start popping babies like a Citadel girl."

"Jaen, stop," said Hilloa. "That's not nice."

"Well, I'm sorry, but as long as those Citadel girls keep acting as if getting a partner was the end-all and be-all of their existence, those stupid Singer boys are never going to get over themselves."

Hilloa and Bethe nodded. "And I don't even think it's because they like sex so much," said Bethe. "They just seem to feel that it's what they're supposed to do."

"Like it's a mark of status," noted Hilloa.

"Wait till they all start getting pregnant. You know they're having sex with Singers and Ayorites. Boys who haven't had initiation. What are we going to do with all those babies?" said Jaen.

"Well, I'm not taking care of them," said Bethe.

There was a pause as the three women ate their barley porridge. Then Jaen said, "Do you think Libyrinth boys will stop taking the initiation?"

"I hope not," said Bethe.

"No," said Hilloa.

Bethe said, "I'm so glad I was raised Libyrarian."

Jaen nodded and Hilloa said, "Yeah, me too. Imagine having to be something extra, just because of your sex.

Either a servant, among the Singers, or a mother, among the Ayorites. . . ."

"Same difference," said Bethe.

"No, it's not, not really," said Hilloa. "I've seen those Ayorite households in operation. The men work just as hard as the women, they just have everything divided up. And I've not seen much in the way of men telling women what to do there, either."

"She's right," agreed Jaen. "They have a lot of stupid ideas about what men are naturally suited for and what women are naturally suited for but you don't get the whole 'women's roles are inferior' piece that you do with the Singers."

"Well, if I had my druthers, I'd be an Ilysian, and let the men wait on me hand and foot," said Bethe, lowering her eyelids and extending her hand as if she were a regal court lady.

"Really? You'd want that? Someone who didn't consider himself your equal? You think that's hot?" said Hilloa.

Bethe flushed. "Well okay, maybe not in the long run, but still, for one night? Especially if he'd rub my feet. These field work days are killing me."

"I heard the Ilysian men are like billy goats," said Hilloa. "Always fighting with one another, and not good for much except scr—" She stopped as she saw Po, who had forgotten himself and was now openly watching them, listening to their conversation with rapt attention.

Hilloa's face fell. She blushed and looked at Jaen and Bethe, who had noticed him, too, and were glaring at her. "Oh, um . . . I'm sure that's just hearsay. Nothing to it at all, I expect."

A glance passed between the three of them. Po was adept at picking up nuances, when they weren't so alien as to be incomprehensible. He knew very well what that glance meant. That from what they'd heard of his behavior, he was single-handedly upholding the stereotype of the overly emotional, sometimes violent, and always childish Ilysian male. His heart sank. And it was true. That was exactly the way he was behaving. And he was trying so hard not to, but . . . It was like blinking. You had to think about it every second in order not to do it.

He looked down at his half-eaten meal. But wasn't that true for most everyone here? Weren't they all trying to overcome their own cultural conditioning? Why was everyone else doing so much better at it than he was? *Because you're a boy*, the automatic answer came, but no, that wasn't the reason. The Singers were all boys, and though they might not be perfect, they weren't creating daily spectacles like he was. Maybe it was just him. Maybe he was just exceptionally stupid and he couldn't change.

He glanced up to find the three Libyrarians still looking at him, though they were pretending not to. A whispered exchange passed among them. At last, Hilloa turned and addressed him. "Excuse me. Po, isn't it?"

Surprised, pleased to be noticed, Po nodded and smiled.

"I just want to say that I'm sorry for the comments I made. You must think I'm very narrow-minded. Maybe I am. Unfortunately, I haven't had a chance to get to know any Ilysian men. It's hard for all of us to overcome the narrow viewpoints we've been raised with."

She was apologizing to him? Po blinked. He remembered to speak. "That's okay."

Hilloa inched closer. "Do you mind if we ask you some

questions? You're the only Ilysian man here. And . . . your culture is quite a bit different from ours."

Yes, it was. That one simple statement made him feel so much better. Just to have that acknowledged did something for him that he couldn't quite define. *Say something,* he reminded himself. They're Libyrarians, they expect you to talk. "Yes. They are different," he agreed. He wanted to say that he was finding it next to impossible to adjust. "I'm not very good at not being Ilysian."

"Why do you fight with other guys so much?"

"Hilloa!" said Bethe. "Don't be rude."

"I'm sorry," Hilloa said to him. Two apologies in as many minutes. Wow. "If I'm being rude, I don't mean to be."

"But she'll keep on being rude anyway, until her curiosity is satisfied," noted Jaen, who elbowed Hilloa in the ribs and shook her head at her. "He's not a social experiment who exists just for your exploration."

Po wasn't entirely sure what that meant but it sounded exciting. Hilloa leaned on the table in a way that accentuated her ample . . . He forced himself to focus on her question, and her eyes. Direct eye-to-eye contact and lots of conversation—that was what these Libyrarian women expected. "It's okay. Um." Po shook his head, trying to explain. "We fight to prove ourselves worthy," he said.

They all stared at him. "Worthy of what?" said Jaen.

"Of, you know . . ." His voice dropped off. Of a woman's regard, were the words that came most readily, but he couldn't bring himself to utter them. It all sounded so ridiculous here. "It's . . . we're very competitive with each other for . . . for the attention of women," he managed at last. "It's part of that."

"But I thought that there are relatively fewer men than women among Ilysians," said Hilloa. "Is that not true?"

"No, it's true," said Po. "Only about one in every three babies born is male."

"Then aren't you guys in pretty high demand?"

He stared at her. She had a point. "I guess so."

"So why do you have to prove yourselves to be worthy?"

Bewildered, he shook his head. It went without question that a man must earn his place as a consort. That he must do everything in his power to make himself appealing and that everything in his life depended on attracting the right woman and siring daughters to provide for him in his old age.

He knew that many women had no consort. He knew that many more shared a consort, but they did not vie over men. Why? "I . . . um . . . I don't know," he admitted. "I guess it's just . . . how things are done."

"So the men in Ilysies really think they're only good for sex and reproduction?" said Hilloa. Jaen and Bethe looked on, awaiting his answer with great interest.

He stared at them, suddenly angry, and he looked down lest they see it in his eyes. "It's not as if we set everything up according to our own wishes."

This was the crux of his problem. At home, no one had consulted with him, or any other male, about what males were supposed to want—it was just given to them. And now here, everyone expected him to want something that he couldn't even really understand or imagine.

"Of course not," said Hilloa. "I didn't mean that. It's just . . . You have to understand. It's shocking to us. We're used to something very different."

He nodded, still looking down at his food. His cheeks were hot. He felt like he was going to cry. He didn't want to cry in front of these women. At home, tears could get him a lot. If he cried the right way and at the right time in front of a woman she would comfort him, she might even place him under her protection; but here it was just considered emotional, which seemed to equal weak, as near as he could tell.

The girls fell silent and returned to their food, and then a little while later their conversation continued on other topics and he was no longer a part of it.

Po finished eating as quickly as he could and walked out of the cool, stone environs of the Libyrinth and into a desert evening, the sand beneath his sandals still warm, but the air cooling rapidly as the sun set in the west. Po enjoyed the lingering food smells from other dining areas and the bleating of goats as they were rounded up into pens for the night. Out here, in what some called Tent Town, things felt a lot less structured, and if he squinted, he could pretend that he was in an Ilysian marketplace, full of life and commerce.

Children ran past, singing the alphabet song, and around a campfire, a group of Ayorites took turns reading to each other from a copy of *The Book of the Night*, the pages of which had been treated with palm-glow to make them readable in the dark.

Though she used to practice out of her office in the Libyrinth, practicality had forced Libyrarian Burke to establish a larger infirmary in a tent located in the center of the settlement. It was lit with the electrical lights the Singers had made. In general, Po preferred the soft, lambent illumination of palm-glow. But he had to admit that the brightness of electrical light was a blessing in this case. It meant that surgical operations could be done at all hours.

As he approached the infirmary, Po saw the motherly figure of Libyrarian Burke inside, walking from one bed to the next. Despite the turmoil of his day and the challenge he knew was to come, he relaxed. Po adored Burke. She embraced all religions, all sciences, all knowledge with equal exuberance and intelligent curiosity. And despite the fact that his kinesiology skills were nearly nonexistent, she welcomed his help.

She was not only a physician; she was also the Libyrarians' high priestess. Among Libyrarians, the one most schooled in the lore of Time and the Seven Tales was also always the doctor. Between her incessant research and her caring for the sick of the community, it was a mystery to Po when she managed to sleep.

Despite her schedule and her responsibilities, Burke was kind and jolly, older and settled. Not for the first time, Po wondered if she had a lover. It would be nice to be the consort of a woman like her. If she liked him, he would feel very secure with her.

Po lifted the flap of the tent and went inside. Beds lined both sides of the tent. There were only two patients at the moment: Nian, who had fallen from a scaffolding while working on a windmill and broken his leg; and Yolle, who was being devoured by the Little Lion Inside and was dying.

Burke stood at the large worktable at the far end of the tent, humming as she mixed ingredients in a mortar and pestle. From the sharp aroma that wafted across the tent, Po knew she was making Ease for Yolle. His shadow, cast by the electric lights, fell over the table and Burke looked up. She smiled. "Po, how nice. How are you today?"

"Fine," he said, returning her smile, and for a moment, in the face of her sunny regard, he really felt like he was.

"I'm just finishing this up. Would you like to work with Nian for a bit? By then the Ease will be ready and you can give Yolle her dose."

Po hesitated.

"Now, Po, just because Nian is another male does not mean he doesn't deserve care." Burke's chiding was gentle, but for once, misplaced.

"No, it's not that."

Burke looked to where Yolle lay clutching the sheet that covered her wasted frame. "Ah."

For a moment Burke and Po simply looked at each other. He saw understanding in her eyes, and determination. "She will ask for you," she said.

Po swallowed and forced a nod, then went to attend to Nian. How ironic that he should prefer to treat the male patient. But poorly adjusted as he might be, Po understood where his duty as a healer lay. Even if they were in Ilysies, where an injured male might lose his consortship to an unscrupulous competitor, Po would not wish to take Nian's place in his wife's household at such a price. At least with an injury such as this, Po's limited skills were useful.

Nevertheless, he avoided conversation with the man as he worked on the pressure points on the soles of Nian's feet, stimulating them to increase circulation. It was impossible to massage the leg itself, now splinted, though that would be an important part of his recovery once the bone mended.

"That feels good," said Nian. "Thank you."

Po nodded, polite if a bit awkward. "You're welcome."

He turned from Nian's bed to find Burke standing there, Yolle's dose in her hands.

Po's heart sank, but he took the cup of medicine from Burke and went to Yolle's bedside. The old woman forced a smile but Po could see the pain in her eyes. He slid an arm under her frail shoulders and helped her up so that she could drink the medicine.

When the cup was drained, Po eased Yolle back onto the bed. If he were a better kinesiologist, he could do more for her. Not cure her, of course, but at least relieve her pain without the need for the drug, Ease. He might even have been able to slow the progress of the disease, if he were as skilled as Adept Ykobos.

"Go ahead and try," said Yolle.

Po drew an unsteady breath. Yolle looked up at him, trust in her eyes. No matter how many times he failed, she always asked him to try again. He wished she wouldn't. He wished Adept Ykobos were here to do this properly. But she was not here. And this old woman, a mother, a grandmother, a person most worthy of respect, was waiting for him to help her.

His humiliation with Princess Selene, his loneliness, his anger with Baris, and his embarrassment with the Libyrarian women all faded to nothing compared with this. He'd been apprenticed to Adept Ykobos at the age of eight and she'd trained him well. Though no one could expect of him the skills of a seasoned adept, he should have at least some capabilities by now.

It wasn't because he hadn't tried. He knew all the massage techniques. The body's pressure points and energy centers were engraved in his mind. Still, the kinesthetic sense, the source of every adept's true healing power, eluded him.

"Please, Po. Just try." Yolle's voice was little more than a whisper.

Shame and hopelessness made it difficult to breathe, but he could not refuse her. He ducked his head to hide his face and placed his hands on the inner part of the old woman's elbows. Closing his eyes, Po fought for the stillness of mind that would allow him to receive impressions from Yolle's body. Adept Ykobos had taught him that such impressions could take many forms—colors, images, sounds, even sensations. But as always, he experienced nothing. He felt Yolle's pulse beneath his thumbs, he matched his breath to hers, he let all the troubles of the day slide away until it was just Yolle and him, breathing together. He sat with her for so long that the settlement grew quiet around them and still, nothing happened.

When at last he let go and opened his eyes, his face was wet. Yolle, at least, was asleep, so he did not have to face her. Not that she'd rebuke him as he deserved. No. Worse, she would thank him for trying.

Queen Thela's Decree

The following morning, Po stood outside of the
Redeemer's office for an hour or more, and would have
been there longer if it hadn't been for Jan.

"What are you doing, Poacher?" Jan had the cot next to
Po's in the boys' dorm tent and he'd come up with that
stupid nickname on the first night. But even Po could rec-
ognize that it was not intended as an insult. It was,
strangely, a term of friendship.

Jan was a couple of years younger than Po and he hadn't
hit his growth spurt yet. He was short and skinny and wiry,
with typical Ayorite freckles, and sandy blond hair that
currently stood up on one side from sleeping. He came
down the hallway and stopped beside him, giving Po's foot
a desultory kick by way of greeting.

In return, Po grabbed Jan around the neck and put him in a headlock. Jan jabbed him in the side with a sharp elbow and wriggled loose. Po tried to grab him again but he dodged and jumped on Po's back and the two of them toppled to the floor in a tangle of arms and legs.

"Cut it out," said Po, getting to his feet and dusting off his robes. "We're not supposed to fight."

Jan laughed. "Look who's talking. Besides, we're not really fighting."

He was right. This was nothing like the fight he'd had with Baris yesterday. That had been for real. This was just practice fighting. They were playing at it, not really harming each other, or at least not meaning to. That could change in an instant, of course, if either of them felt the other had insulted him, or if they were in competition for a woman's attention.

Jan got up and straightened his robe. "But seriously, what are you doing here?"

"What are *you* doing here?"

Jan rolled his eyes. "Don't get like that, Poacher. It's my turn to milk the goats and I'm taking the shortcut. You're just standing outside the Redeemer's office. Why? Are you in trouble?"

Po didn't like Jan's accusatory tone. Now he wished he'd taken the opportunity to really hit him when he'd had the chance. "None of your business."

Jan took in Po's clenched fists and the threatening way he leaned in toward him. He shook his head, and stepped well back before saying, "You're an asshole, you know that?"

"I'm leaving," Po said, not sure why he was spilling his plans or why he should want to explain anything or care what Jan thought of him. "I just have to ask for permission first. I'm waiting now to do that."

Jan's eyebrows rose and he stayed well away from Po. "Leaving . . ." He looked at the door. "How long have you been waiting to talk to her?"

Po shrugged. "About an hour." He gave the words all the defiance they could hold.

Jan nodded and bit his lip. "Have you tried knocking?"

Po gaped at him, and with an act of will, forced his mouth closed. "Of course not! I'm not going to make things worse by disturbing her. I'll just ask to speak with her when she comes out. Or in, if she's not there yet."

"She's there." Jan nodded to the bottom edge of the door. In the early morning gloom of the hallway, the light spilling from beneath it glowed, golden and warm. Jan heaved a great sigh and shook his head. "You're pathetic, Poacher." He reached over and rapped on the door. The sound was loud, preemptory, rude. This was their Redeemer, for the Mother's sake.

As Jan walked away, Po stared after him. Jan was a servant here by birth and yet he had less regard for the Redeemer's peace and station than even the most cosseted stud would have for a common farmer back home. Before Po could formulate a rebuke to Jan, the door opened.

Halcyon the Redeemer stood in the doorway, smiling at him. It struck him that she was no more than a year or so older than himself, but she had so much responsibility. And here he was, to tell her he could not be part of her dream.

Po dropped to his hands and knees and put his head to the floor at her feet. "I'm sorry. I didn't mean to disturb you. It wasn't me who knocked, but I should have stopped him anyway."

Warm hands gripped his shoulders. "Stand up, Po. It's good that you, or somebody, knocked. You can come here any time and knock on the door. You don't have to worry about disturbing me."

Po obeyed her and let her guide him inside, her hand on his elbow gentle but firm. His face felt hot. He couldn't look at her. How was he going to get the words out that he needed to say?

The Redeemer sat him down in a chair and moved off to a sideboard where she had a glow warmer and a teakettle. She poured water from a pitcher into the kettle and put it on the burner.

The office was small, lit with glow torches that cast shadows on the stone walls and floor. The Redeemer's desk faced the door. Its surface was littered with papers and books. Shelves filled with more books lined the wall to the right of the desk. Behind the desk a long sideboard held more papers, more books and, at the far end was the glow warmer. A cupboard on the left-hand wall was stocked with baskets of tea, mugs, and other supplies.

Silence reigned as she prepared tea. Po watched her, feeling that he should offer to do that for her but unable to speak. At last, she placed the teapot, two mugs, and a basket on a platter and set them down on the desk. But she did not return to her seat behind it. Two chairs sat in front of the desk. She pulled the other one closer to his, and sat facing him, no more that a foot or two away.

The silence stretched out until it was unbearable. At last Po glanced up and found her looking at him, smiling. Waiting. "It will take a little time to steep," she said.

The tea. Right.

"Thank you for coming to see me, Po."

He couldn't look at her and say the words, and if he didn't say the words soon he wouldn't be able to get them out at all. He stared at his knee. There was a bit of straw from yesterday still stuck in the weave. "Redeemer, forgive me. I can't do this. I can't be a member of this community. I'm here to ask permission to return to Ilysies."

Some part of him wanted to crawl out of his own mouth and snatch the words out of the air and stuff them back down his throat. But it was too late now. He'd said them.

The Redeemer said nothing. She stood and turned her back to him. The bit of straw on his knee wavered and grew fuzzy. When she turned again he braced himself for her rebuke. Perhaps she would hit him. It would be a relief to pay for displeasing her with something so simple as pain or blood. He closed his eyes, felt the hot tears on his face, and waited.

She took his hand and wrapped it around a mug of hot tea. "Breathe, Po, and drink this."

She sat down again, drawing her chair even closer to his, until their knees touched. She put a hand on his shoulder.

He lifted the cup to his lips and drank the hot, bittersweet tea. His tears dried and he took deep breaths, feeling oddly empty now.

"I want you to look at me."

He did as she asked. Her eyes, which seemed to look right into him, were sad, and yet there was light in them. Her smile, too, was partly sad and partly—it took him a moment to place it, but when he did he felt oddly relieved—amused. "I can't pretend to understand what it's like for you here," she said. "I'm sorry that it's so hard that you wish to return to a place where you can never be more than a second-class citizen. Don't"—she grabbed his face with both hands and forced him to keep looking at her—"don't apologize. It's not your fault."

He swallowed and tucked those words away for later, when he might have time to work on believing them.

"Though I think it would be a mistake for you to go back, it doesn't matter what you or I think. It's not possible for you to return to Ilysies now." She released him and lifted a scroll from her desk and handed it to him. "This came yesterday."

He read the words, in Queen Thela's own hand, that branded him a traitor and barred him from ever returning to the one place where he understood what was expected of him. A distant green valley beyond the mountains became more distant with every breath. The paper rustled in his hands and he wanted to crush it. He wanted to tear it and throw it across the room but he was in the presence of a woman, and such behavior was impossible.

"Po."

He looked up. Again there was that smile, those eyes. "I'm sorry. And . . . for what it's worth, I'm glad we get to keep you. I know it's selfish of me, but . . ."

Po grew reckless. Maybe it was the hollow feeling inside, the sense that all of this was happening to someone else. The Redeemer fell silent in mid-sentence and he took the chance that she was finished. "I don't think the Redemption worked on me."

Now she looked like she was going to cry. "Of course it did. But it's not easy for anyone. It's not even easy for me, and I hear the Song all the time."

That shocked him. For a moment, the green valley was gone from his mind and he looked at her and saw a sixteen-year-old woman who was in over her head. Was that possible? "You?"

"Yeah."

He took a breath. "I go to the performances of the Song. And when I hear it, I remember what it was like that day. Other times, too, I remember. But . . . that's not the same as . . . as . . ."

"As really feeling it in the here and now."

Astonished, he nodded. "You do know."

"You may be the only Ilysian male here, and I won't argue that it's not a special challenge, but everybody is experiencing this. We're all trying to get back to the way we felt that day, before we had to worry about feeding ourselves. Before we had to worry about how to get along with one another." She leaned closer. She wasn't coming on to him. He knew that. This was something else, something much rarer. "I'll tell you something nobody else knows. Something I haven't even told Gyneth. I'm not sure we're going to make it, Po. I think this whole thing could fall apart."

Mother. "That's why I should—"

"What, wander out into the plain? Starve in the desert? Return to Ilysies and get killed for your trouble? No. If we fail, Po, it will be for many reasons, but it won't be because of you."

Her words unlocked a secret door inside him, where his deepest fear had hidden itself. That he would ruin this—not just for himself, but for everyone. He hadn't even known, until this moment, that it was the real reason he wanted to leave. But now she had exposed it and brought it into the light, and called it baseless. Just then, it didn't matter if he felt what she said to be true. The fact that she said it, and believed it, was more than enough. He reached for her, and she took him in her arms, and they held on to each other.

5

Initiation

Po was late for breakfast. By the time he got to the dining hall, nearly everyone was seated and there was no line. He took a bowl from the rack and held it out so Vale, a Libyrarian boy a year or two older than him, could ladle barley porridge into it. He nodded his thanks and turned, scanning the hall for a seat.

The large room was loud and busy with people talking, laughing, moving about from table to table, visiting, eating. How could they be so carefree, when so much was uncertain? Even the Redeemer doubted that the community could survive.

His conversation with Haly had left him with two utterly contradictory feelings. On the one hand, he was more terrified than ever, and on the other, a nameless hope now dwelled inside him, that he was not such a disaster as he'd thought. They left little room for his heartache over Queen Thela's banishment.

"Po, come sit with us!"

Po looked in the direction of the voice and found Hilloa, Jaen, and Bethe waving him over. Pleasure at their invitation warmed him, despite his jumbled feelings.

"We heard that Queen Thela has forbidden any expat Ilysians from returning," said Bethe.

"Not that you'd ever want to go back there anyway, being a boy," said Hilloa. "But some of the Ilysian women are probably pretty upset about it."

Po stirred his porridge. His chest was so tight with tangled objections, he couldn't even begin to voice them.

"I bet they wish they'd let men into their army now."

"Seven Tales, Bethe, is dating all you ever think about?" said Hilloa.

Bethe shrugged. "So I have a healthy libido, what's wrong with that?"

"There are other things in the world," noted Jaen.

"I'm just saying, if I were an Ilysian woman, and I knew I couldn't go home, and I was facing the prospect of dating Singers . . ." She shuddered.

"Gross," said Jaen. "They don't even take initiation."

"Well, and what makes you think they won't nab all the Libyrarian boys?" said Hilloa, and she and Jaen laughed at the look on Bethe's face.

"Maybe they don't care. Ilysian boys aren't initiated, are they?" said Bethe.

All three of them looked at him for an answer.

"Initiation?"

"Yeah, at the onset of adulthood. So you can't accidentally make babies."

"What?"

"It's a surgical procedure."

Po couldn't conceal his horror. "You mean they're castrated?" He'd had no idea.

"No, no, nothing like that. It's just a small incision and a little plug is inserted to block the sperm."

Po tried not to show his shock. Suddenly he felt sorry for Libyrarian males. They couldn't sire daughters. "What happens to the men if they have no daughters to provide for them when they're old?"

The women looked at him as if he'd said something surprising. Hilloa spoke. "Same thing everyone else does when they get old. Their clerks take care of them."

"But then how do you reproduce?" Were they all ring-tails, like in Kip's story?

"There's a procedure to reverse it, if the man's been approved to reproduce."

So many different elements of that statement horrified Po that he didn't know where to begin, but it was the least overt and most sinister that found his voice. "If he's been approved?"

"Don't you practice birth control in Ilysies? I assumed, with women being in charge and all . . ."

"If a woman doesn't want to bear a child she just doesn't let her male copulate with her. There are a lot of ways for women to experience pleasure," *to the heartbreak of their males*, he didn't add. "Some women give birth and then a sister or mother or aunt raises the child. But such things are rare. Babies are prized in Ilysies, and motherhood is the most honored status a woman can achieve. No male would interfere with his own fertility. It would ruin him."

The three women exchanged a look. Po could tell that they carefully kept their faces neutral, but there was no mistaking the pity in Bethe's eyes, or the humor in Jaen's. Hilloa turned her head, and he couldn't see her face at all.

But as he left the dining hall, she came up alongside him. "Po." She put a hand on his arm. "I'm sorry if any of us hurt your feelings."

He shook his head. "No, that's okay. I want to do better. I do."

She gave him a funny kind of smile and tilted her head. "You know, some of the Singer boys are taking the Libyrarian initiation. Because us Libyrarian girls won't have anything to do with them if they don't. We couldn't risk getting pregnant, you see? An unplanned pregnancy is . . . Well, I guess it's like hitting a woman would be to you."

Icy shock ran through him at the words. "That bad?"

She nodded. "Yeah. For centuries we've been a small population in a resource-sparse environment. Reproduction not only has to be limited, but monitored. Not everyone is fit to have children together, no matter how much they might love each other and want to make a child. From the beginning, we've been disciplined about it. We have to be in order to survive."

"What about now? With all the extra people, and once the fields start to produce, there'll be enough food, right?"

She gave him a crooked smile. "Do you think we're going to grow enough food? I hope so. But even then . . . I hope we don't lose our way. I think it's a good way. Maybe . . . people could have more choice in who they have a child with, but . . . I hope boys don't stop getting initiated. I'd hate to have to worry about getting pregnant when I'm having fun. I want to study. I want to read and learn and then write about what I've learned. I want to help unravel the secrets of the Ancients. I can't do all of that with a screaming infant on my hip."

Po blinked. "Why not?"

"What?"

"Why can't you do everything you want and still have babies? The women back home do. While the child's an infant, she carries it with her. And then when they're older, they trail after her or they're looked after by a sibling or a sire or an aunt. Children are everywhere in Ilysies. Having children is expected. It's part of life. There are no places children can't go and so no places mothers can't go. It would be unthinkable. Mothers are the ultimate authority. Motherhood makes a woman wise and powerful. Why would anyone want to limit that?

"I've noticed here, the babies are all in a crèche. Parents make time to visit them but other people actually take care of them. That's very strange, I think."

She stared at him a long time and Po realized he'd gone too far. Wasn't he supposed to be more forthcoming? Less deferential? Wasn't that what she wanted? Where had he gone wrong?

At last, she cleared her throat and said, "Well, anyway, I just wanted you to know that initiation is an option for you. If you want it. If, you know, you wanted to make yourself acceptable to Libyrarian girls."

Oh. Po blinked. Oh, she . . . she wanted him. Pleasure and relief made him dizzy and he forced himself to swallow. She liked him and she wanted him as a consort. He wasn't beyond hope after all.

Only she wanted him to render himself infertile for her. Po's stomach lurched. Could he even refuse? What if hers was the only offer he got? What was he going to do? "Thank you," he said. "I . . . I work in the infirmary tonight. I'll . . . I'll talk to Libyrarian Burke about it."

She brightened. "Really? Great!" She gave him a grin and leaned in for a sideways hug. Her warmth and her scent made him giddy.

They came out into the Great Hall. High above them soared a vast dome pierced by skylights. Morning light filtered through to reflect on the polished stone surface of the floor. The large round chamber was lined with books, and interspersed about the perimeter were alcoves, one for each of the Seven Tales. At the second-story level a balcony ran all the way around the room, and in the center of the hall was a ring-shaped counter—the console where one could request books.

The Great Hall was a hub of activity at any time of day. Now, between breakfast and the first work shift, it was a bustling microcosm of the community as a whole. Though many people of all origins milled about in the open areas, there was an undeniable tendency for certain groups to cluster together. In the Alcove of the Fly stood Rossiter, Baris, and several other former members of Subaltern Chorus Number Five, the adolescent Singers who had accompanied the Redeemer to the Libyrinth after her imprisonment in their Corvariate Citadel.

The older Singer males and the citizens of the Corvariate Citadel congregated in the Alcove of the Fish, where they often played instruments and sang. At the moment, a red-headed Singer was strumming a hand-held harp and several women sat around him, listening. Po liked the music, though the worshipful looks on the women's faces made him uncomfortable.

At the opposite side of the Great Hall, in the Alcove of the Lion, Vorain and a number of the other Ilysian women stood about trading jokes with several village Ayorites. The women of his country got on well with the people from the villages of the plain. All of the Ilysian women had been soldiers, and most of them came from farming families, so they had that in common. And the Ayorite attitude regarding men and women was not in such sharp contrast with theirs, as was, for instance, that of the patriarchal Singers.

The Libyrinth Ayorites, those who were servants here prior to the Redemption, gathered in the Alcove of the Dog, and the Libyrarians clustered around the central console, along with several others who were close advisors of the Redeemer.

Now Haly herself stood there, holding hands with her consort, a Singer boy named Gyneth. Burke and Peliac were there as well, all of them listening to that old Singer, Siblea.

Po watched the old man hold forth. He was obviously comfortable talking in front of other people. There wasn't a hint in his posture or his face to indicate any awareness of himself as a pompous old windbag. But of course he was much more, and much worse, than that. Po's gaze strayed to the scar on Haly's cheek. Back at the Corvariate Citadel, Siblea had been Censor Siblea, a high-ranking priest in their hierarchy. It had been his job to punish people for disobeying the Singer laws. Rumor had it that he'd given Haly that scar.

The deranged perversity that put a man in an occupation that would feed his violent tendencies was exceeded only by the injustice of the fact that he still lived. At home, a man like that, who had done harm to a woman, would be dead and his family in disgrace. But, Po reminded himself, his home was no longer his home. He was stuck here, where a degenerate like Siblea was not only forgiven his crimes, but listened to with respect by the Redeemer herself. His stomach turned.

Hilloa squeezed his arm and nodded toward the group at the console. "Come on, I've got something to show them. They've been on to the concept of dimensions lately, and last night I had an idea!"

Unable to refuse, Po's stomach tightened as Hilloa dragged him ever closer to Siblea and the others.

". . . and what this book says is that seconds after the Big Bang—which they say is how the universe began—the expansion of matter created a standing gravity wave that emanated a sound," said Siblea.

"Do you think that was the Song?" asked Haly, her voice tinged with awe. It made the hair on Po's arms stand on end, to hear her speak so to such a man.

"What else?" said Siblea.

"Wow," said Hilloa, joining the circle. "That's amazing."

Siblea glanced at her in surprise and then looked back at the others. But now everyone was greeting Hilloa. To his relief Po, who hung back, was largely ignored, apart from Haly, who smiled at him and gave him a little wave.

Hilloa continued. "I wonder if what Siblea is saying connects with . . . I had an idea last night for a way to visualize the concept of dimension." She reached into her satchel and drew out an empty sack of the kind used to store barley, and three silverleaf twigs fastened together at their mid-points, each perpendicular to the others. "Hang on."

"Sound is a form of vibration." Siblea kept on talking as if Hilloa wasn't even there. Others in the group shifted uneasily, but he went on. "Perhaps everything we perceive, all the myriad parts of the universe, are no more than the same kinds of particles oscillating at different frequencies."

"Right," said Hilloa. "That's one way to look at it. Particles and wavelengths. But you can also think of it geometrically. Or I mean, a geometrical approach can put the wavelengths in context."

Siblea stared at her, clearly affronted. "I hardly think that geometry is relevant here."

Po stepped forward at the dismissive tone Siblea used to address Hilloa. "Why don't you give your mouth a rest and listen to what she wants to tell you?"

Everyone turned to stare at Po. What? What had he done now? He hadn't even called Siblea an old man, though he deserved it, and so much more. Silence fell over the group as he and Siblea stared at each other. Inside, Po begged Siblea to react the way any normal male would. One step, one single threatening movement from Siblea was all the excuse he needed to take the old man apart the way he'd wanted to ever since he'd heard of him. Maybe he didn't have to wait.

And then, just as he was about to abandon waiting, Haly laughed. "Po is being a bit confrontational about it, but the essence of his suggestion is solid, Siblea," she said. "Let's all hear what Hilloa has to say."

And just like that, the tension in the group evaporated.

Well, almost. Po kept staring at Siblea, who now pretended that he did not exist. "Of course, Holy One," said the old goat. And he turned to Hilloa. "Please proceed."

She hesitated just a moment, and then her enthusiasm came back to the fore. "Okay, see, what we normally think of as space is made up of three dimensions. Each of these sticks is one such dimension—height, width, and depth. Only I think those are arbitrary designations that we lock ourselves into, conceptually. She picked up the sack. "Now this is nothing right now. We know the bag can hold stuff, but it's empty, flat, without space. This is the fabric of existence with no dimensions to fill it.

"But if we put the sticks in the bag . . ." She did so and then pulled the fabric tight around the sticks, showing everyone the bulge in the bag. "Now, it has space. Say this is a universe. It exists because it has dimension. And that's all any universe really is. It's a bundle of sticks, creating a space within the fabric of existence.

"And where all this connects with the Song is that these sticks can be made out of anything. We call them height, width, and depth, but what does that really mean? Couldn't they just as easily be sounds, or ideas? They could be stories, like Time and the Seven Tales, or they could be the Song, or the Name of the Ocean." She looked at Po as she said that last part, and winked at him. He grinned.

"Wow," said Burke. "That is something. I am going to be thinking about that all day. That could be a way to bring the Seven Tales into context with the rest of what we know about physics and the nature of existence. Thank you, Hilloa."

"Yes, thank you," said Haly. "This is why we are going to be okay," she said. She looked at Siblea, who stood quite still, his face carefully neutral. "Because we have so many smart people using their minds."

The group broke up as people dispersed to their various work shifts. Hilloa went off without a backward glance, but Haly came up to Po as he was turning away and said, "I understand why you spoke as you did to Siblea. I'm not blind to what he was doing, and I will address it with him. But I want you to do me a favor, and leave it to me, okay?"

The rest of the day, Po's thoughts ran in circles. A beautiful Libyrarian girl wanted him. But she expected him to render himself infertile for her. What if it wasn't temporary? He'd be ruined. Why would she want a male that she couldn't get babies off of? She said that was exactly what she wanted, but surely she'd change her mind. Then what would he do?

"Po?" Libyrarian Burke's voice broke him out of his reverie. "I think that long grass is ready by now."

He looked down at the mortar and pestle he'd been using. The pale green long grass leaves were nothing but pulp. He and Burke sat at the worktable in the infirmary. It was late. He'd already given Yolle her dose of Ease and attempted kinesiology on her, an effort aided not at all by his distracted state. Now they were preparing aspirin. Outside, the settlement was quieting down for the night.

Burke's smile was kind. "What's on your mind tonight, Po?"

"Do you have a consort, Libyrarian?"

Burke blinked. "A . . . well, I suppose, in a manner of speaking. Libyrarian Talian and I have been companions to each other for many years."

"Oh." Po couldn't keep the disappointment out of his voice. He'd hoped that she would say no. He'd hoped she would ask him to be her consort. But that was ridiculous. Someone like Burke, a woman of eminence and maturity, would not need to resort to a calfling like him. A little voice inside him suggested that he accept Hilloa's offer while he still could. "Is Libyrarian Talian initiated?"

"Of course."

"But you still like him? You're not . . . disappointed that you can't get a child off of him?"

Burke laughed. "Oh, I am long past my time for having babies, Po. And I've already had two. More than most Libyrarians can hope for."

"Off of Talian?"

"One of them, my son, Glai."

"But you haven't put Talian aside, even though you didn't get a daughter?"

"Of course not."

They worked in silence as Po absorbed this. "Hilloa wants me to take the Libyrarian initiation."

"Ah."

"So it is true, then? That you do an operation on the boys to make them infertile?" It had occurred to him that Hilloa and her friends might have been playing a joke on him. The whole thing sounded so outlandish.

"Yes. Would you like to know more about it?" she asked. He nodded.

She turned to a bookshelf. She took down a much-worn volume, a leather-wrapped, single-fold book, its binding marking it as a Libyrarian-written book even before she opened it to reveal the hand-lettered pages. "Here," she said, opening it to a particular page. "These are diagrams of the procedure. Why don't you look them over and then I'll answer your questions." She returned to her work.

Po looked at the pictures. To his dismay, it was exactly as Hilloa had described it. The dry, line-drawing illustrations could not hide the truth of the matter. Of how painful it must be. Of the simple fact that they rendered their males infertile.

And if he did not have this done to himself, he would be unacceptable to Libyrarian women. What was he going to do?

At length he closed the book and returned it to its shelf. Burke looked at him kindly. "Do not think that just because you are Ilysian, you are the only male to be horrified by the procedure. Even our Libyrarian boys, who are brought up to expect it, are afraid. If it was not frightening, indeed, if were not painful, it would not be an initiation."

"But I thought boys and girls were equal," he said.

"We are."

"Then why don't girls have to go through something frightening and painful in order to become women?"

Burke nodded understanding. "They do. You are forgetting that menstrual periods are painful, not to mention childbirth itself."

Of course, he thought. How could he have been so stupid as to forget about periods? Much was made of their difficulty, back home. And of course there was nothing more painful and perilous than childbirth itself. He nodded.

"I have performed many initiations in my time," said Burke, "and I have answered many nervous questions beforehand. I think I can guess at a couple that may be on your mind now. May I?"

He nodded again.

"First of all, it does hurt, yes. It is not an unbearable pain, but it is not trivial, either. It is as bad as any significant cut to a sensitive area would be. You would be sore for many days afterward, and you would have to rest for at least two days immediately following the initiation.

"But once you recovered you would find that it does not interfere with your sexual functioning in any way apart from the fact that you cannot father children without a second procedure to reverse the first one."

"And what about that? Can you really make them fertile again?"

"Usually."

Po gaped. "Usually? You mean sometimes it doesn't work? I might wind up infertile forever?"

She nodded. "It's a possibility. Keep in mind that as Libyrarians, we regard reproduction as a privilege, not a right or a duty. Not all Libyrarians are afforded the privilege anyway. Ever. Those that are, and who find themselves unable to father children due to scarring, well, they are disappointed, of course. But reproducing is never anyone's end-all or be-all among us. It is a misfortune, but not an unendurable one."

Scarring. Po's mouth was dry and he forced himself to swallow. "I see." For a moment there was silence between them.

"I think perhaps you might be best to do without a Libyrarian initiation, Po," said Burke at last. "Given your background, and the primacy your society of origin places on fertility in males."

He took a deep breath. "But Libyrarian women. They won't have anything to do with me if I don't take the initiation, will they?"

Burke gave him a closed-lipped smile and shrugged. "Probably not."

6

Disgrace

The following morning at breakfast, Po was too nervous to follow the conversation between Hilloa, Bethe, and Jaen. He had decided that before taking any irreversible action, he should make sure Hilloa was serious. He'd noticed that the Libyrarians changed partners a lot. If he was going to be initiated so they could be together, then by rights she should offer him a permanent place in her household. Just the idea of making such a bold demand made his heart race. He had rehearsed five different ways of asking her, and he kept comparing them, trying to decide which one was best. Wrapped up in these thoughts, he very nearly missed his opportunity.

Jaen and Beth were standing up and Hilloa was already

in the aisle, heading toward the Great Hall. He scrambled after her. "Hilloa!"

She turned and smiled at him. "You've been even quieter than usual today."

He nodded.

She leaned in to him, letting her arm and the side of her breast press against his chest a moment, before stepping back again. "Have you thought about initiation?"

Po fought his nerves. It was unheard of for a male to be so direct about such things, but he had no choice. "I would do it," he told her.

She grinned.

Po was tempted to leave it at that but he wasn't quite as stupid as his behavior led everyone to believe. "But it's a big deal for someone like me. I'm . . . not Libyrarian by birth. I'm Ilysian, and we . . ." He thought of what Burke had said. "We put a great deal of emphasis on male fertility, so . . . I'd need to know that this wasn't just a passing interest on your part."

She nodded, but her expression had gone neutral and her eyes were wary. Not a good sign.

"If I were to render myself infertile for you, possibly permanently, then I'd need to know that my future was secure. That you intended to . . ."

She widened her eyes.

"To marry me," he blurted out at last.

The look on her face told him all he needed to know. He fervently wished for the floor to open up and swallow him whole.

"I'm sorry," she said. "That's not . . . You're right, my interest is much more casual than that." She looked at him like he had a second nose in the middle of his forehead or something. Like he was an incomprehensible freak. Which was exactly what he was—to her, to everyone here.

He nodded, longing for her to leave and for this agony to be over. "I understand. That's why I . . . I just can't."

"Okay," she said, forcing a smile. There was an awkward silence, and then she reached out and put a hand on his arm and squeezed it. "Well, we can still be friends, right?"

That afternoon was Po's shift doing farmwork. They all did every job, in turn. It was not the most efficient system but it was one way to keep everybody on par with one another. No one was relegated to the scut work. It seemed a bit unrealistic to Po, but no one asked his opinion, and that was just as well.

He didn't mind the farming. Hard physical work was traditional for males and he felt more comfortable plowing the fields than discussing a book. And it was an opportunity to spend some more time with Zam. The elephant had proven invaluable for plowing and for moving the larger of the rocks they uncovered.

Besides Selene, the other members of Po's workgroup were Ock, an Ayorite man of middle years; Arche, a Libyrarian woman about four years older than Po; and Baris. Po had assumed the task of fitting Zam with her tack and bringing her to the field. Today they were working in the far west section of the area that was under cultivation.

The elephant rumbled as he entered her stall, and greeted him with a clumsy caress with her trunk. Po laughed and wiped a streak of saliva from the side of his face. "Hey, Zam . . . If you were human, you'd marry me, wouldn't you?" he said. He felt mixed relief and anxiety over

Hilloa's response. He was glad he didn't have to go through with the Libyrarian initiation, but on the other hand, he was beginning to wonder if he was *ever* going to find a mate. He pushed the thoughts from his mind and concentrated on getting Zam hooked up to the yoke.

She rested her trunk on his shoulder as he led her to the field. When he got there, the other members of his workgroup were already there, picking up surface stones and loading them into a cart. They would be used for making new dwellings. Ock stood near a toolshed, cleaning off the blades of the plow. "Hey, Po," he said. "Back her around here so I can hitch this."

Po knew enough by now not to challenge Ock's right to tell him what to do. Still, inwardly he bristled at taking direction from another male. He quelled the reaction and helped Ock hitch the plow to Zam's harness. "Who wants the first ride?" said Ock as the others left off rock collecting and came to stand in a semicircle beside the elephant.

"I will," said Baris. "I missed my turn last time."

Anger rose in Po. Baris thought nothing of speaking up before the two women in the group and putting his own desires first. Po turned and fetched a rake from the shed, concentrating on the feel of the worn, wooden handle in his hands to calm himself. Of course, no one else thought there was anything improper in Baris's behavior and Po carefully controlled his reaction as Baris climbed up to sit behind Zam's head. The plow was a ten-foot-long beam of hard wood with two-foot-long blades protruding from it, and in the middle, a small platform and hand rails for the rider. Ock took up position there and flicked the reins, and Zam ambled on down the field, dragging Ock and the plow behind her. The rest of them followed in their wake, using

rakes and picks to break up stubborn clods of dirt, collecting more rocks, and spreading manure. Even here, they
traded off jobs. Every hour someone else took the plow, and
the person spreading fertilizer handed their bag to someone
else and started collecting rocks or wielding an adze.

It bothered Po to see women doing the kind of jobs only
men should have to do. But the hardest part was working
side by side with the Pri—with Selene herself, and not trying to do everything for her. For a while, he had feared
he'd be moved to another group, because she had to tell
him, time and again, to do his own work and not to try to
do hers as well. Now he could stand by, collecting rocks
while she sprinkled goat dung over the upturned soil,
though it still pained him.

It was a hot day. The days were always hot, and the
nights were cold. They were in one of the outlying fields
that now surrounded the Libyrinth. Closest to the Libyrinth
itself were the dwellings of the people for whom there was
no room inside the Libyrinth—mostly tents—though more
permanent structures were being built all the time. It
wouldn't be long before it looked like a proper town—after
the Ayorite fashion, anyway. Here, beyond the dwellings,
were the fields. They had worked very hard, digging up
rocks, plowing the ground, and mixing the soil with manure
to make it fertile. Water was always a problem. Wells were
dug, water was carried, irrigation ditches were dug. It was a
never-ending battle with the elements, trying to get this
land to produce food.

Po lifted the hoe and drove it down into the ground,
trying to break up a particularly resistant clump of earth.
Sweat dripped down his face and back and legs. The work
made him strong. And he was not the only one who was

aware of it. He glanced over and saw Arche's eyes upon him. Maybe she liked what she saw, he thought, and even as his spirits rose, one thought dashed them. She was a Libyrarian. She'd expect him to take the initiation, just as Hilloa had.

He moved down the field, wielding his hoe, turning up the soil and picking out rocks and throwing them into the wheelbarrow to be taken to the masonry. Princess Selene was ahead of him and she looked thirsty, but he resisted the urge to fetch her a cup of water from the pail. He'd been told that if she wanted a drink, she would get it herself.

What would her mother think, he wondered, if she could see her daughter now, sweating and dirt-smeared, her brown robe discarded in the heat, dressed now only in her small clothes, which stuck to her body as she sweated. Po swallowed and looked down and concentrated on his work. When this shift was over, he could find some private corner and gratify himself with the memory, but for now, such arousal was an inconvenience and—he saw Baris smirking at him—an embarrassment. Boys didn't flaunt their arousal around here. That much he'd noticed right away. Such a display was considered obscene by these people. *These people.* Which of *these* did he mean? The Singers? Yes, the Singers were definitely anti-sex. The Libyrarians and the Ayorites were less so, though still, compared to the Ilysian attitude they bordered on prudish.

They took a break and gathered around the water pail.

"This is almost the last field," said Selene. "Most crews are already planting. By the end of next week, we'll have the whole crop in."

"Thank the Tales," said Arche. "My back is killing me."

Po breathed in sharply at those words. An instant later, he checked himself. If Princess Selene had meant nothing with such words, then Arche, a Libyrarian, surely had no notion of their import.

"Oh, that won't be the end of it," Ock assured Arche. The Ayorites spearheaded the Libyrinth's agricultural efforts, being the most experienced in the matter. "Once the barley is planted, it'll have to be watered and kept free of weeds, and protected from birds and other animals. We'll still be out here at least three times a week, I'm sure. And then, if we're lucky, the harvest. You think your back hurts now. Just wait."

If they were lucky. Conversation died off for a moment as they all contemplated that. Po eyed the women and then turned to Baris. Under his breath, he said, "What happens if we're not lucky?"

"If we're not lucky?" Baris repeated his question out loud for everyone to hear. Po blushed and glared at him. Baris had something coming for that deliberate humiliation.

"If the crop fails, the settlement fails," said Selene. "With nothing to eat, we either starve or disperse to other areas. Most people will return to their villages. Those of us who have lived at the Libyrinth all our lives . . ." Arche and Selene exchanged glances. "Hopefully the villagers will help us."

Po shook his head.

"What?" said Ock.

Po turned to Selene. "Do you think Queen Thela might change her mind, and help us?"

"I doubt it. Now that she's closed the Ilysian border to us, my guess is that our perishing would please her very much."

Despite the water he'd just drunk, Po's mouth was dry. How was that possible? Queen Thela was a mother to every Ilysian here, and Selene was her biological daughter. He said the words under his breath, but they carried, "A mother would not let her children starve."

"You do not know my mother." Selene's rebuke was gentle, sad. She went on in a brisker tone. "And in the unlikely event that she offered us aid, it would be the end of the Libyrinth as an independent community."

"She only does what benefits her," said Arche. "She might feed us, but we'd have to give her control over all our research. We might just as well load up all the books and ship them to her palace."

As the others nodded in agreement, Po stared at the ground between his feet, shocked past all comprehension. Even when Haly had told him he could not go home again, it had not occurred to him that Queen Thela was their enemy. He still thought of himself as an Ilysian. He'd taken the banishment as a punishment. She was not pleased with them—that he could understand. But how could the mother of all Ilysies abandon her children to starvation, or usurp their efforts for her own gain?

"Yammon's tonsils, are you crying *again*?" said Baris. "Honestly, we should stick a spigot in you. You could irrigate the whole Plain of Ayor."

Po threw down his cup and launched himself at the fat Singer. Baris, taken by surprise, had only enough time to raise his hands. Po wrapped an arm around his neck and dragged him down to the ground. He backhanded the other boy across the face and while he was still reeling from that, straddled his chest. He raised his fist to hit him again.

Strong, wiry arms grabbed him and pulled him up and off Baris. He was held tight against a woman's chest. "No," said Selene, her breath hot in his ear. "We don't do that here."

Po's mortification somehow did not yet overwhelm his outrage. Baris had baited him. Not once but twice. He was asking for it. His voice low, barely a whisper, Po said, "But Your Majesty, he—"

"Don't call me that. I'm Selene. And it doesn't matter what he did. If males start acting like they do among each other in Ilysies, we have no hope of making this community work. It's the reason I advocated that you go home. We can't have this."

She didn't want him here? Po sagged, and she released him. Baris was on his feet again, dusting himself off. Arche stood between him and Po, but Po could still see the smug look of satisfaction on his face. There was no justice to this, no rhyme or reason to anything. Baris had baited Po, and Po had responded the way any self-respecting male would, but somehow Po, was the one now in disgrace. Worse than disgrace. The Princess herself had just told him she did not want him here. And Queen Thela . . .

He turned and knelt before Selene. "Your Majesty. I am at your command. I will leave the settlement if that is your wish."

"Oh for the sake of the Seven Tales, Po, stand up."

He had only angered her further. He threw himself forward and pressed his face into the dirt at her feet. He wanted to beg her forgiveness but he was afraid to say another word. He would await her displeasure, and when that was done, he'd leave. He'd just walk out into the plain. He'd just keep walking all the way to the Lian Mountains, and if he could not reenter Ilysies, he'd find a cave some-where and he'd become a recluse. Maybe he'd go into Ilysies anyway and let them kill him for a traitor. Why not let his blood bring bounty to the land? That was something, wasn't it? He was no good to anybody here. He couldn't get a woman. His life was over.

There was silence above him for a moment or two, and then he heard cups rattling in the basket and footsteps trudging off. He peeked out from beneath one arm. They'd all gone back to work. Including Princess Selene. She was hoeing not far away, her back to him, utterly ignoring him. He wasn't even worth punishing. He stood up, wiped off his face, took his hoe, and went back to work.

7

Ithalia

Po kept on working after his shift was over and the others had left. He let Ock take Zam back to the stable; he didn't even want the comfort of her presence. He lifted rocks and broke up the soil until his back ached and his arms felt numb. At last he stumbled wearily to the pump, standing in a muddy patch of bare ground between a tent where the farm equipment was kept and the corral for the wagons. As he washed himself, his mind was curiously blank. He watched the clear water run over his hands and arms, as if it were someone else to whom these things were happening.

"It must be hard," said a voice, "being the only Ilysian male at the Libyrinth."

Po started. He hadn't known anyone was there. It was near sunset and almost everyone was off to dinner. He turned to see a woman standing there, leaning upon an adze, one foot braced on its blade. She was dressed for work in the fields, with a scarf over her nose and mouth to protect her from the dust. She looked like she might be Ilysian. She had dark curly hair coated with dust, pale blue eyes and, from what he could see, an aquiline nose. Her eyes smiled at him, and he couldn't help but smile as well. He gave her a shrug.

She rested her adze against the side of a wagon and sat down on one of the large rocks arranged in a loose circle about the pump so people could rest while they took a drink of water. "You must feel like you're the only one who doesn't get it."

Po started. In astonishment, he nodded.

She gave him a wink, uncorked a flask, and brought it under her scarf to drink. "Sit down beside me and I'll let you in on a little secret." She patted the stone beside her.

Po did as she asked and she handed him the flask. "Thank you," he said, before drinking. The water was cool and sweet—as soothing to his thirst as her words were to his heart.

"Nobody gets it," she said.

Po blinked.

She nodded assurance. "It's true. Everybody here is struggling to let go of their cultural conditioning. And no one is comfortable with it. The ones who say they're fine are lying. The ones who seem the most together are the ones who are messed up the most inside."

Po absorbed this. Could it be true?

"Look at someone like Selene Tadamos, for instance.

For years, long before the Redemption, she claimed to cast her Ilysian heritage aside. But has she really?"

Po blushed and looked at his feet. "She's been very angry with me. I keep messing up."

"She's embarrassed because you make her feel the natural things that any Ilysian woman would feel around a male like you. What's your name, anyway?"

"Po," he told her.

"I'm Ithalia. My mother is Bea, Niacinth's daughter. We're from Dorax south of Uumphos." Her traditional manners set him at ease. He felt like he didn't have to pretend with her. Like he could just be himself. "How did you know I'm Ilysian?" he asked. Not everyone realized it just by looking at him.

"Well, granted, you don't have the classic features, though you're awfully cute. But I saw you earlier with Selene. Only an Ilysian male would prostrate himself like that. A pity your gesture wasn't appreciated."

Po nodded, feeling himself blush with mingled embarrassment and pleasure. Cute. He felt himself stir. "Pri—Selene is angry with me. I keep making mistakes. Now she—" His voice caught.

"Hey," said Ithalia, putting a hand on his shoulder. "Come here."

His throat thick with tears, Po let himself be drawn beside Ithalia. She put an arm around his shoulders and he sank against her, resting his head on her shoulder. "Is she being unfair to you? Tell me about it."

"She thinks I should leave, that I'm a disruption," said Po. "And she's right. I'm doing everything wrong. Fighting all the time . . . I would leave. But now I can't go back to Ilysies because the queen—" Po found himself at the end of words. He let himself cry and Ithalia held him closer, cradling his streaming face against her neck. The comfort of her arms and her soft bosom undid what remained of his restraint and he sobbed. "I don't know what to do."

"There, there," she said, stroking his hair. "There, there, it's all right. It's not your fault, Po. You are as the Mother made you. You've done nothing wrong."

"B-b-but Pri—Selene—"

"Selene is being very unfair to you. You make her uncomfortable because you remind her of her own heritage, which she rejects. It has nothing to do with you. Remember what I said, about the ones who seem to get it being the most troubled of all?"

Selene? "B-but she seems so perfect."

"No one is perfect, Po. Least of all Selene. Are you consorting with her?"

He shook his head. "No. She doesn't want—"

"Then she's even more of a fool than I thought."

Ithalia's words warmed Po through and through. He relaxed. He felt more comfortable and secure than he could remember being in a long, long time. Maybe even since he'd left his mother's village. His tears abated.

Ithalia gave him a squeeze, and released him. He sat up, rubbing at his eyes. He took in the tear-and-dirt-smudged shoulder of Ithalia's tunic. "I'm sorry."

"What, this?" she said. "It's nothing but a work tunic, made for sweat and tears. And you're entitled to cry. It's been a long time since I've had the opportunity to comfort a weeping male. It's nice. I don't think the men around here realize what they're depriving themselves and the women of, by being so stoic all the time. Sometimes, a good cry is just what you need."

Po smiled. Her words were like nectar. "So you don't think it makes me weak?"

Ithalia raised her eyebrows and looked him up and down. "I'd have to be blind to think you weak, Po."

Comforted, Po took a deep breath. "Thank you, Ithalia. I can't tell you how much— Thank you." Now if only he could be of some assistance to her. "You must be tired from working," he said. "Is there anything I can do for you?"

"I am tired," she said, "and sore." She stretched her arms above her head and arched her back, pushing her legs straight out in front of her. Above the scarf that still covered most of her face, her eyes glittered with sly amusement. "Would it be hopelessly regressive of me to ask for a foot rub?" she said.

"No! I was an adept's apprentice, back in Ilysies," he said. "I give really good foot rubs."

Her voice was full of warmth. "I bet you do."

First he fetched a bucket of water from the pump and washed her feet. Then he took her left foot in his lap and stroked it, heel to toe and ankle to pinky. Out of habit, he closed his eyes and focused his awareness in his hands. As usual, nothing happened, but her moans of appreciation more than compensated for his sense of failure. Here, too, as in their previous conversation, he did not need to be anything other than what he was. He found a knot just below her instep, in a spot that he knew from his training corresponded with her heart. He worked on it, gently unwinding the tense muscle.

She sighed. "You are a wonder."

Pleasure brought a glow to his cheeks and an ache to his groin. He kept his focus on his breath and took her other foot in his lap and repeated the process. There was no need for him to act on his desire, no nerve-wracking question of making the first move. He could rest comfortably in the knowledge that she was aware of her effect on him and would take the next step if she so desired.

When he had finished, she embraced him. "That was wonderful. I must go now, Po. But we will meet again soon, I hope."

Dizzy from her touch, Po nodded. It wasn't until she'd gone that he thought to ask her where, or when.

The next day Po saw Ithalia in the "copytorium," which was really the dining hall, when it was being used for meals. They were making copies of some of the books in order to share them with the neighboring villages.

He had been copying for about an hour or so but his hand, unused to such extended periods of writing, cramped up and he switched to working the paper press, squeezing the water from the mixture of palm-glow and silverleaf pulp they used to make paper, and then setting the sheets, still encased in their screens, upon the rack to dry. It was fairly monotonous work, and he stared at the few people in the room, their heads bent over their work. Between the squeak of the press, he could hear the scratching of their pens.

Ithalia entered the room just as Po had expelled the last of the water from a new sheet. She stood at the top of the broad, shallow stairs that led from the hallway and surveyed the room. Their eyes met. Po conquered his nervousness and smiled at her.

Ithalia still wore her field clothes, with her scarf drawn over her nose and mouth to protect her lungs from the dust, but her black hair was clean and it hung loose, gleaming in the light from the electric light fixtures above. She was so beautiful—tall and slender in the classic Ilysian way. The gleam in her eye, the confident way she stood with one hand on her hip and eyed him up and down made his whole body rush with pleasure, that pleasure then sharpening, sweetening, intensifying almost painfully.

He barely remembered to remove the sheet from the press before it dried and was ruined. When he looked up again from that task, she had taken a seat at one of the tables and was copying; though she glanced up, caught him staring at her, and winked.

Po swallowed against the dryness in his mouth. Should he abandon the press and go speak with her? No. If she wished to talk to him, she would have done so. Then why hadn't she? Yesterday, she had seemed interested in him, and he had hoped . . . Perhaps she had changed her mind. But she glanced at him frequently, with looks that he would have to be blind to misinterpret. It was a game. She was teasing him to prolong their dance of seduction. He smiled back at her and turned, tugging at his robe in such a way that she would be able to see his desire for her.

Po returned to his work, warmed by her regard. He could hear the scratch of her pen and it seemed to him that the creak of the press as he turned it made a nice steady accompaniment to the sound. There were only a few other people working in here this afternoon. He almost felt as if they were alone together.

Suddenly he heard her shout, and then a clatter. She had jumped up, knocking over her chair. Now she ran toward him, her eyes wide. "What are they?" She pointed along the opposite wall, where Po saw a group of Nods.

"It's all right," he told her, putting his arms around her and positioning himself between her and the perceived danger. "They won't harm us."

Ithalia huddled close to him. He wondered if they had truly unnerved her, or if this was more of her game. But then, he felt her tremble. Po's heart thumped as he held her close. She had sought physical protection from him. He couldn't ever remember feeling so proud. It didn't matter that the danger was nonexistent. She didn't know that. "Have you not seen a Nod before?" he asked her.

She shook her head. Evidently, she had not spent much time inside the Libyrinth itself. Nods were a shock to those who had not been born at the Libyrinth, though one grew accustomed to them quickly enough. Little was known about them, even by the Libyrarians. In fact, until the Redemption the Libyrarians had been unaware that there was more than one Nod.

The little group of them clustered together in an alcove near the steps. They appeared to be climbing on one another, but for what purpose he had no idea. The other transcribers paused in their activity and watched as a lot of unsettling squeaks and twitters emanated from the tight ball of little red bodies.

"What *are* they?" Ithalia whispered, beside him.

No one really knew, Po realized. Even the Libyrarians, who were most accustomed do them, did not really know or understand what the Nods were.

At last the knot of Nods broke apart. He couldn't be sure, but there seemed to be more of them now. He knew he saw one Nod go off with an arm that had previously belonged to another, though neither Nod was lacking any appendages. He felt a shudder coming on and he stifled it for Ithalia's sake. As a male he was expected to be emotional, but also courageous where physical danger was concerned. Though it was obvious they were in no real danger and never had been. The Nods dispersed and everyone else went back to their work.

"So strange," said Ithalia, who had regained her composure.

Po nodded agreement.

"Is there anyplace you have to be right now, Po?" asked Ithalia as they left. "I find I do not wish to be alone."

Po swallowed. He'd been hoping for an invitation of this sort. "No," he said. "My time is discretionary this afternoon, until dinnertime."

Ithalia took his hand.

"Where are we going?" he asked.

"To my tent."

They left through the stableyard entrance, Zam lifting her trunk over her stall in question as they passed. He wanted to stop and pet her, say hello, but Ithalia had him by the hand and had no intention of stopping. Suddenly Po felt childish for the impulse.

They walked to the center of town through the maze of tents and impromptu sheds that pretty much made up the community. At last she held up the flap of a small, dun-colored tent and gestured him inside.

Ithalia's tent was dim, hot, and stuffy at midday, but it had rugs to lie upon; and most important of all, it was empty. He looked about in the dim light, searching for an ewer of wine or water to offer her, but he found none. There was little here but piles of rugs, and over in the corner, a satchel hanging from a tent pole.

Ithalia sat down on one of the piles of rugs and craned

her neck this way and that, rubbing at the junction of her neck and shoulder, as if it pained her.

"Sore neck?" he asked her, standing close.

She nodded. "It's all this damn farm work. Still, I suppose it can't be helped."

"I can help," he said, and was shocked at his own boldness.

The edges of her scarf rose as her smile, unseen, made her high cheekbones rise and nearly eclipse her laughing eyes. She lifted her hair.

Po knelt behind her and ran his hands up and down her shoulders, up and down her back. He began to work at the knotted muscles at the juncture of her neck and shoulders, eliciting a groan of appreciation. It felt so good to do this for her.

She leaned back so that her head rested against his chest, and she peered up at him. Her face was relaxed, suffused with pleasure. He could tell. It made him feel like everything was going to be all right now. Like he was where he was supposed to be, finally, doing what he was supposed to do.

She let one hand drop, and ran it up the back of his thigh. "My squadron sisters won't be back for another couple of hours."

Her touch made him stir. Made him want to offer himself to her. And wasn't that just what she was suggesting? "Are you . . . do you wish . . ."

She blinked once, slow and lazy. Her hand squeezed the back of his thigh. She turned and lifted her other hand to his neck, where she stroked up and down with the back of her index finger. "You're a fine male, Po. It's too bad those

Libyrinth girls don't know what to do with you. Too bad
for them, anyway. But I do."

Po's breath was shallow, unsteady. He licked his lips.
Desire filled him. He could fall into her eyes for days and
days and never come out, and that would be okay. He knew
what she expected from him and it was something he was
only too willing to give. He wouldn't have to worry, for
once, if what he was doing was okay. He could just relax.
He smiled, and bent forward, and kissed her through her
scarf. "It would be my privilege to offer myself to you,
Ithalia," he said, hardly able to believe that this was finally
happening.

She stood and he reached for her scarf, to remove it so
he could kiss her again, properly, but she stopped him. She
turned him so his back was to her, her hands resting upon
his shoulders. "Be still a moment, Po. You will enjoy this."

He heard a rustle of cloth, and then her scarf, silken soft
and somewhat dusty, smelling like the field and like
Ithalia herself, settled over his eyes, blocking out the light.
Ah, she wanted him blindfolded. He smiled. Even an inex-
perienced calf like himself had heard of this game. By taking
away one sense, the others became sharper, and a male is
more biddable and enduring when he must rely on touch,
taste, and sound. Enduring—that reminded him of something. "Ithalia."

"Yes, my Po?" She had taken the hem of his robe and
was lifting it up, pushing the coarse fabric up his thighs.
Po gasped. His phallus leaped with eagerness at the sensation. "Easy, my calf."

"That's just it, Ithalia. I . . . I'm—"

She gave a low, satisfied chuckle. He relaxed even before

she uttered the next words. "A virgin? I had only dared hope."

He blushed brighter. "I might—I wish to please you, Ithalia."

She held him to her, her breasts full against his chest, and then she kissed him on the lips. She tasted like barley and . . . licorice. She guided him down onto the rugs. "You please me, Po. Your innocence pleases me. Your earnestness pleases me." She reached down, where he was aflame. "Your eagerness and your desire are all that I ask of you."

Po gave a long sigh, and relaxed into her touch.

He fell asleep in Ithalia's arms, but when he awoke, he was alone. He pulled the blindfold off and looked around him. The tent was empty.

8

The Bloom

For the rest of that day and all of the next, Po alternated between blissful satisfaction and gnawing anxiety. The simple fact of no longer being a virgin was such a relief that it alone nearly crowded out all other considerations. At the time and immediately afterward, Ithalia had given him every indication that she, too, was pleased with his performance.

But then why did she leave before he awoke? Why had he not seen her since? Women were kind. It was not unusual for a woman who was disappointed in her consort to avoid him, rather than hurt his feelings with a direct rejection. Even more commonly, a female relative or friend would act as go-between, informing the unlucky man that his company was no longer desired.

As Po walked toward the Redeemer's office for book study, he saw Vorain, a former captain in the Ilysian army and childhood friend of Princess Selene, walking toward him. He tensed. Was she approaching him with a message from Ithalia? His stomach knotted.

"Morning, bull calf," said Vorain cheerfully. Then she caught herself. "I'm sorry. Po. Your name is Po, right?"

His mouth too dry for words, Po nodded.

"Right. Listen, don't tell Selene I called you that, all right? I'm trying, you know?"

He nodded again. "Of course," he managed.

"Anyway, I've just come from mucking out the goat pen and I reek. I've got to change before book study. In that tiny room, we'll all faint from the fumes if I don't. So please give my respects to everyone, and my apologies, and I'll get there as soon as I can. Okay?"

Po's chest expanded with relief. "That's all?"

Vorain cocked her head at him. "Yeah. That's it."

Po grinned. "Okay. I'll tell them. Thanks!"

Vorain found his reaction funny, but she nodded kindly as he ran off.

Six months ago, on the day that Haly stood before the gates of the Libyrinth and declared the ground rules, she'd had them all count off, one after another, in a long, long line. It had taken an hour and a half and they'd had to go up to five hundred before starting over at one, but ever since then, thirty-threes had met with thirty-threes, ninety-eights with ninety-eights, and so on, for the purpose of studying *The Book of the Night*. Po was a forty-seven, and so was the Redeemer. Out of consideration for her busy schedule, they met in her office. Every week she, Po, Vorain, Mara, Jess, Tob, and Vinnais gathered to read from and discuss *The Book of the Night*. Or to argue, more often than not.

Where Po came from, these kinds of conversations did not tend to occur so openly. Only intimates engaged in direct confrontation, as a rule. Though among themselves males were violently confrontational, that itself was the main feature of their inferior intellectual status. Certainly, a male would not be included in a discussion of ideas among women.

When he arrived at the Redeemer's office, most of the others were already gathered. Haly caught his eye and smiled at him. He fought his impulse to lower his eyes and he smiled back at her. Haly scanned the group. "Where is Vorain?"

"She's running late, Redeemer," said Po, surprising himself and the others by directly answering the question. "She said for us to start without her."

Haly nodded. "Very well. Po, will you read today's selection, pages forty-five and forty-six?"

Because he rarely participated in the discussion, Haly made sure that Po was always the one to read aloud from *The Book of the Night*. He stood and opened his copy to the specified section.

"She tells me that once this whole world was green. Not just in Ilysies or the other river valleys, but everywhere. Imagine the entire Plain of Ayor an unbroken stretch of green grass and wildflowers. It must have been so beautiful. I ask her why it is dry now, why the tallgrass is yellow and the great stands of silverleaf trees grow smaller every year.

"She tells me that she and her friends broke this world. 'It was our toy,' she says. 'We thought we could remake it to suit ourselves, but we are not engineers. We were never supposed to be able to do that in the first place, and we damaged the structures that make life here possible.

" 'It will get worse,' she says. 'Every year brings this place closer to what it came from. If you do not kill each other off, if you live long enough, this world will continue to erode and your people will starve. You know what that's like. You must teach them to refresh it for themselves.'

" 'But how?' I ask her. 'We do not even know how to make Eggs and you will not tell me.'

" 'Eggs! Enough about Eggs, Theselaides. Eggs are completely beside the point. You must stop taking everything so literally. Forget about Eggs. Only imagination can save you.' "

Po stopped. "That's the end of the entry," he said.

He looked at the others, searching their faces. All of them seemed to be as transported as he was by the image of the Plain of Ayor covered in green. "If what Endymion said is true—" Tob started, but Jess interrupted him before he could finish.

"If the land was green once, then it could be green again."

"She said they damaged the structures that make life here possible," said Vinnais. "What does that mean?"

"It implies that whatever was here to begin with was lifeless by nature, and something was done to it to support life," noted Jess.

Haly and several others nodded. "I have read about terraforming," said Haly. "The idea is that you can take a barren rock floating in space, and make of it a lush world full of life."

"Nothing grows in rock," said Vinnais. "It's impossible."

"When it comes to the Ancients, I should think we'd

all know better by now than to expect them to stop at what is possible," said Haly.

"Redeemer, do you think the Ancients created this world out of an asteroid?" asked Mara.

"I don't know."

"How do we know she was telling him the truth?" said Tob. "How do we know the green world is not a lie?"

Mara said, "We Ayorites have a story about a time when the whole of the Plain of Ayor was green. It is said that there was a special flower that grew in rock, which made all the other plants grow. But then one day the lion ate them all and since then, the land has been brown and dry, just like the lion's pelt."

At this Po started. He opened his mouth, then changed his mind. "Po," said Haly. "What? What were you about to say?"

He stared at her wide-eyed. He bit his lip, staring at the rest of them. "It's nothing. It's just a story an old man told me once. I'm sure it's not important."

"Let us decide that, Po," said Haly.

"Yeah, let us decide," added Mara.

Po took a deep breath. "Once, there were only women, and all the world was as green as a lowland Ilysian barley farm in spring. The reason the land was so lush was that a flower called the Lion's Bloom gave off a pollen that fertilized everything it touched. These flowers grew everywhere; but one day, they fell in love with the women, and they dug themselves out of the ground and turned into men. Without the Lion's Bloom to keep the land fertile, it became dry and barren. According to this story, the reason Ilysies is still green is because every year a man is sacrificed, and that returns the generative properties he possessed as a plant back to the land."

When he finished, everyone was silent for a moment, thinking it over. "Sacrificed?" said Mara.

Po nodded. Didn't they know of this?

Vorain blushed fiercely; Vinnais and Tob looked uncomfortable; and Haly, Mara, and Jess exchanged a look that Po could not quite decipher. At length, Haly said, "Thank you, Po. You've given us all a lot to think about."

Would Haly decide to adopt the ritual of sacrifice in order to make the land fertile here? She caught his look. "I do not think we want to take the story too literally," she said. "But there are some remarkable similarities between this tale and Mara's. If, as has been suggested, this world was once an asteroid, and underwent terra-forming, then this Lion's Bloom may be a reference to that. For next week, everyone scour their copies of *The Book of the Night* for any references to terra-forming, the lion, flowers, or the Lion's Bloom." She stood. "Thank you all again, and have a good week."

For the rest of the day, Po was aglow with the knowledge that he'd contributed something the Redeemer felt was useful. The idea of turning the barren plain fertile captivated his imagination, as it did the rest of those who had been present at the meeting, and by dinnertime, the entire dining hall was buzzing with the news.

Po scanned the room, searching for Ithalia. It was silly, because if she was here and she didn't approach him, what was he going to do? Just because he'd repeated an old goat's tale to the Redeemer and it had turned out to be useful didn't mean he was about to start pressing his company on women. But there was no sign of her, at any rate.

"Po!"

It was Hilloa, waving him over to where she sat with her friends. He smiled and joined them. It was nice to talk with them now, without the pressure of trying to impress them as a potential consort. They were full of questions about the book discussion, and about the Ilysian practice of male sacrifice.

"It's just once a year," he explained to them. That didn't seem to make them feel better about it. "And the male is showered with luxuries for the whole year leading up to it."

"Like a goat fattened for slaughter," said Hilloa.

"Exactly!" said Po.

They all stared at him. Hilloa said, "What about this idea of terra-forming?"

"I've been reading that section," said Bethe. "And these books, too." She pointed to the stack at her elbow. "Most of the references anybody's found to the practice are fictional, but this"—she lifted a thick manual entitled *Guidelines and Methodologies for the Settlement of Mars*—"is not. It's proof that it's been done before."

"But what did she mean when she said this world needs to be renewed?"

"Well, sacrifice is a way of renewing the land," Po surprised himself by offering.

Hilloa rolled her eyes. "Come on, Po. You don't really believe that, do you?"

If it wasn't true, then all those men died for no reason. It had to be true. But he said, "Of course not."

"Come on," said Jaen. "Siblea is giving a recital on nano-technology in the Great Hall. If we dawdle, we'll miss the beginning."

They all got up. Hilloa turned to him. "Are you coming?"

He hesitated. It was nice to be asked. But he hated Siblea, and he had no interest in a long, boring song about molecular machines and, he suspected, neither would Ithalia. If he set off for the infirmary now, he'd be passing through the Ilysian quarter at just the time that most women hung out by their fires, drinking and chatting. Maybe he would "accidentally" run into her. "Um. No, thank you. But . . . thanks for asking."

9

Village Life

He was nearly at the infirmary, on the very outskirts of the Ilysian section of Tent Town, when he felt a hand on his shoulder. "Hey, cute boy, got a minute for an old soldier?"

His heart, which had been steadily sinking as he walked through the town and found no sign of Ithalia, rose up and he turned, grinning.

It was dark. They were in a little space between tents and there was only enough light to catch the gleam of her eye and the white of her teeth, but it was her. He knew by her voice and her fragrance. "Ithalia."

"I'm sorry I've been scarce, calfling. I'm on the crew for the windmill project and they've got us working around the clock. I don't have much time, but I didn't want you to think I'd thrown you over."

Her arms encircled his waist and he felt wrapped in glory. His doubts and fears seemed so silly now. How foolish of him to doubt the generosity of a universe that held one such as Ithalia in it, and which gifted him with her regard. He hugged her back and she kissed him. The taste of her made his head swim. He was aflame for her. He stroked her back and held her close, one hand twined in her hair. She shifted, adjusting their positions to savor the full extent of his desire. She took his hand from her back and eased it between them, and down. "Quick now, my love, but later, after your work is done, come to my tent again, and we will take our time with each other."

When Po entered the infirmary, he felt as if the joy burning inside him must overshadow even the electric lights overhead. He'd only felt this way once before in his life, at the Redemption. Now it all came back to him, and he wondered how he could have forgotten. There was nothing between himself and everything he might ever want in the world. All obstacles had been removed by the simple expedient of him being happy with who he already was. It was easy because it was now a demonstrated fact that he was a perfectly good thing to be. Better than good— wonderful. Everything that had once seemed difficult was now simple.

Burke looked up and saw him. Her eyes widened in surprise and then she answered his grin with her own. "Hello, Po."

When he took Yolle's feet in his hands and prepared to

attempt kinesiology, he thought, *Just try. That's all you have to do.*

He breathed with her. For a long time, that was all he did. When his mind drifted, he returned his attention to their breath, and he visualized his hands merging with her feet.

Something squeezed his abdomen. The pressure made it hard for him to breathe. At the same time, a dull ache throbbed just below his rib cage. It was her pain and he fought the impulse to back off from it, to break contact with Yolle. He kept breathing with her, the slow, labored breaths now in keeping with the pressure he felt, as if heavy weights pressed down on his rib cage and belly. To his mind's eye came an image of sickly yellow flowers covering an ancient tree. The flowers twined around the trunk and branches of the tree and squeezed, choking the life out of it. The leaves of the tree turned brown and fell to the ground. Its limbs withered.

Po searched for something to kill the vine, but the ground around the tree was bare. There was nothing. He reached out and grasped the vine. When he tried to pull it off the tree, the bark came away with it and hot red pain lanced through them. He stopped. He went back to the breath again, and just sat, observing. Nothing else came.

From a distance, he felt something on his shoulder, a bird that was resting there. It chirped. "Po. Po. Po." All at once the bird grew, and the tree and the vine faded away, and with them the pain. Po blinked. He was in the infirmary tent, kneeling at Yolle's feet, and Burke stood over him. Behind her, through the open doorway of the infirmary tent, the sky was the deep blue of early dawn. "Po," she said. "Are you all right?"

Po took a deep breath and released Yolle's feet. He looked at her. She watched him, a faint smile on her face. "You did it," she said.

He shook his head. "I . . . I couldn't . . . There's nothing."

"I know that," she said, "but you were with me."

Burke looked between the two of them. "Did you—?"

"Yes," said Yolle.

The full realization hit him. He had performed kinesiology. His lips curved in a smile at the knowledge, and he quickly suppressed it. His abilities had manifested at last, but there was still no cure for Yolle.

She reached for him and he gave her his hand. "Be glad. You will be able to help many, many people."

"You seemed to be in a trance," said Burke. "I didn't want to disturb you. I lay down and I must have fallen asleep. Then I heard you cry out."

That was when he had tried to destroy the little lion inside.

"I hurt you," said Po. "I'm sorry."

Yolle shook her head. "Don't worry about that."

Po blinked. His surroundings wobbled. Sudden exhaustion swept over him like an incoming tide. He sat down abruptly. Outside, the community began to stir. Ithalia. She'd been waiting for him. He hadn't come. He'd better find her and explain. He struggled to get to his feet.

Burke took his arm and steadied him. "Over here," she said, steering him toward the cot next to Yolle's.

Po shook his head. "I have to find Ithalia. She was waiting. I don't want her to think I stayed away on purpose."

"Whoever that is, you can tell her later," said Burke. "You're dead on your feet. Lie down."

He didn't have the wherewithal to resist her. He sat on the bed and she brought him a cup of water. He drank it.

"I don't know much about kinesiology," said Burke, "but Ykobos did tell me how physically taxing it can be. This was your first time, and you were in a trance for hours. I don't think you're supposed to try to do so much right off the bat. Lie down. Get some rest. I'll send word to Selene that you're missing your work shift this morning, and why."

Po wanted to resist. He wanted to go find Ithalia, to tell her the good news and to make sure she understood why he hadn't come to her. But somehow, he wound up lying on his side, and Burke pulled a blanket over him. He let his eyes close.

When he woke, it was late afternoon. Po scrambled up, straightened his disheveled robe, and made for the door. He would like to bathe before seeking Ithalia out, but he did not want to delay his explanation a moment longer than he already had.

"Po," said Burke, looking up from a book she was reading. "Why are you rushing off?"

He stopped in the doorway. "I had an appointment with my . . . my consort last night." Was it okay to refer to Ithalia as his consort? That's what she was, right? "I have to find her and explain what happened."

"You have a . . . girlfriend now?"

Po hesitated. "I don't know if I'd use that term. . . ."

Burke laughed. "Never mind. Go to her. I told your afternoon work-shift members what happened and that you are recuperating. You're free from any duties today."

"Thank you."

She smiled. "Don't worry. I'm going to be getting a lot of work out of you now."

His chest expanded with a warm glow. This was what it felt like to be useful. He ran out in search of Ithalia.

And he found her just outside her tent. She had her back to him and she was mending an adze. "Ithalia," he called, running up to her. "I'm so sorry about last night, Ithalia. I . . . Something happened. My kinesthetic sense came in!"

She turned. Once again, she wore the scarf over her face. She looked at him blankly for a moment and then her cheeks rose in a smile. What did her mouth look like when she did that? "Ah. Is that why—"

"Why I didn't come last night? Yes. I went into a trance. I lost track of the time. When I came out of it, it was almost dawn and I wanted to come to you right away, but Burke made me lie down and I fell asleep and I slept all the way through until right now." He dropped to his knees. "Ithalia, I am so sorry."

She tilted her head and looked down at him, fondness shining in her eyes. "Oh, Po. If that is why you did not come to me last night, then do not give it another thought. And let me be among the first to congratulate you. You really are a most remarkable male." She reached down and took his arm. "An adept, even a male one, should not kneel to a simple soldier. Not for such cause as this."

For the first time, Po felt something other than unadulterated joy at the arrival of his kinesthetic sense. Was this going to change things with Ithalia? They'd only just gotten started. "I . . . I don't want to be treated any differently," he said. "I'm still your . . . I mean . . . am I your consort?"

She pulled him to her and held him close. Her breath was warm against his ear. "Of course. Come inside, and I'll show you."

She led him inside the tent. As before, she turned him so his back was to her, and she wrapped her scarf over his eyes. He wanted to look at her. He wanted to see her face when they made love. But if this was her wish . . .

Afterward, they lay in the waning light of late afternoon. Ithalia had her back to him. He held her against him. He stroked her hair, and trailed his fingers over her shoulder and down her arm. "My hands know you better than my eyes do," he said.

"Do you wonder why I blindfold you?"

"Because that is the way of your desire."

"It's not that."

Po bent his head and kissed her shoulder. "It's not my place to question you."

"My brother struck my sister. I was six years old. My mother, sisters, and I were all branded."

Despite the warmth of her body beside his, he felt cold. He just managed not to recoil from her. His heart pounded. The air, which a moment ago was perfumed with the scent of their desire, now smelled sour. Her body, a delight to him, was now a trap. He had not known.

She had made sure he did not know. She kept her face hidden. He should have known. Why would she cover her face when she was in the Libyrinth, unless it were to hide the evidence of her shame?

He became aware that he had frozen, his hand motionless on her arm, and she was very quiet. Awkwardly, he took his hand away from her arm and rolled onto his back.

She sat up. The blindfold let in enough light that he

could see that she faced him, though he could not make out the features of her face. "I'm sorry," she said, her voice thick. "I tricked you."

He wished he didn't know. "Why did you tell me?"

"Because . . . I really love you, Po. And I won't keep you under false pretenses."

He didn't know what to do. Part of him wanted to jump up and run from the tent, and do what he could to salvage his reputation. The other part ached at the tremor in her voice and wanted nothing more than to hold her, comfort her, and tell her he would gladly ruin himself if it meant they could be together.

Perhaps it was his nascent kinesthetic sense asserting itself, but as he lay there, pinned between those two possibilities, he felt something slicing through his heart from within. As each unacceptable alternative stretched his heart in opposite directions, it seemed to part, and light poured out of it. And the name of this light was . . . "It doesn't matter," he said.

The sudden realization forced him to sit up and grab her hands. "It doesn't matter, Ithalia! We're not in Ilysies. No one here cares."

"No?"

"No! This is the whole point of this place! You were six. It had nothing to do with you but you were punished anyway. That's how it's done and it may be what's right in Ilysies, but it doesn't have to be that way here. What matters here is you. What kind of person you are. You are a hard worker, a strong, caring woman. No one here cares about a brand on your face and what it might mean in another country. A country that has disowned us, anyway."

"You don't care?"

Po took a moment to really think about it. He saw her point. It might be academic to non-Ilysians, but he was most definitely Ilysian and demonstrably stuck in his ways. At home he'd have been appalled, not least because of the ramifications for his future. But even there, would it really change how he felt about Ithalia? The answer came immediately. No. For the first time, he understood why Dexter had been willing to ruin himself for Carys in the famous novel, *The Fledgling*. Love, when it was real, could not be abrogated, not even by shame. But he was not ashamed of Ithalia. Not here. Some of the other Ilysian women here might look askance at them, but he didn't care. "Not so long as you're at my side. It doesn't matter to me." He raised his hand to remove the blindfold.

"No," she said. "I'm not ready."

"I don't care, Ithalia. I love you. I know your beauty. The mark cannot erase it from my heart. It doesn't matter."

She brought his arm down and around to her hip and she leaned in and kissed him. "But it matters to me. It is one thing for you to know. But I cannot make love with you when you can see it. I just can't."

He nodded, and acquiesced.

Night had come. Ithalia lay with her head resting on his stomach, tapping her own belly. "I grew up in a little village in the highlands," she said. "Townsfolk would say it was a backward place. Despite what you might think, I miss it. Life there was simple, slow. Here, it seems like we are always rushing, and just barely keeping up with what needs to be done."

Po nodded. "I was born in a village like that, too, a dusty little hamlet in the hills. Most of the residents were vintners. I left when I was eight. I was apprenticed to the adept of the palace."

Ithalia rolled to her side so she could look at him. She'd taken the blindfold off him and now wore it over her nose and mouth once more. She raised an eyebrow. "You must have been very talented."

Po shrugged. "Connected, more like. Ymin Ykobos is my mother's cousin. There was . . . my mother felt she needed to get me out of the village." He did not elaborate.

She looked at him in silence. It was not necessary for her to point out that she had shared the most private, most compromising secret there could be with him. The fact of it, and the fact that he owed her some sort of confidence in return, was a living presence between them.

Po had never told anybody about what had happened in the village that led to his leaving. But he could tell her. She had trusted him.

"My mother's family was not prosperous, and she was a youngest daughter. She lived with her eldest sister and helped work her land, and helped with the household, but finding a consort for her was nobody's priority but her own."

"What about your aunt? Did she have a male?"

"Yes, but she wouldn't share him."

Ithalia drew her head back.

Po acknowledged her surprise. "I know. But Aunt Minerva was in love with Valce, and she was possessive. She kept him locked up when she was away. And she had told him that she would kill him if he slept with anyone but herself."

"That's most unusual."

Po nodded. "In a larger, more prosperous family, it would not have been tolerated. But my grandmother and great-grandmother were dead. Minerva was in charge and there was nothing anyone could do.

"Our town had several males with no fixed household. They prowled the streets hoping to attract the interest of single women."

"I know how village billys are."

Of course she did. Everyone knew. Po blushed, but the urge to confess was too strong. "It was one of these creatures that my mother brought to her bed, and her disappointment at being delivered of a son, which led to his expulsion. They didn't tell me. I didn't know who my sire was, and I wasn't supposed to know. But on the night of the King's Crowning I stayed out to watch the dance. On my way home I turned a corner and found two males squaring off against each other in an alley."

"Typical," said Ithalia.

Po nodded. "Yes. They were obviously of mating age and dressed to draw attention to their masculine charms."

Ithalia grinned. "Those codpieces."

"Oh, I know. Do they really think anyone believes their boasts?"

"It must work with some women or they wouldn't do it," said Ithalia.

"Anyway, they were all done up for the festival, so you can imagine. And they'd gotten into some wine and they were drunk, and now they were fighting."

"I suppose they usually kill each other off before they have a chance to get old and lose their virility, which may be a blessing in disguise. Have you ever seen an old billy in a gauze shirt, trying to hide the slackening of his torso? Sad. Go on."

"Well, these billys were in their prime."

"You were in danger."

He nodded. "I knew a boy, the son of my neighbor. Village billys caught him one night and killed him."

Ithalia shook her head. "A shame."

"Anyway, I tried to sneak away but one of them spotted me. He was whipcord lean, partly due to the excessive exercise, and partly due to hunger, I'm sure. He had black eyes and a fine hawk nose. The other one was bigger, broader, but he had green eyes and the bridge of his nose was flat for an Ilysian. He said, 'Look, a kid. Let's not waste ourselves fighting each other; let's play with him instead.' I started to run. Behind me I heard him shout, 'Boy!'

"They overtook me easily, the larger of the two tackling me and knocking me facedown in the dirt. I hit my nose and the fizzing pain scattered my thoughts. The next thing I knew this billy straddled my back, lifted my head, and slammed it into the ground again. I tried to wriggle free but the man was too heavy.

"I thought he was going to kill me, and he would have, but then, we all heard a woman's voice say, 'What are you men doing?' It was the town magistrate.

"The big male got off me. I got to my feet and backed away from the men. They both tried to pretend nothing was going on.

"Magistrate Milinas was in middle age, a woman in her prime. She was solid and stolid with a phlegmatic personality that was well suited to her job of keeping order.

" 'This boy stole my coin,' said the big male. 'I was trying to get it back.'

" 'A likely story,' Magistrate Milinas said. She looked at the other man. 'And you, Nev, what are you doing here?'

" 'I was helping my friend,' he said.

" 'Your friend,' she said, then laughed. 'You two are as much friends as I'm the queen of Ilysies. You meant this boy harm, both of you, and don't think you're fooling anyone.' Then she turned to me, and I was afraid I was in trouble, but she just said, 'Run along home, Po. Don't you know better than to wander around out here alone at night? You're asking for trouble.'

"As I turned and ran, I heard her say to the man with the flat nose, 'For shame, Chal. He's your own son.' "

Ithalia's eyes went wide. "He was your father."

Po nodded. "That's how I got this frog face. He must have been part Ayorite. Anyway, after that my mother and my aunts decided it wasn't safe for me to stay in the village. And I think they knew that with my resemblance to my sire, I wouldn't have much chance of getting a decent consortship there. So they wrote to cousin Ymin, and she brought me to the palace."

Ithalia stroked the side of his face. "I'm glad. If you hadn't been—even if you had survived—you wouldn't be here now and we'd never have met."

He smiled and she drew him into her arms. They rested together as night deepened and the town grew quiet around them.

10

Ithalia's Brand

O ur food stores will last us another six weeks, at the outside," said Gyneth, his head bent over a ledger book.

"Then we just may manage," said Ock. "The first crops should be ready in one month's time."

Haly sighed and swirled the cooling tea in her cup. The three of them were in her office, strategizing. "Two weeks is not a lot of margin for error."

"But it's better than no margin at all," said Ock.

Haly supposed that was true. "I wish we could find out something more definite about this terra-forming business."

"Everyone is researching it like mad," said Gyneth. "If

it's a real possibility, someone will uncover something soon."

Ock opened his mouth to say something but was interrupted by a knock on the door. "I'm sorry," said Haly. "That'll be the first arrivals for book study. Anyway, it sounds like we're on track, as best as can be."

She rose, and they followed suit. When Gyneth opened the door, they were all taken aback to see Po standing there. "Po," said Haly. "You knocked."

Inwardly she cringed at her words. The last thing she wanted to do was embarrass him, especially in front of two other men, but again, Po surprised her. He grinned. "I thought I'd see if I could help you with the chairs, Redeemer."

Haly took a good look at him. He'd changed since she'd seen him last. He stood straighter, and he looked her in the eye. Seven Tales, he even acknowledged Gyneth and Ock with a polite nod for each. She returned his smile and said, "Thank you, that's very thoughtful. Come on in."

The other two left and Haly left the door open for the other arrivals as she and Po arranged chairs in a circle for the meeting. "Burke told me that you've developed your kinesthetic sense," she said.

He blushed at this, but appeared more pleased than shy. "Yes."

"She's keeping you busy now, I imagine."

He nodded. "I don't mind. So long as I still have time for my consort."

She leaned on the back of the chair she had just positioned and stared at him. "Your consort?"

He nodded again, looking even more pleased, if that

was possible. "Or I guess you could say 'girlfriend.' It's the same thing here, right?"

She wasn't sure if it was or not. But while she mulled over a response, he went on.

"That's why my sense came in. I'm not a virgin anymore. And it's not just a casual thing, either. She loves me." He gave a little bounce. "We're in love."

"You going on about your lady friend again, Po?" said Tob, walking in and helping himself to a cup of tea. Tob was a village Ayorite just a year or two older than Po.

Haly tensed in anticipation of Po's reaction, and was floored when he simply shrugged and said, "You're just jealous."

"I might be," said Tob, "if I were ever to actually see her. When are you going to bring Ithalia to the group and introduce her?"

"She's got her own work to do, Tob. Don't worry, you'll meet her one of these days."

Ithalia . . . It was a common name among the women of Ilysies. Off the top of her head, Haly could think of five Ithalias living in the community. "She's Ilysian, then."

Po shook his head. His smile was broad. He practically glowed. "Not anymore. We're both Libyrarians now."

Po rested against Ithalia, drowsy in the aftermath of lovemaking. It was early morning, and outside the tent the faint stirrings of the waking town could be heard. Ithalia stirred and Po murmured a wordless protest, stroking her back and nuzzling at her neck. He loved this sleepy time almost as much as the act of love itself, and he didn't want it to end.

Their bodies knew each other now. Her fragrance was

embedded in his senses. He would know her anywhere, even though he had still not seen her face. At the thought, a subtle pain, unnamed but impossible to ignore, threaded its way into his heart.

Ithalia disentangled herself from his arms and sat up. He blinked up at her. Her hair stuck out on one side, and on her forehead were deep grooves where the stippled texture of the carpets they slept on had impressed itself. He smiled at the irony of her not wishing him to see her brand. "You are beautiful, Ithalia, and I love you. Nothing could ever change that."

She regarded him in silence. He did not need to use his kinesthetic sense to know that she was carefully considering his unspoken request, weighing the positives and the negatives. He dared not move, speak, or break eye contact with her. He waited, as dawn came and the tent filled with light. At last she nodded. "You're right, Po; it's time," she said, and drew her scarf from her face.

She was not branded. This came as such a surprise that his realization of the greater truth was delayed a moment. But when it came it took away everything. Po struggled for breath in the suddenly airless tent. He sat up, surprised to find the earth beneath him still, when all he had trusted had vanished in an instant. His mouth worked as he sought words, and then he realized that words were no longer appropriate—had, in fact, never been appropriate from him. He scrambled to his knees and prostrated himself before her. "Your Majesty," he murmured.

He heard the thunk of a small object hitting the rug nearby. He took a glance in that direction and saw a curved clay form roughly the size of his thumb. It was slick with saliva. "Ah. That thing has been driving me crazy," said

Queen Thela, in a voice higher and more resonant than Ithalia's had been. "Of course, I'll have to put it on again soon. But it's nice to have a break."

He trembled. He closed his eyes, wishing this to be a dream and for him to awake from it. But the rug against his face remained persistent. The mold she had used to alter her voice still lay beside him, and above him, the queen of Ilysies sighed. "Oh, Po, are you very upset?"

He didn't know how to answer that. It wasn't for him to be upset about what she chose to do, was it? Why did she care? Why was she here and why for the love of the Mother had she taken him into her bed? He tasted bile in his throat and the need to keep from vomiting in front of her overrode all else.

She seemed to be aware of this, for it was not until he had himself under some measure of control that she took him by the shoulders and lifted him up into a kneeling position. He kept his head bent but she raised his face to hers with one elegant finger beneath his chin. "There's no need for that," she said. "Even a queen wants her consort to look upon her, as long as it's with love."

Po stared into the depths of her eyes. Her beautiful, gray-blue eyes. With the rest of her face denied to him, he had spent a great deal of time studying them, in all their changing beauty. They were the same eyes. "Love."

She nodded. "Yes. I love you, Po. That hasn't changed. Do . . ." She swallowed. "Do you still love me?"

His mouth was dry. He felt cold inside. He couldn't think. Did he love her? He must. "Yes."

She smiled. How odd, that this was the first time he'd ever seen it. He drank in the curve of her lips and the gleam of her teeth, but soon glanced up to the comforting familiarity of her eyes and the crinkles at their corners.

"You must have many questions," she said.

He nodded.

"Ask me anything, Po. It's important to me that you understand. There has been too much misunderstanding between the Libyrinth and Ilysies already. I hope to remedy that, but first, I must make certain that you and I are on terms befitting a woman and her consort."

A woman. She was more even than that, but the knowledge that she saw things that way heartened him. And somewhere in the back of his mind an image flickered to life: himself as an old man, reclining in a bower with dates and olives in bowls at his hand. Surrounding him were his daughters, young women with dark hair and aquiline noses, and just a dusting of freckles and a golden glint to their hair. It was a grand version of the dream he had avoided desiring, because he had always thought it out of reach, but there it was—the affection and protection of daughters, a satisfied heart, and a secure future. Safety. Comfort.

But beside that vision stood Princess Selene, severe in her Libyrarians' robes, telling him that the queen of Ilysies was not to be trusted.

Looking on Ithal—Queen Thela now, it seemed impossible that she could be all that Selene said she was. They had made love. He knew her, did he not? All the same, the question came. "Why are you here?"

She nodded, as if she had expected he would begin there. "It's a good question. You are no doubt thinking of the fact that I have rescinded my offer of aid, and decreed that those Ilysians at the Libyrinth are barred from returning home. It was not until I arrived here that I realized how that had been received by the people of the Libyrinth. I did it because I want the Libyrinth to succeed. Did you know that I was present at the Redemption?"

He shook his head. "You came after . . ."

"But I was on the plain when the blessed event occurred, on a low rise in the distance, and I saw it all—the fighting and the arrival of the wing, the miraculous light. I was witness to all of it, though I did not experience Redemption."

Po caught his breath at the sadness in her eyes. What must that be like, to be so close to Integration, and not experience it?

"At first, I admit, I was jealous," she went on. "I wanted to take the Libyrinth for my own and subvert Haly's plan. I wanted to punish you all for having what I was denied. But . . . recently I realized how wrong that is. And I realized that if the Libyrinth were to accept Ilysian aid, it could never achieve its true promise. That is why I rescinded my offer, and that is why I barred Ilysian Libyrarians from returning to their country of origin. You must make it on your own. Do you understand?"

He nodded. Yes, it made sense once she explained it. "I'm sorry you were not Redeemed, Your Majesty."

"Please, call me Thela."

He gaped at her.

"If you were a resident of my bower, you would use my first name."

Sudden realization doused the glowing image of himself as a father. "I can't go back with you."

She shook her head. "I'm sorry. Not yet. But you will. As to why I came here now . . ." She shrugged. "I was curious. I had hopes that if I lived among you, as one of you, I might learn the secret to Integration—excuse me, Redemption."

"It is the same thing. Have you?"

"Only that it is tenuous, even for those who have experienced it firsthand. No. What I have learned is that my place is in Ilysies, taking care of my own people."

His heart felt as if it were slowly being pried in two. "You're leaving?"

She nodded and reached a hand out to cup the side of his face. "Soon. I'm sorry."

Tears came and he let them fall. "Can't I go with you?"

"Not yet, Po." Her smile was sad. "You are an adept now. Your community needs you."

"But it is only because of you that I can do it in the first place." The knowledge ate at him like acid.

She stroked his cheek. "That is as it may be. But it changes nothing."

He felt as if he were choking on heartache. He shook his head. "Why did you choose me?" This hurt so much, more than a little part of him wished she never had.

His words seemed to startle her. "Darling, even a queen has needs."

"B-but, why me? Why not another male?"

"Here? Those others are not proper males, Po, you know that. They know nothing about pleasing a woman, and I am too old and impatient to teach them. But you are a fine consort indeed, Po. I know this is hard for you, but don't be too downhearted. You are young. The community will get on its feet and then I will send for you, and you will be first among my consorts."

That sounded a long way off, but it was better than never seeing her again. "I will?"

She stroked the side of his neck with the back of her index finger. "Of course. Relax, Po. Everything will be all right."

She cupped the back of his head and drew him down to kiss her. Despite his sadness, her agile tongue made him stir. A small groan escaped him. She drew back. "You are a delight," she said, almost regretfully, as she ran long, elegant fingers down his chest to his navel.

It was sweet and painful in equal measure. Po held her tight, giving himself over to the kiss even as tears leaked down the sides of his face. When she broke the kiss, he gasped, "I don't want you to leave."

A small, sad smile played upon her lips. "Neither do I, but we both have responsibilities."

His body cared nothing for his breaking heart. She caressed his chest and pulled him in for another kiss. Her fingers danced lower. "I need you to be strong for me now, Po, and patient. I'm leaving today."

So soon? "No, please."

"Shh. You may tell whom you wish that I have been here, but consider the impact that knowledge will have. Think of your community, Po. I know you will do what is best for your people. And we won't be parted forever. The waiting will be worth it—I promise you."

11

Fire

P o told no one that Thela had been among them in the community. At first his heartbreak was too over-whelming, and it was all he could do to go through the motions of each day—working, eating, treating patients. He was surprised to discover that his kinesthetic sense cared not one whit for his feelings. He was able to treat Yolle, who was declining quickly, and Nian.

As the days passed and his sadness retreated to a dull but ever-present ache, he realized that no good could come of imparting such information—that doing so could in fact cause a great deal of harm.

Queen Thela had gone now. All talking about it would do is make people worry, and for no reason. There would be arguing—if, that is, they believed him in the first place. He had no proof that Thela had been here.

Whether they thought he was making it up or whether they believed he'd consorted with Queen Thela, no one in the community would ever trust him again.

"What's wrong, Po?" said Burke after he had completed his current session with Yolle. She was failing fast now; he could barely see the tree for all the yellow flowers blooming on the vine that all but choked the life out of it. He no longer rebuked himself for being unable to cure her. No one, not even Adept Ykobos, could have saved her, ever. But at least he was able to bring her comfort, and facilitate her body's absorption of Burke's Ease.

Po shook his head. "Libyrarian? I don't know what you mean."

Burke tilted her head and gave him a smile of wry exasperation. "Yes, you do. For the past several days you have gone about as if you were under some sort of death sentence. What's happened? You seemed to be so happy before, with your kinesthetic sense coming in, and your new paramour." At his intake of breath, Burke raised an eyebrow. "Oh. Have the two of you broken up? Is that it?"

Po stared at her, trying to decide what to say. With Thela gone, he was lonely. He wanted to tell Burke everything so that she could comfort him in his loss, but is that what would happen? No. Absolutely not. At the least, Burke would not believe him that Ithalia was in fact Queen Thela. And at worst, she would believe him, but not Thela's reasons for coming here. She'd be suspicious, not only of the queen's motivations, but of him. The thought of losing her respect, on top of everything else, was just too much. He nodded. "She discarded me."

Burke looked on him with compassion, and he pretended that she knew the whole story. That she was comforting him for what truly bothered him, not for the reason he gave. "Oh, Po, I am sorry. I know you were very happy to have a romantic relationship with a woman from your own country." She put a hand on his shoulder. "But you don't need anybody else to be happy and fulfilled, you know."

He shrugged.

Burke sighed. "You'll see. It hurts now, but the pain will fade. The best thing to do is keep busy."

He nodded and forced himself to smile. "I'm sure you're right, Libyrarian. Is there anything I can do for you now?"

Burke tilted her head to one side. "Well, I am running low on silverleaf. Maybe you could go gather some?"

The idea of getting out of the community for a little while was very appealing. Genuine relief crept into his smile, and he nodded. "Of course."

Haly woke to the smell of smoke and Gyneth shaking her arm.

"Haly! Wake up!"

She blinked and forced her eyes into focus. One look at Gyneth's grief-stricken face galvanized her and she jumped out of bed. "What is it?"

"The fields!" Gyneth pointed out the window of the tower room they shared. From here only the sky was visible, and it was a dirty gray.

She rushed to the window and looked out. The Community at the Libyrinth was ringed by fire. The fields were burning.

* * *

After three days of gathering silverleaf and sleeping under the stars, Po at last turned his steps back toward the Libyrinth. It was dawn, and a spectacular sunrise painted the sky red and gold. Since he was west of the community, he walked directly toward it. He couldn't ever remember seeing such a vivid sky. It wasn't until he began to smell smoke that he questioned its cause.

He broke into a trot. A half-mile later his heart hammered in his chest and he staggered to a halt, unwilling to believe what he saw. Flames devoured the once-green barley fields surrounding the Libyrinth, turning them black and belching thick smoke into the air. Heat pressed against him like a living wall. Smoke made him cough and he could not see. He ran to the top of one of the low hills that surrounded the community, searching for a way through the burning fields, hoping that some part of the crop had been spared. But no. The entire community was surrounded by burning fields. There wasn't a stalk of barley or a vegetable patch left untouched.

What could have caused this catastrophe? His mind raced. There had been no storms. No lightning to spark a dry twig and ignite a blaze. He stared and stared, trying to make sense of it. Everything they had worked so hard for had been obliterated in a single night. How?

That first day, Haly had all she could possibly cope with, mobilizing the community into water brigades, passing bucket after bucket from the wells to the outskirts of the settlement, putting out the blaze before it could devour the entire town.

It was a near thing. They lost a tent full of silverleaf twigs and another that housed a family of seven, but by the

end of that first day, the fire was vanquished. Soot-stained
and coughing, everyone went to bed, darkness mercifully
cloaking the ruin of their fields.

Haly was too weary to go back to the Libyrinth and climb
the stairs to her room. She lay down in the girls' dormitory
tent and fell asleep almost instantly.

She awoke just before dawn, got up, and walked out to
the edge of town, watching as the sun rose over the blackened, smoking fields. She wasn't even aware that she was
crying until her tears dripped onto the front of her soot-
stained robe. Her frantic mind, her broken heart, taunted
her with memories of how these fields had looked just
a day ago, green and lush, the barley stalks furred with
ripening grains. She longed for some way to reach into
the past and pull that former reality into the present. It
was so vivid, it really did seem as if she should be able to
grasp it, reclaim it. The wind shifted, bringing with it the
fetid smell of wet, charred vegetation. How had this happened?

"Who could have done this?" said a voice at her side.

She turned to see Siblea standing there, looking every
bit as devastated as she felt. "Who?"

He gave her a disparaging look. Despite the fact that
she was the leader of the community, he still regarded her
as a pupil. "The fields were green, not dry, there's been no
lightning. This was not an accident of nature, Holy One.
Someone set this fire."

Cold wrapped around her heart. He was right. Yesterday had been one long scramble to keep from losing more
than they already had and there'd been no time to think
about the whys and wherefores. But Siblea was right. She
could think of no natural cause for this fire. As she stood,

contemplating this, she spotted a figure in the distance, walking toward them across the blackened field.

"What is more important than how this happened, is what we are going to do now," said Haly.

"Of course," said Siblea. "What do you suggest?"

The figure was nearer now. It was a man in robes, tall, broad shouldered, with a bag slung over one shoulder.

A sob burst forth from her, unexpected and appalling. She bit her lips and fought for control. "I don't know," she whispered.

Siblea sighed and put a hand on her shoulder. "Perhaps, this Lion's Bloom . . ."

She nodded, her throat raw with smoke and unshed tears. "But it seems so tenuous."

"It is. But it is better than nothing. The grain will last another two months. We can get another crop in as soon as we may; we can seek aid from the villages of the plain." He squeezed her shoulder. "You must not give in to despair. As long as you have hope, the others will as well."

The man in the field hastened his stride and in moments she saw that it was Po, with a bag of silverleaf at his side. He looked every bit as soot-streaked and lost as everyone else, but he had not been with them during the fire, she realized. Where had he been?

B ut who would do such a thing?" protested Burke. It was the morning of the second day since the fire and an impromptu meeting was in progress in Haly's office. People had just started showing up after breakfast.

"My mother, that's who," said Selene.

"Queen Thela?" asked Peliac.

"Do you think that she is content to sit at home while we grow and flourish?"

"But she offered us aid."

"Yes, as a means to control us. And now that we have refused, she will bring us to heel by other methods."

Haly sighed. "But if it was Thela, how did she do it?"

"She almost certainly has agents in Thesia and the Corvariate Citadel. It would be naive to think she did not have spies here as well."

The room was silent a moment as they all pondered that. "What is more dangerous than spies," said Haly, "is the suspicion of spies. We are all we have now. We cannot afford mistrust."

"Perhaps," said Siblea. "But someone set that fire."

Haly could see it all so clearly. It would not be starvation that would destroy them. They would tear themselves apart with accusations long before the grain ran out. "And finding that person and punishing them will bring us no closer to ensuring our survival. I suggest we turn our attention to more useful pursuits, like investigating terraforming and the Lion's Bloom."

"I may have something on that, Holy One," said Rossiter. "There is an obscure object from Singer history known as Endymion's rose—an object of great power and terror. It bears some striking similarities to the Lion's Bloom. Some say it was what made the ancients all-powerful, and that when it was lost, that was when they were overthrown."

"What happened to it?"

"No one knows, but by all accounts, it disappeared in the Corvariate Citadel."

The Lion's Bloom. Endymion's rose. Ultimate power. Transformation. Fragments were beginning to accrete. "I think some of us should go there," said Haly. She looked to Siblea. "You and Selene should take the Chorus of the Word. You can stop in villages on your way and try to elicit support for us. Then, when you get there, see what you can find out about this object and its function."

Siblea had been glaring at Rossiter the entire time he spoke. "Holy One, I assure you there is no such thing as Endymion's rose. It is a tale told to frighten children." He turned to Rossiter. "I'm surprised a young man of your caliber would even deign to repeat it."

Rossiter colored, but did not back down.

Haly looked at Siblea. Her irritation must have shown. Siblea blinked, and then said, "Of course, it would not be a bad idea to create some goodwill among the villages; and as for the citadel—there may be some things there we can utilize."

"Fine. Gather the members of the chorus and make preparations for the journey. There's no time to lose. In the meantime, Peliac, you meet with Ock about getting another crop in as quickly as possible."

"And I'll take the wing out and search for food," said Clauda.

"Yes!" Haly embraced her oldest and best friend. "Good idea."

The meeting broke up. For some reason, even though nothing concrete had been accomplished, Haly felt better. It was the difference between being overwhelmed by calamity and taking action to remedy said calamity. She hoped their efforts would be enough.

12

Traitor

The leaves of the tree were withered, the bark dry and flaking. Po carried water from the stream and poured it over the roots of the parched silverleaf tree. Then he had a better idea. He summoned a shovel, and he dug a trench from the bank of the stream to the tree, supplying it with a steady stream of refreshment.

Po opened his eyes and removed his hands from the pulse points at Ock's knees. He had been among the first to discover the fire, and in his desperate efforts to vanquish the blaze, he'd been badly burned. He lay in the infirmary, dosed with Ease to keep the worst of the pain at bay, his burns coated with salve and bandaged. Po hoped that his efforts would bolster his body's ability to heal the damage, but no matter what he did, there would be scars, and it was unlikely that his hair would ever grow back.

Po stood, and was about to turn to Burke to see what he could do next when someone grabbed him by the arm and bent it behind his back. Pain lanced up his shoulder and at the same time, he felt hot breath in his ear. "Traitor, you're coming with me," said Siblea.

For a moment, it was all so sudden that Po had no reaction at all. He heard Burke at the other end of the tent say, "Siblea? What—?"

Then, Po realized what must have happened. Somehow, Siblea had learned of his relationship with Thela. Po stamped his foot down on Siblea's instep and jammed his free elbow into Siblea's solar plexus. The older man groaned and his grip loosened. Po freed himself and spun around to face him. "I haven't done anything wrong. She had every right to be here."

Bent at the waist, his arm to his chest, Siblea panted and glared. "She? Who are you talking about?"

Uncertainty made Po blink. By now, Burke had hurried over to them. "Siblea, what are you doing?"

Siblea straightened and pointed a long finger at Po. "He set the fire."

"What?" Po shook his head in confusion. "What are you talking about?"

Others in the infirmary had heard the exchange. Ock said, "Po?" in a tone of disbelief. Other murmurs and questions could be heard, some of them bewildered, others angry. Burke looked between Po and Siblea and shook her head. "No. There's some mistake." She looked at Po. "Don't worry, dear, we'll get to the bottom of this."

"Yes, we will," said Siblea. "Who were you talking about just now, Po? Who has every right to be here?"

Po's mouth went dry. Burke and Siblea both stared at him and the rest of the tent went silent. Everyone was waiting for his answer. He couldn't say it. "That's none of your business, Siblea. Why are you accusing me of setting the fire?"

A low murmur of suspicion ran through the tent at Po's nonanswer. Burke was watching him very carefully, her eyes narrowed. Siblea bared his teeth in a rictus grin. "I'm going to make it my business. Now come with me."

Po shook his head and folded his arms. "I don't have to go anywhere with you."

"Po, perhaps you should—" Burke began, but before she could finish, Siblea shot his arm out and made a grab for Po's ear.

Po stepped inside the old man's reach and threw a punch. His fist connected with the side of Siblea's face with a smack and a sting in his knuckles.

Siblea made a low, growling sound and tackled Po to the ground. Po grunted under the man's surprising weight. He threw his head forward, hitting Siblea in the nose with his forehead. "Gah!" the old man yelled.

"Po! Siblea! Stop this at once!" said Burke.

Po knew Siblea would not listen to her. He took advantage of the other man's pain to roll them both. Now he was on top of Siblea, straddling his waist and pinning his arms to the ground. They glared at each other, chests heaving.

"Po!" It was Burke, and she was angry. He looked up to see her staring at him as if he were something entirely alien to her. "Whatever this is about, you are not helping.

Siblea, your use of force is unacceptable. Now whatever you think Po has done, you are not entitled to push him about like an unruly goat."

"He is a traitor."

"I doubt it, but you will have your opportunity to make your case before the Redeemer."

"I have proof—in the boys' dormitory," said Siblea.

Rossiter had materialized at Burke's side sometime during the fight. He stared at Po with open suspicion.

"Rossiter, go and fetch the Redeemer," said Burke. "Po, get off Siblea. Siblea, do not attempt to lay hands on Po again. I will escort both of you to the boys' dorm and we will see what this is all about."

Po looked down at Siblea, who stared back at him, utterly undaunted, implacable. Whatever the outcome of Burke's intercession, they were enemies now. Nothing would change that until one had succeeded in killing the other. Po never broke their mutual gaze as he slowly got off of Siblea and stood up.

Burke took him by the hand, squeezing it tight. She took Siblea's arm in her other hand, and the three of them walked out of the infirmary tent and headed for the boys' dorm.

A crowd surrounded it. As they approached, someone spotted them. "There he is!" Others shouted, "The traitor!" and, "He set the fire!" The crowd began to break away from the tent and sweep toward them.

Burke's hand tightened on his. He couldn't let her wind up in the middle of this. "Wait!" said Po. He released Burke's hand. "Please, Libyrarian, go help Rossiter look for the Redeemer," he told her, and then he turned to Siblea. "Show me what you've found."

He permitted the old Singer to grab him by the arm. Despite Siblea's age, his grip was like iron. He pushed Po through the angry mob and into the tent, where more people milled about. Jan stood between his cot and Po's. The look he gave Po as they approached was one of baffled betrayal.

A tight, hot knot grew in Po's gut. "Show him," said Siblea.

Jan tilted Po's cot onto its side to reveal a long, narrow box made of woven silverleaf twigs. He opened the lid.

Empty pots, the kind used to hold cooking oil, filled the box, as well as numerous fragments of barley stalk. In one corner, resting on top of one jar, sat a flint and iron.

Po stared at the box, trying to make sense of it. Since Thela had gone, he'd been sleeping on his cot again, but he'd not seen this here. The coverlet would hide it, he supposed. "How long has that been here?" he asked Jan.

Jan shook his head in disbelief. "Suck a goat, Po."

Siblea's grip on his arm tightened. "How dare you?"

The tent was packed with angry people—Ayorites, Libyrarians, Singers, and Ilysians. They gathered close. The air in the tent was hot, and thick with impending violence. Po wanted to protest his innocence, but so many of those accusatory looks and menacing stances came from other males. He would not justify himself to them. He said nothing.

The crowd parted, and Haly, Burke, and Selene approached them. At the sight of them, Po fell to his knees. "Holy One!"

She looked from the box to Po to Siblea. "What is this?"

"He set the fire, Holy One," said Siblea. "Here is the proof."

Haly looked at Po. "Is this true?"

Po shook his head. "No! I don't know where these came from. I didn't put them here. I didn't set the fire!"

Haly shut the lid of the box and stood on top of it. Speaking directly to Siblea, but loud enough for all to hear, Haly said, "I wish you would have brought your concerns to me before taking matters into your own hands, Siblea." She looked out over the gathered throng. "However the fire happened, this kind of witch hunt can only make our already dire situation worse. We all have work to do. Rest assured that I will get to the bottom of this, and when I do, everyone will know what I've learned. But no matter what is discovered, there will be no mob justice in this community. That is worse than fire, and worse than famine. The first two will merely kill us. Vengeance betrays our souls."

Po had never really seen Haly angry before. He was guessing most of the others here had not, either. The tent was silent.

"Go back to work now," said Haly.

The crowd dispersed. Many appeared shamefaced, but a few cast backward glances at Po, clearly wishful of revenge despite the Redeemer's words. Haly looked at Po and Siblea. "Take your hands off him."

Siblea released him.

"I would like both of you to come with me now, and you as well, Jan. Burke, Selene—I'd appreciate your presence also."

They formed a little procession from the boys' dorm tent to Haly's office in the Libyrinth. As they passed, most people stopped what they were doing and watched. Po read speculation on some of those faces, suspicion on others, and hatred on a great many.

W ho did you speak of when you said, 'She had every right to be here?'" Siblea demanded the instant the door was shut behind them.

Po felt as if the fire had followed them inside. The air was hot and dense; it pressed in upon him from every side.

They were all staring at him, waiting for his answer.

"Ithalia?" said Jan.

Po opened his mouth, hoping words would come. None did.

"Where did she go?" Jan demanded. "I thought you made her up. I never met her."

"She left," said Po. "But that was over a week ago. This has nothing to do with her."

"Left? For where? If she's Ilysian, she can't go back home," said Selene.

Po stared at her, at a loss.

"When I called you traitor, the first thing you said was, 'She had every right to be here,'" Siblea persisted. "Why did you say that? Who is she, and why would her right to be here be in question?"

Po swallowed. He looked to Haly, his eyes pleading. "The community is for anyone, right?"

"Yes," said Haly, a question in her voice.

"She just wanted to see what it was like, that was all. She . . . she missed the Redemption, but she saw it happen and she wanted to see how it was here for herself. That's all, and it was long before the fire. It couldn't . . . She couldn't have . . ."

Selene stared at him fixedly. "Who, Po? Just tell us."

Pressure at the back of his throat and behind his eyes made it difficult for him to speak. He longed to keep the words inside. He knew that the moment he let them out, everything would change. He knew that once spoken, they would reveal truths he did not wish to know, and shatter dreams that he cherished. But Haly, Selene, and Burke were waiting. "The woman I thought to be a soldier named Ithalia was really Queen Thela in disguise."

Selene's eyes flashed. Haly's shoulders drooped. Burke tried to stifle a gasp. Po felt as if he had run for days across a rocky plain. The admission left him exhausted, his heart flayed. "I only learned of it on her last day in the community," he added.

"Her last day? When was that?" said Haly, her tone clipped. She was struggling for control.

"Nine days ago."

"Well before the fire," noted Burke.

Selene shook her head. "That means nothing. She may have just hidden away somewhere."

"So you think she set the fire?" asked Haly.

Selene looked at Po, and then at Haly and Burke. "Do you really think he did it?"

They both shook their heads. Po thought that would make him feel better, but it didn't, not really. If Thela set the fire, he could have prevented it by telling someone about her.

"It could have been someone besides Thela," said Burke.

"Possible, but highly unlikely," said Siblea. "If she was here . . ."

Haly turned to Po. "Why, in the name of all we hold

dear, did you not tell someone that Thela was here, Po? Why?"

Po sought for words. "I . . . She was leaving . . . I didn't think it mattered, and I knew that it would just stir up trouble. I knew no one would trust me if they knew of it."

Burke and Haly looked heartbroken. Selene stared at him shrewdly, and Siblea's gaze was full of open hostility. Po turned to Selene. "Libyrarian, do you really think she set the fire?"

"And framed you for it, Po. Yes. You were her consort for a few weeks, but I have been her daughter all my life. This is perfectly within her capabilities, and very much her style. She betrayed you, and counted on your naiveté and your lack of confidence to keep her secret, and to give her time to destroy the crop."

"But you don't understand! She wasn't here to harm us! She told me that she rescinded aid and forbid Ilysians from returning for our own good. She wants us to succeed!"

Selene's disappointment was withering. "Oh, Po."

He shook his head. "That's why I didn't tell anyone that she'd been here. I knew it would cause a big uproar, and that . . . that no one would trust me ever again if they knew I'd been her consort."

"Don't you see—she used you," said Selene. "She perceived you as the weak link in the community and she seduced you so she could frame you for the fire that she set. That way, our crop is destroyed and we are torn by conflict over what to do about you. It's perfect. She has not lost her touch."

Po swallowed against the heaviness in his chest and stomach. Was it true? Had she just been using him? "She said she wanted me to come back to her once the community was on its feet." His voice was weak, pathetic. Even he did not believe those words now.

"I wish you had told me," said Burke.

The fact that he had disappointed Burke was even worse than Selene's confidence of Thela's betrayal. He wished he could die, right now. He got to his knees.

"Po, don't—" Haly began.

"In Ilysies, a male is sacrificed every year for the fertility of the fields. Please, Holy One, I beg you. Make me your sacrifice. I don't deserve the honor, but at least let my blood bring forth the plants. Let me be of some use."

"Don't be ridiculous," Haly said, sounding angrier now than he'd ever heard her before. "We will never resort to such misguided barbarity here. If we do, we have truly failed. Now stand up, please."

Po obeyed her, and she took him by the shoulders. She embraced him and then held him out at arm's length, looking on him with kindness, with pity. It made him feel lower than low. "I'm sending you out with the Chorus of the Word," she said. "For your safety, as well as for the good of the community."

Numb, Po nodded.

"Do you understand? You can't stay here now. Another incident like today's is bound to happen. You could be killed and the community would tear itself apart. No matter who believes what, your position here is intolerable to them. Either you set the fire, or you colluded with Queen Thela. You see?"

"Yes." Po glanced at Siblea, whose mouth was set in a grim line. He'd been looking at Haly in dismay at her decision, but when he noticed Po looking at him, he glared back. Going away with the chorus meant being under the direct supervision of Siblea. Po looked back at Haly.

"You may not have noticed yet, Po, but life almost never gives you what you expect or what you think you want. The key is in what you do with the things that do come your way. That is something we must all learn, if we are to survive."

Perhaps, if he helped them find the bloom . . . "When do we go?"

"Tomorrow morning, at dawn."

13

The Chorus of the Word

The Chorus of the Word was small, its numbers denuded by the needs of the Libyrinth community. For instance, Burke and Rossiter could not be spared from the infirmary tent, especially with Po now departing, and several of the other members elected to stay behind and help with getting the next crop in. That left six of them in all: Po, Jan, Selene, Siblea, Hilloa, and Baris.

They traveled north and east, along a route that would take them to a number of villages before reaching the Corvariate Citadel. It was harsh terrain and the days were long. At night they slept on blankets on the ground and Po lost consciousness the moment his head hit his rolled-up robe. In the morning he seemed to crawl up from sleep as if through a tunnel filled with gray wool. During the day, he felt as if that numbness surrounded him like a barrier. He welcomed it. It was enough to shield him from the glares of the males, but it could not dull the sting of Selene's pity or the ache of Hilloa's reproach. No one spoke to him unless it was necessary, but it was in their eyes. He avoided looking at anyone.

They walked for a week, the land gradually sloping upward to a high, rocky mesa where even silverleaf bushes became scarce.

Late in the afternoon of the eighth day, Po spotted some small humps in the distance. As the group neared, the humps resolved into stone dwellings, none of them larger than a tent back at the community, and many of them much smaller than that. There were fields under cultivation, the land grudgingly giving up meager crops of pulse, onions, and barley. And there were goat paddocks, the animals grazing on the scrawny silverleaf shrubs that everywhere dotted the plain. A girl not much younger than he was, who could have been the legendary Goat Girl personified, herded her flock into a paddock, shut the gate, and came running toward them.

"Are you Singers?" she asked.

"We are the Chorus of the Word, young lady," said Siblea, and Po winced at the condescension in his tone. "Many of us were once Singers, before the Redemption, but now we are all brothers and sisters of song and book. We bear tidings of the Redemption for you and your family, for your whole village, and we bring knowledge from the Libyrinth."

The girl's eyes went wide. "The Redemption?"

It was a remote village of ten or twelve dwellings, a few meager fields, and a herd of about thirty skinny goats. She stared until Po thought her eyes would roll from her head. Then she hopped twice, turned, and pelted for the cluster of stone huts. "Ma! Ma!"

At this time of day, no one was in the huts. They were all out in the fields except for one lone woman, tending a fire in a pit in the middle of the village. She looked up as the girl ran to her. A brief conversation ensued and Po saw the girl pointing excitedly in their direction. The woman stared, shielding her eyes against the glare of the sun behind them. She said something else to her daughter, who ran full tilt toward a work crew that was clearing stones from a field. The woman gave her fire a desultory poke and then, wiping her hands on her skirt, approached them.

She stood before them, her arms crossed. "My daughter says you are Singers but not Singers. She says you have news of the Redemption."

"We do, madam," said Siblea, bowing. "It is our honor and our joy to bring you tidings of the Redemption of the Word." He paused.

She squinted. Her arms still crossed, she seemed to brace herself as if she would repel them all by herself.

"We come in peace," he said, turning to point at their wagon. "Feel free to investigate the wagon; you will find nothing there but food, medicine, and books."

She pulled her head back at that and tilted it to the side, her look incredulous, suspicious. "Books?"

Siblea nodded and spread his hands. "The word is Redeemed, madam. It is our mission now to bring the rich store of knowledge housed in the Libyrinth to every living soul on the Plain of Ayor. We have brought with us copies of the most useful books. They are but a small sampling of what the Libyrinth holds, but we will bring more when possible. In the meantime, we will teach you how to read, and then all of you are invited to come to the Libyrinth to study, any time you wish, for as long as you care to stay."

She gave him a long, penetrating look. She glanced at the wagon again. Not taking her eyes off the chorus, she slowly approached the wagon and lifted the tarp. She stared. She dropped the tarp and turned to them again. "Wait here," she said.

By now, the others were filtering in from the fields—work-worn men and women who were thin and had faces like the plain itself—windswept and spare. Clearly they struggled to feed themselves in this harsh land. And the Chorus of the Word was going to ask them to help feed the Libyrinth should this quest fail? It seemed indecent. The tallest man was barely bigger than Jan, who was short for a male, and not yet fully grown.

They wore goatskins, mostly, leggings and tunics. Their tools were made of rock, the wood handles fashioned from the thickest part of the silverleaf bush, its fibers used to tie haft and blade together. They gathered around the fire pit in the middle of the huts and they talked. Occasionally Po made out a word—Singer, book, Redemption.

At last the woman returned and indicated for them to enter the village circle. Before approaching the village fire, Siblea took out one of the medical kits Burke and Rossiter had assembled. It contained antibiotics, aspirin, Ease, antiseptic, and inoculation patches.

He presented the medicine to the woman who had greeted them. A man had joined her—presumably her husband. The two of them examined the kit, poking at its contents and holding up one of the patches to examine it more closely. Selene prodded Po in the side. "You're our medical expert; explain it to them," she said.

Caught by surprise, Po swallowed and said, "Uh, that's an innoculation patch? For the babies? The medicine sinks in through the skin and they won't get spotted fever."

The couple stared at him. The other villagers had stopped what they were doing and gathered around, all of them staring at Po with suspicion.

"It is the mark of Yammon," said Siblea.

"Oh! The mark!" said the man and smiled, nodding. "Thank you!"

"And that is aspirin," said Jan, pointing out the small round tablets in their packet of woven leaves.

"For headaches and muscle aches," said Hilloa.

"This is Ease," said Baris. "For really bad hurts—but be careful with it. Only use a little bit at a time."

Po stepped back as the other members of the chorus did his job for him. He hardly even cared that Jan and Baris were showing him up. What difference did it make? The important thing was that the people here understood which medicines to use for what—not who taught them.

After a few minutes, the little group around the medical kit broke up and the woman who had first greeted them said, "Welcome to our village, wanderers. I am Hana and this is Dov. We are the heads of the village. Thank you for your gift of medicine. Please, sit and share the evening meal with us. You can sleep here tonight, too, if you wish."

They sat around the fire in a circle. The goat girl and several other young women disappeared into a hut and returned with platters of pulse, oats, and dried goat meat. The oldest woman in the village handed out stoneware bowls, and everyone helped themselves from the platters and ate with their hands. Afterward the young women took the dishes away and returned again with a large, two-handled ewer. Starting with the head woman, Hana, everyone took a drink and then passed it to the next person. When it came around to Po, he peered inside and saw a milk substance. It smelled sour. He took a sip. It had a very high alcohol content.

"Fermented goat's milk," murmured Jan as he took the ewer from Po. "It'll knock you on your ass if you're not careful."

Po tried not to notice how relieved he felt that Jan had spoken to him.

"We haven't had visitors since my grandmother's time," said Hana, after the food and a few more sips from the ewer had relaxed everybody. "You say the Redemption has come. Tell us of it."

Siblea spoke first. "As was foretold by Yammon, when he had his great vision, Song liberated Word, and Word and Song became one."

"A great golden wing came from the east and spoke the Name of the Ocean to the library of Ayor, and everyone present was integrated," said Selene.

"The Last Wind of the World blew a golden ship across the sky to rain blessings down upon all those assembled, and those who received the blessing became as one," said Jan.

"Literacy was freed from its state of tyranny, reunited with the Song and made available for everyone, through us, the Chorus of the Word. *The Book of the Night* returned to us, and we have copied its words and the words of other useful books. We bring them to you, along with the key to understanding them," said Baris.

The villagers all stared at them, puzzled.

"I guess you could say that the Redemption means something different to every person who experienced it," said Hilloa. "The important part is that we have set aside our differences and commited ourselves to working together for the betterment of all."

"What about the fire of purification?" said Hana's husband, Dov.

"That was the light," Siblea said without missing a beat. "The light was the fire and it purified us all without destruction. To continue our mission, to make ourselves worthy of the blessing we've received, we travel, to bring the Word to others."

Dov leaned forward, pointing at Siblea with a piece of dried goat meat. "And what of this key you speak of? The key to understanding *The Book of the Night*?"

"*The Book of the Night* is a tome of many mysteries," said Siblea.

"Do you know how to make Eggs now?" asked an ancient woman on the other side of the fire.

Siblea tilted his head. "That miracle is yet to come. For though the words of the book are plain to those who have been taught how to read them, their meaning is not always as plain. That is another reason why we bring you copies and we hope that many of you will allow us to instruct you in reading them. The more people who read the book, who meditate upon its wisdom, the more chances there are of comprehending its deepest mysteries."

The villagers looked at one another, frowning.

"You want to teach us to read the book so we can figure out for ourselves how to make Eggs?" said Dov, skeptical.

Siblea's eyebrows rose. "That's one way of looking at it," he said.

"Another way is this," said Selene, glancing at a small boy on the fringes of the circle who was leaning forward, craning his neck to get a better view of them. He had a light in his eye. "The Redemption has made us all brothers and sisters. Once the Chorus of the Word has instructed you, you are every bit as important as any Libyrarian, Singer, Thesian noble, or Ilysian queen. Someone right here in this village might be the one to unravel the secrets of the Ancients."

The boy's eyes were wide, his mouth open. The adults glanced among themselves uncomfortably. At last Hana spoke. "That is a nice thing to say. But the queen of Ilysies does not have to plow the fields for her food. How are we to have time for reading? It's all we can do to survive in this barren land."

Selene nodded. "Of course, you must do what is necessary to survive. But you sit around the fire at night and tell stories before you go to sleep, don't you?"

Reluctantly, they nodded.

"Then might not you also read to one another?"

Hana got a thoughtful look. In the back, the boy squirmed. Dov and the old woman and several others scowled, but more of them seemed thoughtful. Dov glanced around and saw this. "But we have not seen these books," he said. "Perhaps all that you say is a dream tale. Something that would be beautiful, if it were true."

Selene looked at Po, Hilloa, Baris, and Jan, and nodded. They each scrambled up from the ground and ran to the cart, bringing back with them armfuls of books. It was now dusk, and the palm-glow-infused pages shone softly. At the sight of this, Hana, Dov, and several other adults jumped to their feet, and the old woman began herding the children into a nearby hut. Someone whispered "witch-craft" in a low, terror-laden voice.

Po came to a halt, Hilloa and the others doing the same. They stood ten feet from the fire pit, awkward, hearts rac-ing, as the villagers glared at them.

"Do not fear," said Siblea. He and Selene remained seated. They could easily be cut down where they sat, and Po saw the old woman come out of the hut with a scythe. But the two oldest members of the chorus just sat there, holding their hands up in reassurance. They would do nothing to protect the others either, if they were attacked. "It is only palm-glow. We know that you must work in the daylight. So we made these for you with the glowing lichen so that you may read them at night."

Everyone stood stock-still, assessing the situation. Sud-denly the boy with the bright eyes ran out of the hut and came straight for Po. "I want one! I want one!"

"Lerrit, no!" shouted Hana. Dov ran to grab him as the old woman broke into a sprint, the scythe high over her head. Po dropped the books and fell to his knees. Just like the Barley King, he closed his eyes and bent his head, waiting for the death stroke.

"Pir! Stop!"

Po opened his eyes again to see Hana restraining the old woman and Lerrit bent over Dov's knee, getting the spank-ing of his life. "Don't you ever disobey your grandmother!"

"Mother, it's all right. Go back in the house. Stay with the children," said Hana.

Pir looked at the glowing books all tumbled around

Po's knees, at the other members of the chorus sitting quietly by the fire, and finally at her daughter. "You are too bold, Hana."

"That's what you've always said." Hana's voice carried resignation, and affection. "But you know I won't let harm befall us."

The old woman nodded at last and retreated inside the hut.

"We apologize for causing concern," said Selene, standing now at last. "We should have explained about the palm-glow."

The rest of the villagers still eyed the books and the chorus members with suspicion. But Hana came to where Po knelt. "Are you all right, boy? My mother is a terror, isn't she?"

Po swallowed and managed a breathy laugh and nodded.

"Palm-glow, they say. We've never seen it. But we've heard of the glowing lichen. That's what makes these pages glow?"

Why she was asking him, and not Selene, or Siblea, Po had no notion. But he nodded. "Yes, ma'am. The paper is made from silverleaf, with a little of the lichen mixed into it, so it glows. So you can read what's written on it at night, like"—for once he got it right—"Selene says." With a new burst of confidence, he went on. "It's harmless. Can I show you?"

She nodded. Po picked up a book and got to his feet. He opened it and ran his hands over the softly glowing pages. He held his hand out to her. "See? It doesn't burn or anything. It just glows. Look." And he buried his face in the book, rubbing the pages against his cheeks. "Harmless."

Hana nodded. She held out her hand and Po gave her the book. She touched one finger to the page. "It's not even warm," she said. She looked at Po. "You have an honest face, boy, and you did not run from Pir when she came at you with the scythe. You were willing to die rather than dishonor your cause. I believe you."

She turned to the others. "It must be as they say," she said. "The Redemption has come to pass and now the books glow, purified. We would be fools to turn our backs on the blessing these people offer us."

That night they slept near the fire pit for warmth. "How could you just kneel like that?" whispered Baris as they rolled out their pallets. "She was really going to cut you down."

Po glanced at him. For once Baris seemed to be genuinely curious, not mocking him. "What else was I going to do?"

"Not make it easier for her to lop your head off! Run, or fight her. She's a crone, for Song's sake; even you could take her."

Po stared at Baris. He honestly had no idea what blasphemy he spoke. "It would be unthinkable for me to strike a woman. And she is an old woman. Most worthy of respect."

Baris snorted. "Unthinkable? Nothing's unthinkable. I've always wondered why you Ilysian guys don't rebel. Most of you are bigger and stronger than most of the women. Why do you put up with playing second fiddle?"

"First of all, our role is important and we're honored to fulfill it. Secondly, what you describe would require cooperation, and as you may have noticed, males don't do that very well among themselves. Third—" He stopped.

"What?" Baris whispered. Everyone else had bedded down and the clearing was quiet now. "What's third?"

Po lay listening to everyone's breathing. When they all sounded like they were asleep, he said, in a voice just barely audible, "There is nothing worse a man can do than harm a woman. One who does that dishonors not only himself but his entire family."

"So? What does that mean, dishonor? Could it really be worse than living like a slave?"

"The man himself is killed, of course. So are his sire, and any brothers and sons he may have. But of course it is understood that the women of his family are the ones truly responsible. His mother, his sisters and daughters, even his grandmother, are branded, and may never have consorts again. It is the end for the entire line."

"You sound more troubled by what happens to them than to the men."

"It's very like you to frame it as if men and women can be separated from one another. As if our interests are independent and competing. You don't understand."

"Maybe not. But none of this explains why you knelt."

Po couldn't explain that, except that in that moment, with the embodiment of the Destroyer herself coming at him with the ritual implement, he'd truly felt like the chosen Barley King, blessed with the honor of spilling his blood to bring fertility to the land.

They stayed in the village a week. By the end of that time, Lerrit and Hana, their two most enthusiastic pupils, understood the alphabet well enough to read most of *The Book of the Night* and to teach the others. When they finally left, everyone gathered to see them off, waving and asking when they'd be back.

14

A Fly Story

At the next village, the chorus received a very different welcome. While most of the villagers kept to their huts, the head man came and spoke to them. He had a pitchfork in his hand, and from one of the nearby doorways Po caught the gleam of an adze held in readiness. "We don't want any more trouble," the head man said.

"More trouble?" said Selene. "I'm sorry, we don't know what you mean."

"Oh, yes you do. Another group of you people were through here two months ago," said the man. "First you told us that the Singers had been overthrown, and that reading and writing were good now. And then you said we had to learn, but when we got things wrong you got mad and beat us with mind lancets. Then you stole our food.

The Singers used to help us, not like you lits. If this is
what the Redemption's done, then you can keep it."

"I don't know who it was who came to your village
before," said Siblea, "but it wasn't the Chorus of the Word.
We would never strike a student. We are here to help you.
We have medicine and books for you. Look." He showed
him the contents of the wagon. Fortunately, in the brightness of midday, the palm-glow didn't show.

All the same, the man recoiled. "Are you insane? Those
aren't approved. Get them out of here before we get in
trouble!"

"Approved?"

"Yes. You should know. There's a list of books we're
supposed to read and copy, and if we stray from the list,
they'll come back with their mind lancets. My boy is still
ill from what your people did to him."

They all gaped at the man.

"I tell you, sir, we are the first expedition of the Chorus
of the Word from the Libyrinth. Whoever these other
people are, we will do our best to help you fend them off if
they return."

"You dress the same."

"That may be."

"We might be able to help your son," said Hilloa. She
glanced at Po. "We have some experience treating the shaking sickness."

The man looked at them warily. "I don't see any mind
lancets. Are you hiding them?"

Siblea stepped aside and gestured at the wagon. "You
may search for them. You will not find any weapons."

The man did so, pausing as he uncovered the food. "Is
that peabea?"

"Yes," said Siblea. "We will be happy to share it with you." He exchanged a glance with Selene. Any hope of the villagers helping to feed the Libyrinth was misplaced.

The man pursed his lips and scanned the gathered chorus. "Wait here," he said, and went into one of the huts. They heard arguing, though they couldn't make out what was said. Finally he emerged again, accompanied by a woman. "Which of you are healers?" she said.

Po stepped forward. He grabbed Jan by the arm and pulled him along with him.

"These two will look at my son and see if they can help him. The rest of you will wait here with your wagon," the head man informed them.

The woman led Po and Jan into one of the huts. "He had another fit this morning. He's sleeping now."

The boy was about eight years old. He lay on a pallet in the corner of the small hut, a thin blanket over him. His skin shone with sweat. "What kind of maniac would hit an eight-year-old with a mind lancet?" muttered Po.

Jan shook his head. "I wish we could wipe those damn things off the face of the earth, anyway."

Po knelt beside the boy and put a hand to the side of his face. His skin was hot to the touch. He smelled the boy's breath. "Fever."

Po placed his thumbs over the inside of the boy's elbows, one on each side, and closed his eyes, allowing his breath to adopt the boy's stuttering rhythm. He hadn't performed kinesiology since the fire. Would he still be able to?

Nothing happened at first. Po kept his focus on his breath as despair tried to distract him. Then the image of a raspberry patch came into his mind. One side of the patch was barren; the other was so overloaded with fruit that the branches broke under the weight. The boy's energy was out of balance, that much was certain. Po began to pluck the berries. He placed them at the base of the barren side of the bush and watered it, so that new seedlings would sprout, refreshing that side of the patch.

When he came out of the trance, the boy was sleeping peacefully, his breath deep and even. Po felt his forehead. It was cooler.

Jan and the boy's mother watched him from the doorway. "I balanced his energy. He should sleep better now and hopefully the fever will continue to go down."

"If we stay here tonight, Po can check him in the morning and see if the work has held," said Jan.

Po blinked at Jan's use of kinesthetic terminology.

"I pay attention, unlike some people," said Jan.

The boy's mother bowed to Po and lifted the curtain over the door for him. "Thank you."

Embarrassed, Po hesitated. Jan put a hand on his back and propelled him through the doorway. Outside, the head man and several other villagers waited. The woman nodded her head.

The man smiled for the first time since they'd arrived. "Thank you for helping my son," he said, and then he turned to the rest of the chorus, standing clustered near the wagon. "Stay tonight and share our fire."

The day was warm, the sun bright. Po swayed as the customary weakness following a trance overcame him.

"Easy there, Poacher," said Jan, steadying him by the arm. "You were in that trance a long time. How about a drink of water?"

"Thanks," said Po, and let Jan lead him to the wagon.

"So why did you want me in there with you, anyway?" asked Jan. "I don't know anything, and I can't do anything. You handled it all."

Po shrugged and took a seat on the back of the wagon. "I didn't know if I was still going to be able to do it, after everything that's happened." He hesitated, staring at Jan. He was the closest thing to a male friend Po had. Now he looked back at him with neutrality. "I panicked," said Po, "and you were nearby, and I thought you might go along."

"Okay, I guess I can see that."

"Do you still think I set the fire?"

"No," said Jan, handing him a water skin and taking a seat next to him on the back of the wagon. "I think you were tricked."

Po drank. "I'm glad you don't think that of me."

"Yeah? Since when do you care what a male thinks?"

He shrugged. Jan had a point. "What does Hilloa think?"

Jan leaned back on his hands and laughed, his face lifted to the sky. "Seven Tales, Po, you are hopeless."

As they had at the previous village, they sat in a circle around the fire pit in the center of the village, only this time the chorus contributed as much to the meal as the villagers did. The conversation drifted to the deteriorating conditions on the plain. "Used to be we'd harvest two crops of barley a year," said a woman who looked to be about Siblea's age. "Now we're lucky if we get one."

"Last year, a dust storm wiped out our seedlings and we had to start all over a month late in the season," said a man.

"The land gets drier and more infertile every year."

Siblea told them about methods of irrigation and fertilization. "If you are willing, we can teach you these things, as well as how to read."

The head man mulled over Siblea's offer. "We will see how my son is in the morning."

The next day, Po checked on the head man's son. He was much improved, sitting up and eating a big bowl of barley gruel. When Po examined him, he needed only minor adjustments. "His system is very resilient," he told the boy's mother. "He just needed a push in the right direction."

She hugged Po.

The boy felt better and was restless. He wanted to join the others in the field, but his mother forbade it. "You must get your strength back," she told him.

"Perhaps if we sat outside . . . ," said Po. "The fresh air might do him some good."

So they sat outside the head man's hut and Po read aloud to the boy from *The Book of the Night*. And soon four or five other children who were too small for the fieldwork were gathered in a circle around them. At midday, when people returned from the fields for a bit to eat and a rest, some of them sat and listened as well.

Po gave the boy another kinesiology session that evening, and confirmed that his pathways were solid and in balance.

After they'd eaten the evening meal, the head man said, "Have you all heard the story of why the Ayorites have curly hair?"

"Because the Goat Girl was struck by lightning trying to out-shout thunder," said Jan.

"No, not the Goat Girl version, the Fly story."

"You know a Fly story?" Jan was skeptical.

"Yes I do," he said with pride. "My grandma told me it, and she was told it by her grandpa, and he was the brother-in-law of the next-door neighbor of the Boy who Outran the Wind."

"Okay, then, let's hear it."

Po was shocked at this confrontational exchange, but from the smiling faces of the villagers, and of Jan, he guessed that this was some sort of traditional call-and-response.

"Yes I do," the head man continued, his chest expanding with pride. "My grandma told me it, and she was told it by her grandpa, and he was the brother-in-law of the next-door neighbor of the Boy Who Outran the Wind."

Jan cocked his head to one side. "Okay, then, let's hear it."

Well, as you know, many many people have wondered why Ayorites have brown and curly hair. And one of them was this boy who could run faster than anyone, even faster than the wind. Well one day, this boy and the Goat Girl were arguing about why Ayorites have brown and curly hair. She had her version, and we've all heard it, but the boy who ran was skeptical, and he decided to go ask the Fly. So he ran out into the desert. He ran so far and so fast that he outpaced not just the wind, but the Last Wind of the World. His feet turned into sand. And still he ran. His knees turned into sand, and he ran on. Finally all of him was sand except his mouth to ask the question and his ears to hear the answer and he found the Fly. Not just any fly, you know, but the Fly, the one who guards all the mysteries of this world. And he asked the Fly, Why do

Ayorites have brown and curly hair? And this is what the fly told him:

A long, long time ago, this world was nothing. There was no life here, and no light, and no air for life to breathe. There was no sky, no sun, no moons, no wind or rain. There wasn't even room for emptiness.

And then some people who knew how to walk sideways through time came along and decided to do something about it. These weren't ordinary people like you or me, just like the Fly isn't an ordinary fly. These were the People Who Walk Sideways in Time. And they could go wherever they wanted, whenever they wanted. Well, who can say, with people like that, why they do the things they do? But whatever the reason, they made a place for their children to play and they took their children's favorite stories and made people, like us, for their kids to play with.

Now this is a long and roundabout way of answering your question, I'm sure, said the Fly to the Boy Who Outran the Wind, and I'm sure you're all thinking the same thing now. What does all of this have to do with Ayorites having curly hair? Well, the answer is simple. One of the favorite characters from the most popular story of the Children of the People Who Walk Sideways in Time had brown and curly hair. So that's why.

The headman sat back and took a sip from his cup. He looked at them with evident satisfaction.

That satisfaction was not mirrored on the others' faces. There was a pause, and then Jan said, "See, this is why I hate Fly stories. They never make any sense."

The head man shrugged. "You think curly hair being caused by a lightning strike makes more sense?"

Their conversation rolled over Po. He couldn't stop thinking about the People Who Walk Sideways in Time. What did that mean?

He never found out, because the next day, the chorus departed at dawn.

Five days later they encountered another village. This time, the moment they were spotted, a call went out and the entire village came running toward them. Siblea and Selene went ahead to meet them. The tall old man held his hands out like a priestess accepting the accolades of the faithful. "Greetings, people of the plain," he said.

The crowd did not slow down. Po, observing from near the wagon along with Hilloa, Jan, and Baris, noticed that the way they held their pitchforks and adzes was anything but casual. He glanced at Hilloa. She shook her head. As one, they ran forward. "Libyrarian!" Po shouted. "Selene! Come back!"

"Siblea! Siblea!"

Behind them, Baris and Jan hastened to catch up. "What is it?"

The first of the villagers were now within shouting distance. "Get away from here, lit scum!" shouted the angry villagers. "We've had enough of your raiding!"

"Peace, brothers and sisters of the plain," said Selene. "We are the Chorus of the Word and we bring you news of the Redemption."

"You took all our grain!" The man in the lead raised a cudgel and struck Selene over the head with it. She crumpled to the ground.

"Fuck you and your books!"

Siblea fell beneath a blow from another. Po grabbed Selene under the arms and started dragging her away. Someone struck him across the shoulders with the haft of an adze and he staggered. Jan fended the man off with a kick to his groin. "Hurry, get her to the wagon!" he shouted.

Hilloa wrested an adze from a villager and struck him with it while Baris helped Siblea, who was bleeding from a cut to his forehead, retreat. They all piled back into the wagon and Po, the largest of them, grabbed the handles of the cart and ran as the villagers shouted and pelted rocks at them.

By the time he dared to stop, Selene had revived and Jan had bandaged the wound to Siblea's forehead. They made camp high up on a plateau. Po performed kinesiology on Selene, treating her concussion and coming away with a lasting headache. No one asked him to treat Siblea and Po was glad. He took his bedroll from the wagon and went to sleep.

"I think someone's trying to make us look bad," said Jan, long after Po thought everyone had gone to sleep.

"But how would they even know about us?" said Hilloa. "It's more likely it's just some bandits running a scam on these people."

"In any case," said Selene, "we must be on the lookout for this group, and for any other villagers who've been harmed by them. I think for now, we had better head straight for the Corvariate Citadel. No more villages."

She got no arguments.

15

Ayma

There was no sound but the wind. The silence of the plain echoed in the empty, burning blue dome of the sky. Po wiped the sweat off the back of his neck with a rag long since soaked with it and now starting to crust up around the edges.

They had just descended a ridge and a wide, flat plain of red sandstone lay before them, bits of its broken surface scattered like waves on the ocean. How he missed the sea.

"There," said Baris, pointing to the far horizon.

For a moment Po saw water, but it was only the memory of it still cherished by his eyes. No, it was a low, mounded form, shadowy and blue with distance. "The Corvariate Citadel," said Siblea.

As they neared the citadel, they found that rocks and

pebbles were not all that lay strewn upon the ground. Corn husks, broken sandals, scarves, socks: all manner of human debris scattered the plain that was now furrowed by cartwheels. "What is all this?" asked Jan.

"It must be stuff people dropped along the way on the pilgrimage to the Redemption," said Siblea.

It was eerie to see such abundant evidence of people, and yet except themselves, there was not another soul in evidence. Even when they reached the citadel itself, with its massive walls of gray stone rising up before them, its great arched gate standing partway open, there was no one—no sound, no movement save the wind fluttering in a red kerchief that had snagged upon a silverleaf bush sprouting up from the base of the wall.

"I don't know about this," said Selene. "Something feels wrong."

Siblea nodded. "The place is deserted. Not all of the people left for the Redemption. What's happened to them?"

"I think, as a precaution, we'd better leave the wagon here for now," said Selene, and Siblea agreed. Po wheeled it up a rise and into the shelter of a rock overhang. When he returned, the rest of the chorus was already following Siblea through the gate.

It towered fifty feet above them, and even half-shut as it was, there was ample room for him, Jan, Hilloa, and Baris to walk through side by side.

Once inside, Po did not know which was more shocking: the sheer size of the place or its apparent utter desertion. They stood on a broad avenue that was lined with buildings similar in design to the Libyrinth—domes and towers— only these were made from gray stone, not sandstone. The avenue ran the length of the citadel to a building on the far side of the city that was at least as big as the Libyrinth itself. Its front was fashioned to resemble an enormous gray face with its mouth wide open. "The Temple of Yammon," said Siblea.

Streetlights stood on either side of the street. They were not the kind Po knew from Ilysies, which used palmglow. These were made to run on electricity. Some of them were still lit, but others appeared to be broken, their lightbulbs shattered. It seemed a shame for such glory and opulence to fall into disrepair.

Smaller streets ran off of this main avenue in a regular, grid-shaped pattern. Po spotted a young woman peering at them from the shadow of a doorway in one of these narrower tributaries. Just as he was about to point her out, she disappeared inside. The street was lifeless again. Nothing moved.

Po was about to say something about the young woman when Siblea muttered, "By the Song and the Seven Tales," and hurried toward a row of streetlights that Po had assumed to be jury-rigged with hanging lanterns of some sort. But they weren't lanterns that hung suspended from the lampposts. Black-robed figures hung by their necks, lifeless and in varying stages of decomposition, on both sides of the street, one after another, seemingly all the way to the temple itself.

Baris went pale and was sick in the street. For once, Po felt sorry for him.

"Yammon's tonsils," swore Siblea. "What has happened here?"

"Where is everybody else?" Selene wondered aloud. "They can't all have come on pilgrimage or been . . ."

"I saw someone just now, but she ran away as soon as I spotted her," said Po.

"Talis?" said Baris, wiping his mouth as he looked up at one of the more recently hanged victims. "It's Talis!" He turned to Siblea, pleading, as if somehow Siblea could make it not true. "Who did this?" His voice rang out along the street and echoed back at them.

Moved, Po reached out a hand to comfort Baris. The other boy slapped it away, grimaced, and then struck Po a heavy blow on the side of his face. Caught off guard, Po swayed. Baris took advantage of his disorientation and rushed him, grabbing him by the waist and bringing him down. Baris straddled his chest and cocked his fist to punch him in the face with it.

"Baris!" shouted Siblea.

Baris shook his head. Then, suddenly there came a crashing, cacophonous sound, so abrupt and harsh in the surrounding silence that they all jumped. Po pushed Baris off him and got to his feet. "What is that?" said Jan.

Selene shook her head. The sound grew louder and Po made out a few words: "I positively hoped, that my aspect was not so—what shall I say?—so—unappetizing: a touch of fantastic vanity which fitted well with the dream sensation that pervaded all my days at that time." They were interspersed by a clash and clatter, a noise that set Po's teeth on edge.

"You. Over here." This was another voice, much softer, and it came from the alley near which they stood. It was the young woman Po had seen a moment before. He tugged at Selene's sleeve and pointed.

The girl motioned frantically for them to join her, and by now, Siblea and the others had noticed her, too. With anxious glances in the direction of the clanging and shouting, they hurried toward her. She was about Po's age and she wore a skirt and blouse that had seen better days. She had large brown eyes and long, lush, dark hair. She was short and round and curved in every possible way and Po loved her on sight. "Follow me," she whispered. "You don't want to be caught out here by them."

Siblea narrowed his eyes. "And who are you?"

"I'm nobody, but unless you want to wind up like them," she nodded at the bodies hanging from the lamp posts, "you'd better follow me."

Siblea turned to Selene. "It could be a trap," he said.

"One can't live with one's finger constantly on one's pulse," shouted the voice from up the street, louder now. Siblea was right, of course. The stranger very well could be leading them into a trap, but that voice and the sounds that accompanied it were so menacing, Po could not help but edge closer to her, and he noticed that Baris, Jan, and Hilloa did the same. Selene shook her head at Siblea and said, "We must get out of the street."

They followed their guide up a narrow alley between two buildings. She opened a door and led them into a dim, cool place that smelled of beer and wood shavings. As his eyes adjusted, Po found himself in a large room with numerous tables and a long counter along one wall. It was a tavern.

Shuttered windows ran along the wall facing the street. Siblea and Po went to them and peered out through the cracks in their slats. The noise grew louder still, and then, rounding a corner three blocks away, came the oddest procession Po had ever seen. People dressed in dark robes much like their own carried odd, curving sheets of metal which they shook to make a noise like a thunderstorm. Their faces and hands were covered with spirals and curving lines, like songlines. Po started. They looked like the scar Haly bore on her face—the one everyone said Siblea had given her.

After the people carrying the noisemakers came a group bearing a litter carved all over with words. On the litter sat a man upon a throne. The back of the throne was taller than he was, and worked to resemble a star burst.

He held a book in his hand, from which he read in a voice loud enough to be heard even over the sounds of his retinue. At the sight of him, Siblea gasped. Po looked at him. He'd never seen Siblea so frightened. "Thescarion," Siblea breathed. And then he looked back through the shutters. The others gathered around Po and Siblea. Breathless, they all watched as the procession passed.

"What is it, Siblea?" asked Selene when the procession had disappeared and the noise had finally faded away. "What is going on?"

"As to that, I have no idea, but I can tell you that that man"—he pointed out the window, his hand shaking—" was the most notorious criminal we ever had. He called himself the Lit King. He was caught harboring over a hundred and fifty books stashed all over the city. He had memorized them and was teaching his daughter to read—she's the one who turned him in. Even after he was brought into custody, he kept trying to write down the books he'd memorized, using anything he could find for the task. He was without a doubt the most recalcitrant subject I ever encountered." He turned to the young woman, who had gone behind the bar and was now pouring tankards of ale. "What is he doing out of prison?"

She seemed to shrink in upon herself. "He led the revolt," she replied, her voice little more than a whisper.

"What revolt?" said Selene.

The girl glanced up, and this time there was fire in her eyes. "Why do you dress like a priest?" She turned to Hilloa. "You, too."

The women shook their heads in confusion.

"We are not priests in the sense you're thinking of, my dear," said Siblea in his most condescending tone. "We are members of the Chorus of the Word, come from the Libyrinth to spread the good news of the Redemption, and to do research for the benefit of all. Thank you for guiding us to safety. What is your name?"

Po bristled at Siblea's attitude but the young woman appeared to find comfort in it. "My name is Ayma, Censor. I . . . I remember you." She risked a glance from beneath her brows at all of them. "Are you here to fight him?"

"We are not here to fight," said Selene. "We are here to learn and explore."

The girl gave Selene a stony look, then glanced at Siblea. Po got the distinct impression that she would not believe a word Selene said unless it was verified by Siblea. "We must come to an understanding of the situation before we can determine proper action," said Siblea.

"We have a mission," Selene warned him.

He gave an enigmatic nod. "Indeed. Now Ayma, what can you tell us about what has come to pass in the citadel since the exodus?"

"I will tell you all I can, Censor." She nodded to the mugs. "These are on the house. Please, sit, drink. My father kept the inn well-stocked with beer, but I'm afraid I have no food."

Baris grabbed a tankard and gulped it down, beer running from the corners of his mouth and down his chin. "Ahh. I've missed beer."

The others helped themselves and took seats at the tables. "Thank you, ma'am," said Po. Ayma gave him a quizzical look.

Po drank. The ale was tangy and bitter, rich with hops, refreshing and soothing and fortifying all at once. Ayma stood behind the bar, watching them as if awaiting an order for another round.

"What happened here, Ayma?" said Siblea.

Ayma seemed to return to herself at his words. "After everyone left for the Redemption, all the heretics, witches, and lits in the dungeon rose up. They killed their guards, and then they took over the city. The Lit King is their leader. Some of the people tried to fight them at first, but they were killed, too. Now we just try to stay out of their way."

"Isn't it dangerous for you to be helping us, then?" asked Jan.

She nodded. "But my father was one of the ones who fought."

Oh. Po looked about him. The tavern was large. Once it had been prosperous. Now it had a half-abandoned air about it.

"Will they find us here?" said Selene.

Ayma shrugged. "Maybe."

Selene raised her eyebrows. "Maybe? What kind of an answer is that?"

Ayma's nostrils flared. She looked at Selene as if the Libyrarian was something that had adhered to the sole of her shoe. "A good enough answer for one such as you.

You may dress like a priest but that doesn't make you one."

Selene's eyes went wide and she opened her mouth to retort but Siblea cut her off. "Forgive me, Ayma," he said, standing up. "I've quite forgotten my manners in the shock of all this. I should have introduced you to everyone properly. I am Siblea, not Censor Siblea any longer. As members of the Redeemed Community of the Libyrinth, we do not make distinctions of status among ourselves. If you feel you must use an honorific, 'Libyrarian' will suffice for any one of us. This is Selene. She was a Libyrarian long before I became one. She is very knowledgeable and deserving of your respect."

Ayma looked Selene up and down with a skeptical expression on her face.

"The same goes for Hilloa, here. She is your own age, but brought up with the egalitarian expectations of the Libyrinth. She has no need to defer to any man here."

The glance Ayma gave Hilloa was less hostile and more speculative.

"Baris was a subaltern here at one time, but he, too, has abandoned the notions of his culture of origin and regards women as equals." The way Siblea looked at Baris as he spoke, Po got the sense that his words were as much a warning to Baris as a reassurance for Ayma. "Jan is an Ayorite, and Po here—you may find some common ground with Po. He was an Ilysian before—raised in a society where men serve women."

Ayma's eyes widened at this. She seemed skeptical as she glanced Po's way. He smiled and nodded to her, but she quickly glanced away. She looked about at them, saw them all looking at her, and blushed. "I don't know what I can do to help you, but I'll try."

"You can tell us more about the Lit King and what is happening in the citadel these days," prompted Siblea.

She nodded. "Well, the Lit King is in charge here now. He's nothing more than a lit jailbird, and everyone knows it, but we're afraid of him and his people, so we pretend to love books. His minions are everywhere. We're not allowed to sing anymore. We're all supposed to learn to read and write. That's not going so well, because most of the instructors will get drunk first and forget. And if you get something wrong, that's almost as bad as not being able to read at all." She turned to Siblea, her eyes pleading. "I don't understand, Censor. Books are evil, or they were. But we're supposed to love books now. Which is it? Which is the truth?"

"The Word has been Redeemed, and reunited with the Song, my dear. There is no longer any harm in literacy. In fact, it is to be encouraged."

"So he's right. If we do not learn to read, we'll be damned. I . . . I don't know how to read."

"It's not a question of damnation, Ayma. There is no damnation anymore."

Po saw clearly that she had a question, but did not dare ask it. Instead, she picked up a rag and began to wipe down the bar with it.

"What does the Lit King say about the Libyrinth?" Siblea asked her.

"It is like paradise."

"And what about the Redemption?"

"Any Redemption which he is not a part of, and which

did not immolate all Singers in their own fires of purification is a false Redemption," she recited, as if by rote.

"What kind of control does he have over his followers?"

Ayma shrugged. "Not much. He has most of the food,
and he led them to freedom, so they obey him, or at least
pretend to. They're criminals, most of them. I don't think
all of them really believe in literacy the way he does."

Siblea nodded. "Not everyone we imprisoned was there
for literacy or heresy. Some of them—most of them—
were common miscreants."

"Siblea, all of this is beside the point. We need to get
the bloom and go, as quickly as possible," said Selene.

"And leave innocents such as this at the mercy of an
unruly mob of criminals? What would our Redeemer say
to that?"

"She won't say anything if she's dead of starvation before
we get back."

"Besides," said Hilloa, "what can we do? We are only
six people."

"That is as it may be. If this young girl can defy this
tyrant, then there must be others here who will also stand
against him," said Siblea.

At these words, Ayma looked up, eyes shining.

Selene stood up. "Siblea, we have our own community
to think about. You're getting sidetracked."

"Endymion's rose is an old wive's tale," said Siblea. "If
there is aid for the Libyrinth here, it is in the technologies
of the citadel. In order to make use of those, we must deal
with this usurper." He turned to Ayma again. "Where
does he make his lair?"

Ayma, clearly frightened, said, "The T-t-temple of Yammon, sir."

Siblea and Baris both drew in long, rasping breaths.

In the ensuing silence, Selene groaned. "All of that is beside the point. We have a mission to accomplish."

"What is your mission?" said Ayma. Unlike the lowered eyes and soft tone she employed when speaking to the men, she looked directly at Selene, and her words were blunt, almost confrontational. "We thought we were forsaken. Now you are here, but not . . ." Now she glanced at Siblea and hesitated. "Not to save us, just yet."

"We seek an object that may make life better for everyone. It is called the Lion's Bloom," said Selene.

"Or Endymion's rose," added Jan.

Ayma colored. She stared so hard at the surface of the bar Po half expected twin holes to appear in the polished wood. "I'm sorry. You are quite right to rebuke me. I should not question wise ones such as yourselves. It's just that after the Lit King rose up, we thought the Redeemed had forsaken us."

"No," said Siblea. "We have not forsaken you. We will help you."

"Siblea . . . ," Selene began, in warning.

Siblea stood. "We will stay here tonight, and tomorrow we can take a look around the city, get the lay of the land."

"And search for the rose," stressed Selene.

Siblea gave a noncommittal tilt of his head. "Of course. And of course we may find other things that may aid our cause in the process."

Selene sighed. "We'll talk more about this, Siblea." She yawned. "I'm going to turn in."

"Me too," said Hilloa. "Just think—a real bed!"

Selene, Hilloa, and Siblea filed upstairs. Po, Baris, and

Jan remained. Jan pulled out a book and began to read. Baris reached into his knapsack and drew out a salted roll. Po, who couldn't seem to stop staring at Ayma, caught the look on her face when she saw the food. He remembered her apologizing for not having any food to give them. She caught herself and turned to pour them more beer.

"Here," he said, taking a roll and a jar of peabea from his own bag. "In return for the ale," he said, placing them on the bar.

She licked her lips at the sight of the food, then glanced up at him, a question in her eyes. He smiled, and bowed his head. "Please. It would be my honor."

After a long pause, she reached out slowly, as if anticipating some trick, and took the food. "Thank you."

"She'll be eating something else later tonight," said Baris with a laugh.

As usual, his words made little sense, but it was clear from his tone that they were meant as disrespect to their host. Po whirled around and charged Baris, grabbing him by the front of the robe. "What is that supposed to mean?"

Baris dropped his roll on the floor but rallied with a sickly grin. "She's a tavern slut, Po, come on. I know you're all into venerating women, and I'm trying to be understanding about it, but a girl like that—she's beneath you. At least, she wants to be."

It took him a second to get the joke. Po shoved Baris back into his seat, confusion robbing him of the thrill of righteous anger. Baris was saying that Ayma wanted him for a consort. Was that true? Baris also seemed to be saying that it was contemptible that Ayma should want him. So who was Baris insulting—Po or Ayma? Or both of them?

What was the point in trying to unravel it? He settled for an all-purpose warning. "You leave her alone."

For some reason this made Baris laugh even harder, wheezing as he bent to retrieve his roll. Po turned his back on him and returned to the bar, where Ayma ate with urgent efficiency. She shrank back as he approached, fear in her eyes. It made him want to die. Why was she afraid of him? "Would you like another ale, sir?" she said.

"No thank you, ma'am." He'd had two already and he wasn't used to drinking. There was a warm buzzing sensation in his head and chest, not altogether unpleasant, but a bit strange. "Please, keep eating. Have all you want."

He could not for the life of him decipher the look she gave him then, but she did reach forward, slowly, and took the food back.

"She thinks you're buying her, Po," said Baris.

"Buying her what?" he asked, and Baris and Jan laughed. They were no help.

When Ayma finished eating, she looked up at him solemnly with her big, dark eyes, and asked, "Would you like me to show you to your room, sir?"

Po smiled. "Yes, ma'am."

As he followed her up the stairs, he heard Baris and Jan laughing. They were jealous that she was paying attention to him. Po smiled.

Ayma took him to an empty room furnished with a bed and a chest of drawers. Shutters closed off a window opposite the door. It was dark out now, only a little starlight filtered in through the slats. Ayma lit a candle on the chest of drawers, then stood looking at him, an uncertain expression on her face.

"Thank you for letting us stay here." Po looked at the

bed. "It's big," he said. "Do you mean for me to sleep here by myself?"

She shook her head. "No, of course not. I . . . I wasn't sure if you . . . Of course." He waited for her to tell him he'd be sharing with Jan, or Baris, or both, but instead she sat down on the bed. Her head still bowed, she gave him a sidelong look. "You are Ilysian," she said.

Po nodded. "I was, before I joined the community at the Libyrinth," he explained.

"Are you very different from other men?"

"I don't know. Our ideas about women and men are very different from yours."

"I've heard that in Ilysies, the women are in control of everything."

"I guess."

"So, you are like a woman, then?"

That wasn't how he wanted her to think of him. He shrugged. "I'm male, but . . . I probably have more in common with a citadel woman like you than with any of the men here."

She laughed and her smile reached her eyes as she gazed at him. For a moment, the sun was shining in the middle of the night. She looked down again, the smile still curling at the corners of her mouth, like a sleeping cat. She reached up and undid the tie of her blouse. "But still, you buy a woman."

"What?!" Shock made Po back away. Baris's words came back to him, and with them, a chill flood of understanding. *She thinks you're buying her.* There was no "what" missing from that sentence. He'd meant *her*. Buying her, like a slave. She did not want him. She offered herself to him in exchange for the food he'd given her. It was repulsive past anything Po had imagined possible.

She shook her head, clearly panicking as much as he was. As she sat up, her blouse gaped open and he saw one of her breasts, heavy as cream. "I'm sorry! Sir, sir, I'm sorry!"

"What? No! I don't . . . Buy? You?"

Her look became pleading. "Please. I like you very much. I don't mean to offend you. I only thought . . . You gave me food!"

Po felt ill. "There's been a mistake."

She hurriedly tied her blouse up again. "You don't want me."

"I do! But I don't buy you. I gave you the food because you were hungry, that's all. It wasn't *payment*. I can't pay a woman to make me her consort—that's . . . that's just wrong. I thought you wanted me."

She stared at him in silence for a moment. "I'm sorry. I don't know Ilysian men. I meant no offense."

He nodded. "Okay. I'm not offended. Don't be afraid, please. I would never hurt you."

She nodded. "You fought the blond Singer because he offered me insult. And the way you watch me. I think you still want me, si—Po."

"You're beautiful."

She smiled and leaned back on the bed, tilting her chin and pushing her breasts up. "You can still have me. It doesn't have to be because of the food."

Po swallowed. He was aflame for her, but . . . "But do you want me?"

"Of course. You're strong and kind. You'll protect me

from the others. . . ." She paused, biting her lip. "And when you leave, you can take me with you."

Po turned away. If he didn't look at her, he had some hope of controlling his response to her. She didn't want him. She wanted the things he could provide her with: food, protection, the hope of a better future. With a start he realized that was exactly what he'd hoped to gain from every liaison he'd sought: Selene, Hilloa, Thela herself. Was he ever interested in them beyond what being their consort could provide? Suddenly he felt the very opposite of horny. He felt disgusted—with himself and with Ayma. He blew out the candle and sat down on the floor with his back to the door. "Get some sleep," he told her. "I won't let Baris or anyone else bother you, and once we find the bloom, I'll do everything I can to make sure you come with us to the Libyrinth."

"I've made you angry."

"No." But it was a lie.

When he awoke, he was far from the door, wrapped in a blanket, his head on a pillow. He sat up. The bed was empty. Ayma had gone.

There was a knock on the door and Selene said, "Po, if you don't get downstairs right now, you're going to miss breakfast."

Breakfast. And Ayma would be offered food again, if she had none, and then would she give herself to that person, and would they accept? What if it were Baris? Irrational jealousy propelled him from the floor. Why should he care? She was unnatural, to behave as if she were a commodity. Let her do as she wished.

Still, he hastened into his robe and fairly ran downstairs. There he found that two tables had been pushed together and the chorus sat around it. Ayma sat with them, wedged between Selene and Hilloa, chewing on a piece of bread with a shuttered expression on her face. She looked up as Po entered and for a moment their eyes met. Po flushed with shame, and he saw her blush as well. He looked away. Did she think he had meant to buy her, and then had rejected her? And if so, for which act did she hate him more?

Po did not look at her as he took a seat between Jan and Baris. He reached for a roll and some peabea to smear on it. He felt eyes on him and looked up to find the entire table watching him—except for Ayma, who had stopped eating and now stared at the table, clearly mortified.

Hilloa looked at him with reproach. Selene appeared to be unsuccessfully suppressing humor; Siblea tilted his head upward with superiority. Jan appeared to be exasperated— why, he did not know—and Baris, of all things, looked sympathetic.

"We have explained to Ayma that for as long as we are staying here she will eat with us, and that all of us will treat her with honor and respect," said Siblea.

Po glanced at Baris and Jan. What exactly had they told Siblea? "Of course," he said, looking at Hilloa, since Ayma would not look at him. He wanted to explain, but he didn't know where to begin. He did not really understand what had happened himself. "Of course."

"Since our own food stores are limited, I suggest that our first order of business today be securing more supplies," said Siblea. He leaned toward Ayma. "Will you accompany us to the market?"

She nodded, though reluctantly. "It is dangerous, and

expensive. Some days, there is little there. When there is, there is usually fighting. But you can take some of the beer to trade, if you want."

"Perhaps we can offer the merchants books," said Jan. "Since literacy is encouraged now."

Ayma gave a little shake of her head, caught herself, and then stared at the table again.

"What?" Hilloa said, prodding her gently. "Why is that a bad idea?"

Ayma lifted one shoulder. "If they are the wrong books . . ."

"The wrong books?" said Selene.

Ayma nodded. "The Lit King only likes certain books. *Heart of Darkness*, like he read from yesterday in the procession; *Peer Gynt*; *Moby Dick*; *Roseanne*. There are others, but no one knows all of them and sometimes the list changes. He's . . . mad."

They were all silent a moment. Then Siblea said, "What about *The Book of the Night*? Do you think that would be worth anything to the merchants?"

Ayma's eyes opened wide. "You have *The Book of the Night*?"

"Here." Siblea reached into his satchel and drew out his own copy. "You may have it. We have many copies."

Ayma stared at the book in her hand as if she held a fragile and dangerous thing. "Many copies? Then . . ." She smiled. "Then the Redemption *is* real."

"Of course," said Siblea.

"He said it was a false Redemption. We thought we'd been forsaken for nothing. But . . . this . . ."

"Siblea," said Selene, "food is important, I agree, but we need to consider our mission as well. I'm not at all sure that handing out copies of *The Book of the Night* in the marketplace is going to get us any closer to finding the bloom. In fact, it could draw attention to our presence here in ways we don't want."

"She's right," said Hilloa. "We should try to make do with what we have for now. Once we get the bloom and turn the plain green with it, there will be food for everyone."

"If the bloom even exists," countered Siblea. "Besides, just how do you propose we embark on our search? The citadel is a large place, and since this object was not found at any time during our occupation of it, it must truly be secreted away."

"Then that's where we start," said Selene, "at the places that nobody goes to. We've discussed this. The Well of Silence, the old theater, Endymion's tomb." She stood up. "Come on, what are we waiting for? Let's go."

Siblea remained seated.

"Siblea—look, we have food enough for everyone for another day and a half. If we don't find the bloom today, we'll go to the market tomorrow."

"It should be the other way around," he insisted. "Ayma said that the market is depleted. We may not successfully provision today. I would rather we tried that first. Then we have tomorrow to figure out something else if we're unsuccessful."

"Perhaps some of us can go to the Well of Silence and some of us can go to the market," suggested Jan.

"No," said Siblea and Selene in unison.

"Well, at least you agree on one thing," said Hilloa. "Look, Siblea, you're not fooling anyone. We know you have no real interest in finding the bloom. You don't even believe it exists. And since we've arrived, it's obvious that you are upset about the Lit King and want to do something about him. It's understandable, but he will still be here later. The situation at the Libyrinth is critical. I think you've forgotten that."

Silence hung over the table as Siblea looked at the others. All of them, except for Baris and Ayma, nodded in agreement with what Hilloa had said. "I see," he said. "Very well; we'll go to the Well of Silence, then."

"Wait," said Ayma.

Shocked that she'd spoken, they all turned to her.

"You'd better not go out dressed like that," she said, nodding at their robes. "People will think you're priests, and if any of the Lit King's mob sees you . . ." She didn't need to finish the sentence. "There are some clothes upstairs; they belonged to my father."

Half an hour later, the Chorus of the Word assembled in the main hall of the tavern, dressed in the clothing of its former proprietor. Po and Baris both wore homespun wool trousers and tunics. The pants strained at Baris's waistline and stopped about a hand span above Po's ankles; Hilloa and Selene wore skirts and blouses similar to Ayma's, all equally worn and stained. Jan wore a spun silverleaf shirt that was probably only worn on special occasions, and a pair of felt drawstring pants. Siblea had presented the greatest difficulty. He was well enough known to be recognized, and on top of that, Ayma's father was not a tall man like he was. He wore a hooded poncho to help hide his face and a pair of coveralls, their straps extended with rope so they hung low enough to cover his legs.

After showing them the clothes, Ayma had resumed her station behind the bar. Despite the fact that the surface gleamed already, she polished it with her rag, her hand moving in repetitive, slow circles. She had an absent look on her face, as if she had gone somewhere else in her mind.

"Ayma?" said Hilloa.

She started.

"Would you like to come with us?"

She looked dismayed, and directed her gaze to Siblea. "I . . . must I?"

"Of course not," he said. "We just thought you might wish to. That you might be safer, with company."

Her mouth formed a small *O*, as if the notion that they concerned themselves with her safety was a novel one. "Thank you, Censor. But . . . I will remain here. I'll wait for your return."

As they left the tavern, Po looked over his shoulder. She was still behind the bar, still polishing it.

16

The Marketplace

W hat is the Well of Silence, anyway?" Po asked Selene as they made their way down a narrow side street. They were avoiding the main thoroughfares.

Of course, Siblea thought nothing of answering the question, even though it wasn't directed at him.

"It is the place where the Devouring Silences used to bring their victims."

Jan paled. "Are there still any left alive?"

"No. Not since Yammon slew the last one."

"He didn't slay the last one," said Selene. "Haly did, last year."

Siblea shrugged. "Well, we thought they were all dead."

Selene shook her head. "I don't think—"

"If you would rather that we went to the market . . . "

said Siblea, grinning at Selene's reaction. "By virtue of being a shunned place, the well is a perfect hiding place," he continued. He gave her an insincere smile. "Don't be afraid, my dear."

She set her jaw and gave a short nod. "Fine. Lead on."

As they walked, the buildings became smaller and more decrepit. Apparently no one wanted to live near this place. Po had no difficulty keeping up with Siblea's long strides, but as usual, Baris did. Po deliberately slackened his pace so as to fall back to where Baris wheezed along. Baris gave him a quizzical glance but said nothing.

After a time, Po said, "Citadel people hate sex, right?"

Baris laughed. "Hardly."

"But they think it's wrong."

Baris tilted his head to one side. "Sort of. It depends. You're supposed to get married first. But even then, nobody really cares if men do it outside of marriage."

"But it's bad for women."

"Their reputations, you mean? Yeah. They're whores."

"And that's bad?"

Baris snorted. "Yeah. This is about Ayma, isn't it?"

"She offered herself to me, but she didn't want me."

Baris shook his head, laughing openly now. "You crack me up, Po. Of course she did. She wanted what you can offer her—your protection, your food. Besides, she thought you expected it. She was afraid to refuse you."

"Afraid? Why?"

"Well, it's generally easier on the woman if she goes along with it. If she doesn't make the guy force the issue."

For an instant, the neighborhood of shabby homes and pitted stone dissolved in a fizzle of incandescence. In the blink of an eye he was walking down the street beside Baris once more, but everything was different—the buildings, the shadows, even the paving stones held new menace. Force.

The idea that Ayma thought of him as someone who would—he couldn't even think of it—made him feel ill—guilty and at the same time furious at the injustice of the charge. "I'd never—"

"I know. So does the rest of the chorus. Look, she just has a different set of expectations. The mistake you're making is in thinking that it matters what she thinks."

How could it not matter? Po decided not to ask him.

The buildings dwindled and dwindled, becoming mere hovels before finally falling away entirely before a wide open, circular space with a large cavity in the center. They stood at the edge and looked down into a vast, bowl-shaped crater littered with what appeared at first to be thousands upon thousands of steel masks—faces looking up at them. Po's heart tightened and he forced himself to breathe. Dead—they were all dead.

There wasn't a person, Ilysian, Libyrarian, Singer, or Ayorite, who didn't know about the Devouring Silences. They were the nightmare of the Ancients' reign, slave takers. They burrowed underground and surfaced in the middle of a town or village in the dead of night and then deployed their "tongues"—tentacles that stunned people and sent them into a deep stupor. They gathered them inside their body and returned with them, here, where the victims were collected by those who served the Ancients, fresh fodder for their games. On the inside of the pit, Po saw the remnants of corrals and tunnels, where the slaves were collected and taken off to serve their new masters. A few of the Devouring Silences had flipped over, showing the ribbed, flexible undercarriage with which they propelled themselves. And here and there, in between the metal carcasses, Po spotted a few human bones as well.

"What makes you think the bloom can be here?" said Jan.

"If you wanted to hide something, this would be a good place," said Selene. "It's shunned. Look at how loath we ourselves are to go down there."

"What if some of them are still alive?" said Baris.

"They're not. Nothing has moved in this place for generations," said Siblea.

"Come on," said Hilloa. "Let's get it over with."

A rickety ladder led down into the pit on the southern end. They climbed down. It was difficult to get around. The place was crammed with the carcasses of Devouring Silences, each one roughly eleven feet across and twenty feet long. Po and the others climbed and crawled, all the time alert for any sign of life among the ruins. Most pathetic of all were the bones, in and among the Silences and in the corrals carved into the sides of the pit. Po tried to imagine what it must have been like to go to sleep in your village and wake up in the belly of one of these creatures, condemned to a life of slavery.

They searched the place until the sun was low, to no avail. "Let's get out of here before it gets dark," said Selene.

Siblea agreed and they all climbed out of the pit, each of them trying not to appear as anxious to get out of there as they all really were.

The following day it was decided that Selene, Jan, and Baris would continue the search for the bloom, while the others went to the market and tried to get some food.

The marketplace was a large open square filled with

booths and tables. On their journey the previous day, the city had appeared all but deserted. But here, people milled about, haggling or hawking their goods. Still, it was a pathetic, bedraggled market compared with what Po had known in Ilysies.

Apparently it had fallen far from its former glory by citadel standards, too, for Siblea shook his head and clucked at the scattered booths and thin crowd of shoppers.

Hilloa and Po were in charge of rolling Ayma's donated barrel of beer down the street. The tavern keeper had again refused to accompany them. "Why does she polish the bar all the time?" Po wondered aloud as Siblea scouted ahead for a buyer.

"Isn't it obvious?" said Hilloa. "She's been traumatized. Her father was killed by that mob. And if she offered you sex in return for food, who knows what she's been doing in order to survive."

The whole idea was unimaginable to him. "What kind of man would want a woman on terms like that?"

Hilloa laughed and gave him a sideways hug. "Oh, Po. How can you still be so naive? Have you ever *talked* to Baris?"

"That's all bluster."

"In him, yes. But it's real for others. Others who live here."

Po nodded. "I guess I don't have to understand it to see that it's real. I just . . . I don't want it to be."

She leaned into him harder. "Of course you don't. But you'd better be careful around Ayma. I know you mean well, but she's been through a hard time and the potential for misunderstanding between you two is high."

He laughed at that. "Yeah."

Hilloa released him. Her smile dimpled her chin. "Do you like her?"

A confused mix of feelings rose up in him. "I can't tell."

She raised one eyebrow, and Po got the impression that Hilloa thought she knew the answer to her question. Just then, they heard shouting up ahead.

An argument had broken out at one of the stalls. Two men were fighting over a sack of barley as the merchant looked on. A crowd gathered around the men and the chorus joined it.

"I paid him!" yelled one man. "It's mine!"

"He promised it to me!" the other one protested.

Each of them had hold of one end of the sack and were tugging on it. Both were large, muscular men in ragged pants and tunics. The one who claimed to have purchased the grain had dark hair; the other was blond.

"He paid for it!" yelled the merchant.

The blond man glared at him. "You told me you'd save it for me! I have children at home!"

"We all have children at home, Harv," said the dark-haired man. "You didn't get here early enough—that's your misfortune, not mine."

Harv gave a mighty tug on the sack of grain and it tore. Barley flew in all directions, and the crowd scattered with it. Po, Hilloa, and Siblea looked on in dismay as everywhere people were on their hands and knees, grubbing for a few handfuls of grain.

The dark-haired man confronted the merchant. "Give me my money back."

The merchant, a thin man nearly as tall as Siblea, said,

"You received the goods, Ben. It's not my fault what happened after that."

As Ben growled and seized the merchant by the collar, a voice directly behind Po rang out. "Stop!"

It was Siblea. Po turned to see him standing on top of Ayma's barrel of ale. He had thrown back his hood and he held his hands out to the crowd. Someone murmured, "It's Censor Siblea!"

The news traveled through the crowd like wildfire. "The Singers are back! They've returned to help us!"

Po and Hilloa exchanged dismayed glances. Hilloa tugged at Siblea's overalls and whispered, "Siblea! What are you doing?"

But Siblea ignored her as well as the excited whispers of the gathered throng. "People of the Corvariate Citadel," he proclaimed, "you forget yourselves. You are not animals, to fight one another and grovel on the ground for a few morsels of food. For shame! You are men! Citizens of the largest, most advanced city this side of the ocean. Do not let the Lit King take away all that you are! Set aside your differences. Join together to fight the usurper!"

The crowd's reaction was mixed. Some nodded in approval and shouted, "Yes! Death to the lits!" while others shook their heads and looked skeptical. The tall, thin merchant stepped forward from the crowd and said, "Respecting your honor, Censor, you have not been here these past many months. We did fight him, at first. He has many men on his side, and they will stop at nothing. They ride out of town and raid the villages, so the farmers have nothing to bring to market. And the crop this year is bad, too. In the city, those who oppose him are killed. I am sure"—the man looked about him at the others gathered around—"there are many here today who would oppose the Lit King if they could. But how?"

Siblea nodded. "You speak well, sir. Those of us who have been redeemed are at fault. We should have returned to the city instead of focusing all of our efforts on the new community at the Libyrinth. If we had known what was taking place here, we would have come to your aid much sooner than this."

"Siblea! We can't . . . What are you doing? Stop!" said Hilloa, but everyone ignored her.

"But now I have returned," said Siblea. "Those who have the stomach to fight the Lit King, and to put the citadel back to what it once was, follow me!" Siblea jumped down from the barrel and at last turned to Po and Hilloa. "See what you can get for the beer. I will take those who are willing back to the tavern, where we can plan our next move."

"Siblea, you can't—" But he was gone before Hilloa could even finish her sentence. She and Po stood staring at each other in the midst of the rapidly depopulating marketplace.

"Are they all following him back to the tavern?" asked Po. He thought of Ayma and her reaction should half the town arrive and demand beer.

"No," said Hilloa. "Most of them are just running away."

They managed to make a trade with a woman selling beets and pulse. She let them know she would have preferred grain or Ilysian currency, but she was eager to flee the site of Siblea's impromptu uprising.

"Look, Po, you take these back to the tavern, okay?" said Hilloa. "I think I'd better find Selene and let her know what's going on."

17

Siblea's Revolution

When Po got to the tavern, Siblea and six other men were in close conversation. Ayma was nowhere in sight.

"He has a lot of followers in the city, mostly because people are afraid of him," Ben, the dark-haired man from the market, was saying. "The uprising took everyone by surprise."

"It was brutal, Censor," said the barley merchant.

Po walked up to the table of men. "Where is Ayma?" he demanded.

"The wench?" said Ben.

Po leaned toward him. "What does that mean?"

Siblea held up a restraining hand. "Ben means no disrespect. She must be in the back, Po. She was here when we came in." Without taking a breath, he turned back to the other men. "But what about his fellow inmates? How many of them are still with him?"

Po knew Siblea lied. Ben did offer Ayma disrespect, but he didn't want to take the time now to confront him about it. Behind the bar was an archway. It led into a close, warm space with a stove, a sink, a counter, and a chair. Two of the walls were stone—the outer walls of the building. The ones adjacent to the bar were wood, their finish long ago peeled and many of the boards dried and cracked from the heat of the stove. At the far end of the room, between the stove and the wall was a little gap. Po saw one end of a pallet poking out from there. Ayma stood at the sink, washing mugs.

At his footfalls she spun around. The wet tankard in her hand slipped free and crashed to the floor. For a moment, the look on her face was one of stark terror.

Po backed up. "I'm sorry. I startled you."

Ayma blinked and took a deep breath. "You don't have to apologize to me, sir."

It seemed an odd thing to say, but Po did not question her. He knelt and picked up the shards of the broken tankard. "Have you any glue to mend this with?"

"It doesn't matter. There are many more tankards here than will ever be used again. You don't have to do that— let me."

He stood, his hands full of pottery shards. "You want me to hand them to you? I'm afraid you'll get cut."

She laughed and her smile reached her eyes. Shaking her head, she grabbed a pail and held it out for him. He dropped the broken pottery in it and turned to the sink. "You had a bad fright. Let me finish this."

As he began washing mugs, she stared at him, open-mouthed, to all appearances dumbfounded.

He paused in the washing. "Can I get you a beer? You seem . . ." Uncomfortable, he wanted to say, but felt that would be rude.

"Why do you do my work for me?"

Po didn't know how to answer. "Do I do it poorly?"

She shook her head.

Po fetched her a beer and, since she remained in the kitchen, brought it to her there. "Here, please, make yourself comfortable."

Nonplussed, Ayma sat in the chair and allowed him to press the tankard of ale into her hands.

Po washed and dried the mugs, and put them on the shelf behind the bar. He took the sacks of food back into the kitchen. "Hey, guess what? We have food! Beets and pulse, plenty for everyone, see?" Her eyes did light up at that. Then, a moment later, she looked worried again. "Will the others be staying?"

"The others?" Po began scrubbing beets.

"The men who are with Censor Siblea."

Po thought about that. In the back of his mind was the knowledge that Siblea was acting against Selene's wishes, and at cross-purposes to the mission the Redeemer had given them. He wondered if he should do something about it. Yet it didn't seem right to let people like Ayma suffer if they could help them. He decided it was best to wait for Selene and see what she thought should be done. "I don't know. Maybe."

Ayma nodded thoughtfully and took a sip of beer. A line appeared between her eyebrows.

Po remembered the way the one man had spoken of her. "Did one of them offer you insult?" he asked.

Ayma appeared not to know what that meant. "Insult?"

"Were any of them disrespectful to you?"

One side of her mouth rose in a grin and she gave a brief, incredulous laugh. "You say the funniest things, sir."

He was missing something, and it was important. He could tell because the feeling had become very familiar in the past year, and since he'd met Ayma, he'd had it a lot. He turned to face the sink again. He closed his eyes, breathed deeply, and tried to forget about everything he knew. He turned and opened his eyes again, and tried to just see Ayma, as she was right now, and nothing more.

A young woman just barely past girlhood, small, alone, and afraid, sat in a chair holding a mug of beer. She wasn't drinking it. When she looked at him, there was both confusion and hope in her eyes. Outside the kitchen, the men's voices became loud and angry. She flinched.

Po dried his hands and knelt at her feet. "I won't let them hurt you," he said.

She opened her mouth. "Do you mean it?"

He nodded. He took the beer from her hands and she rested them on his shoulders. Her touch made him warm all the way through. This close, she smelled like hops and cinnamon. Her eyes were deep and dark, full of meaning that he could not comprehend. She bent her head and pressed her lips to his.

The kiss was deep and soft. Their lips melded together, their tongues met. Po sighed and abandoned himself to sensory overload. Instantly he was aflame for her.

"You take your time," she said, quite breathless, a few

minutes later. "After your first night here, I thought you didn't like me."

"I desire you very much," he said, gasping.

She grinned and sat forward, drawing his face down to her breasts. It was like falling into clouds. "You'll let the others see that I am with you?"

Po sat up. The sweet taste of their kiss had become sour. What he felt was real, but she—she had other reasons. This was the same as what had happened the other night, only now the coin for which she would enslave herself was his strength. With an effort he stood and backed away from her. "I won't let anyone harm you. I told you, ma'am. You don't have to do anything for that."

He looked away from the devastation in her face, but her words came to him anyway. "You give me food, you do my work, and you offer me your protection. And you take nothing in return. I want to believe you, but you're too good to be true."

Sudden clarity seared Po. How would he feel if a woman offered him every benefit of consortship, but did not let him make love to her? Not only was Po making it impossible for Ayma to believe him, but he was probably hurting her feelings as well, making her feel unwanted.

But the alternative was to allow her to make of him something so abominable he had not even truly comprehended its existence until just now. He could not become that kind of man, not even to please a woman. "You don't have to believe me."

In the main room, a door slammed. "Siblea, what in the Seven Hells do you think you're doing?" It was Selene.

"Uh-oh," said one of the men. "In trouble with the missus?" Others laughed.

Po went out through the archway to see what was going on. Ayma followed him. As they emerged from the kitchen, he took her hand. Let those men think that he was just like them, if it would protect her.

Selene stood with Hilloa at her side and Baris and Jan behind her. They all faced Siblea and his compatriots. "We have a mission," said Selene.

Siblea did not stand. He simply spread his hands out to include all present and said, "Is not our first mission always the welfare of our fellow beings?"

Selene took a deep breath. "And the best way to attend to that is to find the bloom so that we can make the land green and fertile for all. Have you forgotten the welfare of our fellow beings at the Libyrinth? In the villages we visited on our way here? There is more at stake here than your wounded pride in coming home and finding one of your own inmates in charge."

"Now please, don't overreact, Selene. I see no reason why we cannot do both. Am I preventing you from seeking the rose?"

"The rose?" said Herv.

"The rose of Endymion." Siblea spoke quickly, as if he wished not to answer at all.

"The rose of Endymion? That old wives' tale?" crowed the barley merchant. "Don't tell me that's the reason you've come here, Siblea."

"Does it matter why we came?" Siblea's tone was suddenly sharp and the men, who had all been smiling and some of them laughing, sobered. Siblea turned to Selene with a very fake smile. "How was your search today anyway?"

Po had never seen Selene so angry in all his life—not

even when he had made the mistake about the bath. For a time, she stood. Po watched her nostrils flare. Suddenly she stepped forward and started grabbing tankards from the table. Po hurried to help her.

"Hey, I wasn't done with that, lady," said Ben.

"You are now," said Selene. "Get out. All of you. This is not acceptable."

Ben guffawed and grabbed his tankard back from her. "Says who, you?"

"That's right. Siblea has been reckless. He's endangering the safety of the chorus, and of this young woman who has bravely opened her home to us."

The men guffawed. "Oh yeah, she's a real hero, she is."

"She opens her home to everybody, don't you know that?"

Po could not believe his ears or his eyes. "What do you men think you are doing?" he demanded. "What's wrong with you? She's telling you to leave."

Herv sprawled in his chair, holding his tankard in both hands. "We don't want to leave."

"It's not up to you."

"Oh no?"

Selene tried to take his beer away from him again. "You must go."

Herv shoved Selene.

Po, who had gone his entire life without ever seeing a man strike a woman, could not believe that it could look so ordinary. Selene stumbled backward. Po grabbed Herv around the neck, dragged him out of the chair, and kneed him in the stomach. Herv tried to get loose but Po pushed him to the floor, kicked him in the gut again and then straddled his chest, pinning his arms to the floor with his knees while he hit him in the face.

"Po!"

"Song and Silence! All right, we'll go!"

"Po! Stop!"

He realized that the voices had been directed at him for some time. He looked up and saw everyone standing in a circle around him and Herv. The looks on their faces varied from appalled to frightened, to impressed. He looked at the barley merchant. "You men are going now."

The man nodded slowly. "Just let us take Herv with us."

Po got up but stayed close as the men carried their friend out of the tavern. When the door had shut behind them, he bolted it and returned to where Siblea stood beside the table, looking at him with the oddest expression on his face. Po stood close enough to smell Siblea's sweat. He looked him in the eyes. "This is your fault, old man. You brought that man here and you let him disrespect Ayma and the Princess of Ilysies, and then . . . If I ever catch you letting a man get away with something like that again, I'll kill you."

He could see that Siblea believed him.

He turned and found Selene standing there. The look that passed between them was one of recognition. They were both exiles now. He looked down. His hands were bloody. The back of his throat tasted like iron and his face was hot. He thought of Herv's wife, his mother, his sisters—all those lives ruined. But no, that wasn't right. They didn't do that here. Here, no one would be punished. Po wasn't sure which was worse. If only he'd been able to stop it from ever happening in the first place; but he hadn't, and now . . . He was so afraid.

"Po."

At the first touch of Selene's hands on his shoulders, the pressure inside him burst. The sound that escaped from him was like a skull cracking, and then, a world falling into the sea.

"Come here."

She guided him to a chair, then sat beside him and drew him to her, nestling his face in the crook of her neck. She put her arms around him and held him close. Here was all that was left of everything he had always known, and he fell into it in the vain hope that he might never have to leave.

A yma watched the big guy, Po, tremble as he sobbed onto the shoulder of the Ilysian woman, Selene. The others—Jan, Baris, and Hilloa—seemed as embarrassed as they should be. They hovered at the far end of the bar, not looking at him or each other or her. The censor had gone out. Ayma sidled up to the girl, Hilloa. She nudged her and nodded to Po. "What's wrong with him?"

Hilloa gave her a sharp look. "Nothing. It's complicated. He's upset."

Ayma widened her eyes. "I guess so, but why? He took the other guy apart." She took another covert glance at those big shoulders of his. He was really something. The way he'd gone after that man was amazing. If she could figure out how to get him to fall for her, she'd have it made. But that was a fool's dream. Despite the way he treated her, despite that kiss and all the other things he did for her, he knew what she really was and he'd made it clear he wasn't about to forget.

"He's Ilysian. Do you know what that is?" said Baris.

Baris now—she could work something out with him. She should. She was being stupid, letting her heart tell her what to do. Baris knew exactly what she was, but he wouldn't care as long as he got what he wanted. And then, when these people left the citadel again, maybe he'd let her come along.

"It's a country," said Ayma. "Where the women are in charge, right? Is that why that Selene lady tried to tell Siblea's men what to do?"

"Sort of. Anyway, the thing you need to know is, the very worst thing that can happen, as far as an Ilysian man is concerned, is for him to strike a woman."

"Really?"

"Yeah. The guy is killed, like right away, even if it's just a little thing, like that shove just now. But there's more. All of his male relatives are killed, too. And the women in his family . . . They're branded. So they can't have husbands."

Ayma stared at him, then turned back to Hilloa. "He's teasing us."

But Hilloa shook her head and looked very serious. "No, it's true." Baris gave her a surprised glance and she shrugged. "I was listening to you guys the night he told you."

Did this Hilloa like Po, too? She was pretty. In fact, she and Ayma looked a lot alike. How was Ayma going to compete with her if she wanted Po for herself?

But Ayma forgot all that speculation when Po raised his face from Selene's shoulder. Her breath stopped when she saw his face, so naked and raw from crying. And he looked at Selene with such tenderness, such gratitude and admiration. She kissed his forehead, and he closed his eyes, as if he were receiving a benediction from Yammon himself. The moment, the image, caught inside her and became a small, new thing, too full of shattering implication to bear examining. Though she could not think on it, she felt it through and through, and she knew she would carry it with her for the rest of her life.

The evening meal was subdued, if more plentiful than Ayma had had in recent memory. Baris, Hilloa, and Jan clearly did not know what to say to Po. They avoided looking at him. Po himself was withdrawn. He seemed heartbroken, for reasons she could not fathom despite Baris's explanation. And Selene was taut and contained, clearly still furious with Censor Siblea.

The atmosphere made the beets and pulse ball up in her stomach in an uncomfortable way. It was the first decent meal she'd had in weeks. At last, in an effort to dispel some of the tension in the room, she said, "So you truly seek Endymion's rose?"

"Yes," said Jan, with some irritation. "Why is that so difficult for everyone around here to believe?"

She drew back, but then realized he was not really angry with her. And in the meantime, Hilloa had elbowed him and Po gave him a glare of such menace that for an instant, Ayma thought she smelled again the blood of the man he'd beaten. She felt sorry for Jan, then, and hastened to continue. "If you really mean to find it, I can tell you where to look."

They all stared at her. "Why didn't you tell us before?" said Selene.

Ayma lifted one shoulder. "I could not speak of such things in front of the censor. It is something that women talk about, but not in front of men." She glanced at Jan and Baris and Po, hoping they would accept her words as the apology she meant them to be. Po watched her with such rapt attention, it startled her and frightened her a little. And, since she knew he would not really hurt her, she liked that quite a bit. "Certainly, not in front of a priest."

"Please," said Po. The redness from his tears had faded and his eyes now were clear, intense, and the most beautiful shade of gray green. She had never known such a color even existed. "Tell us."

She nodded. "It is said that the Ancients ruled us through their books. I'm sure that's the truth. But . . . this story is about a flower that they had. This flower did not belong to them. One of them stole it from the place where they lived before they came here. They were always fighting over it. Whoever possessed it ruled the others, and the rest of the world as well. Endymion was the last to claim it, and with it she wielded her will like a . . ." Here she faltered. Could she really say it? "You all read, don't you?" she asked.

They had been listening raptly. The question seemed to puzzle them. "Yes. Of course we do," said Hilloa. "Go on."

Ayma looked about, anxious that Siblea might come in at any moment. But they were all waiting, Jan and Baris and Po, their expectation demanding that she speak the heresy. "With the rose, she could wield her will like a pen, writing down what she wanted to happen. And her words were made real." She paused to see what their reaction would be.

They looked at her, not in horror or anger, but interest. It was almost a bit disappointing.

"Interesting," said Selene. "But it doesn't help us find it."

Ayma nodded. "There's more. Endymion liked to throw parties for the other Ancients at the old theater. She would wield the rose and force slaves up onto the stage, where they had to act out whatever she wrote. It is true that the old theater was where the Ancients performed some of the worst atrocities against the slaves, which is the reason it is shunned now. When the Ancients were overthrown, Iscarion interrogated Endymion. Thus he came into possession of the rose. He knew how dangerous it was, how it would corrupt anyone who possessed it, and so, when she died, he buried it with her and told no one but his wife."

"Where was Endymion buried?" asked Selene.

"In a vault beneath the old theater," said Baris.

All was quiet as they looked at one another. Ayma wondered what the rest of them were thinking. Did they believe the tale was true?

"First thing tomorrow morning, we go and get it," said Selene. "And then we're getting out of here."

18

Shame and Its Opposite

After all that had happened, Po could not bear for a woman to clean up after them. As Ayma rose at the end of the meal and reached for Baris's dirty plate, Po stood. "Please," he said, reaching for the dish in her hand. "Let me."

She shook her head. She was blushing again. It was clear that telling them that story had taken something out of her that none of the rest of them could understand. Only he had some idea. He remembered telling the Redeemer and the rest of his book study group Kip's story about the flowers. How embarrassed he'd been.

"That's okay, sir. You don't need to—"

"Oh, for the love of Yammon," said Baris, "would you just let him help you?" He turned to Po. "And you—stop being such a pussy. You just nearly killed a guy, and now you're sucking up to this wench. I can't stand this." He stood up. "You're all driving me crazy." He went behind the bar and began pouring himself another beer.

Po thought about making Baris pay for speaking to Ayma that way, but the idea of beating another person was repellent. He looked to Ayma. She was repressing a smile. Apparently Baris's exasperation amused her. Well, all right, then. He collected the rest of the dishes and followed her into the kitchen.

She had turned on the water in the sink and put the dishes in it. She turned to him. Po tried not to stare at her. He was hovering, he knew—hoping to win her favor. He was acting desperate. Maybe it was because of everything that had happened, or maybe it was just because she was beautiful in every way—the way she moved, the shine of her eyes, her bosom and the curve of her hip. She curtsied to him and stood aside, allowing him to place the rest of the dishes in the sink. "Thank you, sir," she said.

He began to wash, but moments later he heard her gasp. He turned to see her doubled over, retching. She threw up the beets and pulse she had just eaten.

Po went to her, pulling her hair away from her face. When she had done, he helped her to her chair and cleaned up the mess. When he came back from the alley he found her with her face in her hands, her shoulders shaking as she cried. "I'm a healer," he said, kneeling at her feet. I can help you."

She shook her head. "The first decent meal I've had in ages and I can't even keep it down. Oh, Song and Silence, what am I going to do?"

"Let me help." He tentatively put a hand on her knee.

At first he thought she might be pregnant, but now, seeing her reaction, he feared she was truly ill.

"Can you make it so I can keep some food down?"

"I can try. I'm a kinesiologist. I have to touch you on two meridian points, and meditate. It takes a little while."

She nodded. He placed one hand each on the outside of her knees, and he closed his eyes. "Just try to relax and breathe."

He breathed with her. He was getting better at it. It only took him moments before he entered that state of concentration in which the body's energies made themselves manifest in his mind's eye.

A beautiful young maple tree held a bird's nest in the crook of one of its branches. A bird roosted on her egg, chirping and flapping, disturbing the leaves nearby. But otherwise the tree was strong, free of disease and parasites. The turmoil caused was troublesome, but it would pass as Ayma's body adjusted to the pregnancy.

Po sang a song to the bird to soothe and quiet it, then released Ayma's meridians and sat back, smiling. "It's all right," he said. "You're fine. And I have good news. You're pregnant!"

Ayma burst into tears again and hid her face in her hands.

"What's wrong?" Where on earth was her consort? Had he died in the fight against the Lit King? She had not mentioned a consort, only a father.

She dropped her hands and gave him a look of such despair that he reached for her hand, not thinking if it was too forward. She shook her head, her brow furrowed. "How can you ask me that? How can you even look at me now that you know what I am?"

He bent his head. "I'm sorry. You are beautiful. I mean no offense."

She gave a hysterical little laugh at that. "You speak of offending *me*. What manner of man are you?"

Something prompted him to look her in the eye, and allow some portion of his passion to show in his gaze. "I'm an Ilysian man."

That gave her pause. She stared at him for some time, thinking that over. When she finally spoke, it was not what he expected. "Do the others know?"

"I don't think so. Why?"

She stared off into the corner of the room, but Po could plainly see disbelief at his question in her face.

"Why don't you want them to know?"

She shook her head. Po recognized her reaction. He was torturing her without meaning to. Asking something of her that she could not bear to do. And to him it seemed like a perfectly reasonable, ordinary question. Was this what it was like for the others who had asked him to volunteer in discussions and answer direct questions? Had they been just as oblivious and well-intentioned as he was right now? "It's okay. You don't have to answer. I'm sorry if I embarrassed you. I didn't mean to."

She shook her head. She squeezed his hand. "No. You're kind. I . . ." Her voice dropped to a whisper. "I'm glad you know."

Po dared to sidle closer and lean against her chair. He marveled at her hand in his; it was warm and lively like the bird. "For Ilysians, a pregnant woman is a figure of the greatest respect," he said. "A physical incarnation of the Goddess. There is no . . ." He trailed off as he saw a fat droplet splash upon her hand. A tear. She was crying again. Great; now he'd made her cry.

"Shame," she said, her voice a hoarse whisper.

"No shame," he said.

"But this child has no father."

"That would not be of significance where I come from."

She released his hand and stood. She paced to one end of the kitchen, her hands clenched in fists, her shoulders rigid. At last she turned to face him, a wild fury suffusing her face. "But you don't know how it was got on me!" She stopped, her eyes wide, and he saw the fear come back to her. "I'm sorry!" she bowed her head. "I'm so sorry!"

He couldn't stand it. She was . . . cowering . . . like she expected him to hit her for speaking to him in anger. It was intolerable. Po didn't know what to do. He wasn't accustomed to a woman behaving like this—so emotional, so out of control. The realization struck him like a frying pan over the head. She was behaving like a male would, under analogous circumstances. Well, in that case . . .

"It's okay," he said, getting calmly to his feet. He took her by the shoulders. "Come . . . come here." He stroked the tense muscles of her shoulders and gave her a gentle tug. She allowed him to draw her into his arms. "You haven't done anything wrong."

She laughed, the sound ugly and harsh. "You don't know what I've done, sir."

"I'm not a sir," he said. "I'm like you. Someone who says sir or ma'am. Someone who obeys the wishes of others." *And is lost when left to their own devices.* He thought of her wiping the bar down, of him, mooning after every woman in the

Libyrinth, desperate. She snuffled and said nothing. She was still and tense in his arms. "I know," he said. "You don't believe me. You can't, not now. I understand that, too."

She pulled back and looked at him in surprise. He nodded, transfixed as her lips parted. She laughed again, only now it was softer, rueful. "It is so strange . . . So you do not find my condition . . . repellent."

"Quite the opposite."

"But if you knew how I got this way . . ."

Po swallowed. He had a bad feeling about that. He'd seen firsthand that the men here thought nothing of using their physical strength against women. But if that was what had happened to Ayma, surely she would not take the blame on herself like this. Would she? What would he do if a woman mistreated him? Po sighed. What could he tell her that might help? "In Ilysies, a man who does violence to a woman is killed." He did not mention what happened to the rest of the family.

She nodded. "The others told me. That's why you went off on that man today, isn't it?"

"Yes. A male like that is not to be tolerated."

"We must seem strange to you."

He nodded. "If I knew that something like that had happened to you, I would do my best to punish that man appropriately."

Po was good at gauging the emotional reactions of others. The look Ayma gave him now was one he would carry with him all the rest of his days. But then she looked away. "Not *a* man," she said. "And not . . ." She struggled with herself, and at last let out a breath. "They did not force me. They gave me food."

Oh. Poor Ayma. Po took her hand. "It doesn't matter."

She turned to face him, her eyes red. "But it *does*."

Not to him. But of course to her, it did. Po felt helpless. "I don't care," he said. "If you liked me, if you permitted me, I would treat you properly. But no matter what, when we finish our mission here, I will make sure that you come back with us to the Libyrinth, if that is what you wish."

She at last allowed herself to sink against him. "You really don't care that I'm carrying another man's child? That I don't even know who the father is?"

"It is your child. That is all that matters. And it is still early. If you do not want it, there are techniques in kinesiology to safely expel the fetus."

She looked up at him, her eyes glittering with unshed tears and wonder. "Po, is there no end to your perversity?"

The way she said it, he knew she quite liked what she called his perversity. So he smiled. "There's only one way for you to find that out."

She laughed. She tilted her head down and nudged his chest with her shoulder. For once, he was astute enough to realize that that was the absolute limit to which she could go in making an advance toward him. If he wanted more, he would have to initiate it. But first, she needed to eat.

He helped her make herself comfortable on the pallet near the stove. It was what she was accustomed to, and was warmer than the rooms upstairs. Then he served her more beets and pulse. "I'll only throw it back up again," she said.

"Not this time. You feel better since our session, don't you?"

She thought about it. "Yes."

He nodded. "Permit me." He sat on the pallet with his back against the wall and invited her to sit between his outspread legs, with her back resting against his chest. He placed his fingertips on the meridians at her waist, closed his eyes, and breathed. "Eat as much as you like. You won't get sick."

He was a river, flowing past the maple tree. His cool, clear waters soothed the earth around the tree and sent gentle breezes up, amid the branches, to calm the bird that was nesting there. The tree took its nourishment, and the bird sang for him.

When Ayma finished eating, she turned to face him and he took her in his arms.

Ayma had never met a man who delighted her before. Her father had been a good man, a good father. He would have preferred a son, of course, who could work beside him in the business as an equal, and whose virtue he did not have to take such pains to protect. Not that it had been any use in the long run. The men who came to the tavern were all right, most of them. Since the Lit King took over and her father died some of them had helped her, but they all wanted something in return. Ashamed of herself, of what she'd done, she had never imagined that being with a man could be a source of pleasure.

But she was wrong. She was so wonderfully wrong, about so many things. Ayma rolled over, stretching luxuriantly, allowing herself to press up against Po's warm, sleeping body. She could do that without worrying about how he would interpret it, about what he would demand next. They hadn't even gone all the way yet, though Po had shown her some other things that she had never even heard of—things that she'd never been told were wrong and that, once she'd gotten over her initial surprise, she had thoroughly enjoyed.

Po sighed and opened his eyes. Ayma, emboldened, kissed him. He put his arms around her. She loved that.

In the main room, a chair scraped against the floor. The others were stirring. Regretfully, Ayma withdrew from Po and reached for her blouse.

"Will you come with us today?" said Po.

"Do you wish me to?" She realized, too late, that it was the wrong thing to ask him.

"I don't know which is worse. The place we're going sounds like it could be dangerous, but if you stay here, I do not think Selene will let me remain behind. And Siblea did not return tonight. What if the Lit King's mob, or another man like the one who was here yesterday comes? I'm afraid."

They were going to the old theater. No place was more shunned. But there was truth in what Po said about the Lit King's mob. Word of what had occurred at the market yesterday would have spread by now. They might come here looking for the censor and his followers. There would be danger either way, but at least at the theater she'd be with Po.

19

The Old Theater

P o felt Ayma's hand sweating in his as they followed
Selene, Hilloa, Jan, and Baris up the desolate street
toward the old theater. This was the most decrepit part of
town. The theater itself was a multistory building with
the classic dome roof, lined with tiny, crenelated spires all
around the edge of the dome like rays of a sun. Everywhere
else they'd been in the citadel, they'd found an air of aban-
donment, but not of such long standing that the buildings
had fallen into actual disrepair. They were still well-kept,
if vacant. But the theater—its spires were crumbling. Silverleaf bushes had sprouted up around the place and
grown to unheard-of proportions, some of them growing
right up the walls themselves, laying another layer of curving, swirling lines over the songlines that were already

carved into the stone beneath. Refuse clung to the spaces between pillars, and dead leaves and trash filled every nook and cranny. It was, in fact, difficult to determine what was part of the building and what was an almost geological accretion of trash.

"Is it even safe to go inside?" wondered Selene.

"I doubt it," said Jan.

"No one has entered the theater since Yammon overthrew the Ancients. Of all their depravities, the worst were committed here," said Baris. Po noticed sweat trickling down his neck.

But the sooner they went in and got the rose, the sooner they could go home. A tall, wrought-iron fence surrounded the place. Po put a hand to the rusted latch of the gate and it crumbled beneath his fingers. The gate swung inward a couple of feet, and then one of its hinges gave way and it listed to the side, grinding to a halt with a sound like Siblea's victims must have made when he tortured them.

They all stood on the sidewalk, none eager to enter. But Selene went in anyway, her feet scuffing on dead leaves.

Po and the others caught up to Selene by the time she made it to the front steps. They were made of the same gray stone as all the rest of the buildings here. They were worn by countless generations of feet before them, but caked with grime. Untouched for centuries, as Baris said. Po couldn't help but wonder about the people whose feet had worn these grooves. Who were they? Had they been Ancients, too? Or were they their ancestors, the slaves of the Ancients?

A cool wind swept through his hair. They all shivered.

At the top of the steps was a portico lined with pillars

along the front edge. The doors to the theater lay before them, the pointed archway reminding him of the gate of the Libyrinth back home. Home? It surprised him that he now thought of it so, but he pushed the thought aside.

The doors were carved with songlines, finer and more intricate than any he had seen so far; and here, too, silver-leaf bushes had sprouted up from the cracks in the stonework and wound themselves over the doors. Ayma's grip on his hand tightened.

"Maybe the doors are locked." Jan sounded hopeful.

Selene wrapped her fingers around one of the rusted door handles and pulled. The door swung open, grating against an accumulation of dirt and refuse. At the breaking of the seal there was a puff of air that blew into Po's face. It smelled like dust and ancient, dried-up dead things—bitter and a little peppery. It was dark inside.

Selene rummaged in her satchel and took out her copy of the *The Book of the Night*, which had been treated with palm-glow so that the pages gave off light. She took the lead. Inside, the book illuminated a great hall, the ceiling arching above them, too high for the feeble light of their glow to reach. At their feet the floor was tiled, but dust and dirt obscured the pattern of the tiles. They were in an entrance vestibule that ran the width of the building but was only about twenty feet deep. On the wall in front of them were doors, spaced at even intervals. These were wooden—those that remained, anyway. Many, it seemed, had been carried away and the archways gaped open into even deeper darkness beyond. At the end of the hall on each side was a staircase curving upward.

Selene crossed the vestibule and stood in one of the archways. Po and Ayma followed on her heels. He heard

Selene's sharp intake of breath and a second later, he saw the cause.

This was the theater itself. Row upon row of seats swept down before them, and at the far end, the stage stood surrounded by an ornate archway. Above them were balconies and private boxes. Chandeliers hung from the ceiling, frothy concoctions of glass enshrouded in cobwebs. It was beautiful and terrifying that such splendor could flourish and then be so utterly abandoned.

They walked down the center aisle of the theater. Once the seats had been upholstered in fine fabric—perhaps velvet or brocade—but now the fabric had rotted away, the stuffing become nesting material for birds and animals. As they walked, something skittered away in the darkness, and as they neared the stage itself, a bird squawked in indignation, nearly giving them all heart attacks. It swooped out from the proscenium, winging overhead to disappear in the balcony above. "How many Ancients came here?" asked Selene.

"All seven of them," said Baris.

"That's all there were? Seven?" said Jan.

Baris nodded. "They fashioned the place to resemble an Old Earth theater. Thus all these seats. But the shows that took place here were nothing like the plays you've read about in books."

"What were they?"

"They used their powers to control their slaves up on the stage, make them act out their whims."

"How?"

"With their books." He glanced at Ayma. "At least, that's what we always thought. But if Endymion's rose is real, such a device could be used in any number of ways, including forcing people to act against their will. Like a puppet show."

"Only the puppets were living people," said Selene.

Baris nodded. "That's why, of all the sites of the Ancients in the citadel, this one is the most reviled."

It was also a good place to look for the rose, if that was what the Ancients used to control the players. The chorus fanned out and searched the seats, using their copies of *The Book of the Night* to illuminate every shadow. The dark theater looked like a night sky filled with green stars.

But two hours later, every seat and balcony had been examined and nothing but birds' nests and dead mice had been found. "Let's try the stage," said Selene.

"Carefully," said Jan. "The boards may be rotted through."

However, they found the stage to be solid despite its age. They searched through props and set pieces. Po and Ayma were backstage, examining a shoe the size of one of the stone huts of the plain when he heard Selene call out. He and the others gathered around her at center stage.

"Look," she said, kneeling on the floor and using a corner of her robe to wipe away centuries of dirt and grit.

"What's that?" Po asked, pointing to a number of brown stains marring the ancient finish.

"Blood," Baris whispered. He was pale, and a fine sheen of sweat glistened on his forehead.

Someone tapped Po on the shoulder.

Po turned and looked up into the face of a very old woman, her skin engraved with songlines. She cracked a grin.

Po stood, reaching beside him to take Ayma by the

arm. Standing around them in a loose ring were twenty or more men and women, dressed in brown robes, their arms and faces covered to varying degrees with scars in the undulating shapes of songlines. It was the Lit King's mob. And they had mind lancets.

By now the others had noticed them, too. Selene held her hands up and said, "Peace, sisters and brothers of the Word. We come from the Libyrinth with good tidings of the Redemption. We are here to seek Endymion's rose, for the benefit of all the people of the Plain of Ayor."

The old woman laughed. "The Redemption you speak of is false. We are the true people of the Word. Your priest gathers followers to oppose the glorious Lit King. You are no brethren to us. Come, we will escort you to the true Redeemer of the citadel. He shall determine how you may serve the people of Ayor."

Po watched Selene, waiting to see what she would decide to do. She looked at the men and women surrounding them. As she nodded her head, two other things happened at once. Ayma let go of Po's hand, and Baris threw himself at the old woman. "Lit bitch, we're not going anywhere with you!" He grabbed for her mind lancet but she swung it around and struck him across the shoulders with it. He screamed and fell.

Ayma ran toward the part of the circle where the Lit King's people were most sparse. As the rest of the mob moved in, brandishing their mind lancets, Po went after her. She was headed straight for a tall, lean man, who lowered his mind lancet and braced for her attack. Po redoubled his pace and passed her up, reaching the man before her. He slammed right into him, knocking both of them to the ground. For a moment, all was arms and legs.

Po felt the brush of the mind lancet against his arm and it sent a shock rippling through his body. He kicked the man in the stomach and dodged under the swinging lancet. The man tried to hit him with the weapon again but Po grabbed the haft and forced the glowing blue orb back into his opponent's chest.

The man shouted and fell back, writhing, on the floor. Po leaped to his feet. Behind him he heard shouts and screams. Ahead he saw Ayma, still running, another of the Lit King's people right behind her. He took off after them.

They ran backstage and down a staircase, into a dust-choked, low-ceilinged place filled with stage props and bits of scenery. He lost sight of Ayma and her pursuer, but he could hear their footsteps. He dodged around a mushroom that was taller than he was. Ahead of him stood a gigantic head with bright, distorted features and twin flames of red hair jutting out from the sides. He heard the zap of a mind lancet and Ayma's scream. Red poured up from the base of his spine and spilled into his head. He ducked beneath one jutting spike of hair and found Ayma pressed up against the side of a strange-looking horse with a pole through the middle. The man with the mind lancet menaced her. Po cast about for a weapon of some kind and found a length of rope, much gnawed upon, lying in a serpentine heap on the floor. Ayma saw him pick up the rope but she didn't let on.

"You'll come with me," said the man.

Slowly Ayma nodded. "Yes," she said. "I'm sorry for running. I'll come with you." She arched her back, leaned her shoulders against the horse, and tilted her head down. She cocked her right hip. "But . . . we don't have to go back up there this instant, do we?"

Astonishment at what she was doing quickly gave way

to determination. As the man leaned down to take Ayma in his arms, Po crept up behind him with the rope. He stepped on something that gave with a crack and the man spun around, his mind lancet firmly in hand. Po crouched, circling to the left, away from the other man's weapon hand. His opponent lunged to the right and Po dodged.

It was a trick. The man's lancet struck Po hard on the elbow. Po's entire body fizzed with pain and his vision whited out around the edges. He dropped the rope. The next thing he knew, the man grabbed him around the waist and took him to the floor. Po thrashed, but it was hard to coordinate his movements. The blow from the mind lancet had landed right on a nerve cluster and his entire body was on fire. Knees pinned his arms to the floor. Hands grasped his neck, tightened.

Then, suddenly, Ayma came into view behind the man. *Run!* Po wanted to shout, but he had no air. The whiteness around his narrowing field of vision turned gray. Something scratchy thumped into his face momentarily and then he saw the man's eyes bulge. Ayma had the rope and she was strangling him with it. The man reared up, staggering to his feet. Ayma clung to his back. He scrabbled at the rope cutting into his neck with frantic fingers. Po gasped, his vision clearing as oxygen coursed through his system.

The man convulsed and then went still. His eyes closed and he slumped to the floor.

Ayma let go of the rope and came to stand beside Po. For a moment both of them stared down at the body of their slain foe. "Is killing a man to you what harming a woman is for me?" Po asked her.

Ayma shook her head. "We're just not supposed to be able to, that's all."

20

Endymion's Tomb

W hen they went back up the stairs, the theater was empty.

"They've been captured," said Ayma.

"We have to get them out," said Po.

Ayma took him by the hand. "That will be difficult. But if we find Endymion's rose and it does all that legend claims, then we can free them very easily."

It made sense. And they were so close. Even if they could not find the bloom, another hour spent looking for it would not make any difference.

Not far from where the slain man lay, Ayma found a seam in the floor. "What is it?"

They cleared away the dust and debris and found that the seam was a square, and on one end, a metal ring lay in a shallow indentation in the wood. Po looked at Ayma, waiting for her to pull it, and found her staring at him, waiting for him to do the same. It unnerved him the way she looked to him like this. "You're stronger," she said.

"Okay." Po grasped the ring and pulled up. The door resisted at first and then swung open, falling back on its hinges to rest against the floor. Coughing at the dust, Po and Ayma peered through the opening. A ladder led down into the dark.

They descended. It was dark and Po reached into his satchel and pulled out *The Book of the Night*. He opened it. In the pale green glow, thousands of books came to light. Row upon row of them lined the passage down which they descended. They climbed down, through a veritable tunnel of books, a hundred yards or more until they came to the bottom. They were in a small landing area, the bare stone floor dusty beneath their feet. The walls around them, still lined with books, curved in a circle. A small door sat in the wall across from the ladder. It was only as high as Po's chest. Most people would have to bend over to go through it.

It was just a wooden door with an iron handle and latch, but dread washed over him at the sight of it. He looked to Ayma and saw that she was equally frightened. "What is it?" she breathed. "Why is it so . . . ?"

"It's just a door." He realized they were whispering. "But . . . All I want to do is get out of here."

He understated the case. More than anything in the world, he did not want to go through that door. In fact, his body was even more of the opinion that going through there was a bad idea. He discovered they had both edged back toward the ladder, seemingly without recognizing it.

He looked at Ayma. She shook her head. "I'm scared." And there was that look again—panicky, and seeking reassurance, leadership, from him. A sharp jolt of resentment nearly overwhelmed his fear. "You can go back," he said, hoping she didn't notice the irritation in his tone. "Wait for me at the tavern. I'll be there soon." It would almost be better to face this alone than to do it with someone who expected him to take care of her.

Ayma put a foot on the lowest rung of the ladder and then stopped herself. She shook her head, then an expression of determination came over her face. That was more like it. She reminded Po of Selene now. "No," she said. "We'll do it together." She glanced at him, a worry line between her eyes, as if she thought he'd be angry that she asserted her leadership.

"It's just a door," he pointed out. "What's the big deal?"

"What lies on the other side."

Po had understood that people considered this theater haunted because it was the resting place of the last Ancient. But he had chalked that up to superstition. He hadn't been prepared for a physical sensation.

Walking across the room and opening that door felt as unnatural and wrong as striking Ayma or complimenting Baris. But it had to be done. Endymion's rose, if it existed, most likely lay on the other side of that door, in the tomb of the last Ancient. And if he was ever going to see Selene, Hilloa, or Jan again, they had to go and get it.

"Let's just get it over with," said Ayma.

They held hands tightly and ran to the door. Po grasped the handle and pulled it toward him. It resisted, and for a moment his heart was wild with joy at the thought that they could not get in and they would have to try to get the chorus out of the clutches of the Lit King and feed the Plain of Ayor some other way.

And then, with a click, the door opened. He expected it to be dark on the other side, but that was not the case. A faint glow emanated from the opening.

He and Ayma exchanged a look, and then with a deep breath, crossed the threshold.

Once they were on the other side, the feeling of fore-boding actually abated somewhat and they were able to stand up, as well. They were in a landing at the top of a broad, curving, stone staircase. A finely wrought cast-iron handrail graced one side. The walls were stone as well, carved with flowers and vines. Sconces on the walls emit-ted a soft, steady glow. Po and Ayma descended the shallow steps. He noticed that the risers, too, were carved with the floral motif.

The room that came into view was unlike anything Po had ever seen in real life, even at the palace. He'd seen a book at the Libyrinth once—an illustrated history book. It had included a picture of the Old Earth palace of Versailles. That was what this looked like.

Dust lay thick on the carpeted floor and on every avail-able surface, but otherwise the room seemed somehow to have survived the ravages of time better than the rest of the theater. The fabric on the ornate, upholstered chairs had not rotted away, and the tiny, intricately carved tables still stood. The walls appeared to be covered with a pattern of flocked wallpaper. A chandelier festooned with cobwebs hung from the ceiling above, dust not entirely extinguish-ing the glow of its lights.

They walked swiftly around the perimeter of the room. Po noted that the door by which they'd entered was the only one in the room. There were no windows, either, of course, since they must surely be below ground. There was an ornate desk and chair, and an object that he realized was a harpsichord, and in one corner, a shrouded hulk that looked to be a standing candelabra or a coatrack covered with a sheet.

"Where is the last Ancient?" he asked Ayma.

She shook her head. "Perhaps she has withered away to nothing. Perhaps she is the dust on the floor."

Po shivered. He heard something from the far corner of the room where the shrouded object stood: a dry, whispering sound like a stray breeze blowing over dried-out sheets of paper. But there was no breeze in here. He looked to Ayma. "Do you hear that?"

She nodded. She stared at the shape in the corner. They still held hands, palms welded together with sweat. The hair on the back of his neck stood up as they slowly approached it. The corner was dim in shadow. As they neared the shrouded form he realized it was both too short and too wide to be a standing candelabra or a coatrack. The whispering sound continued; it came from beneath the cloth.

All he wanted to do was run away. But a burning field of barley and the thought of his friends in the clutches of the Lit King forced him to continue forward. It was Ayma who reached out and pulled the cloth away.

At first he couldn't make out what he was looking at. He saw a tall, pointed arch at the top, made of ornately wrought metal—tiny wires in intricate filigree, all threaded through with beads and bits of colorful paper. Below this was what appeared to be a carving in sandstone. It was so pitted and grooved that it took a moment for his eyes to resolve what he saw into a high, domed forehead, deeply sunken eyes, high cheekbones, and a nose that jutted forth like a scythe over shriveled lips and a receding chin.

Po took an involuntary step backward. Was it a statue, a piece of eccentric and elaborate art? No, of course not. So this was what an Ancient looked like.

It was seated in a chair. The hands that rested on the chair's arms were encrusted with rings. The hair hanging at each side of that fantastic face was an elaborate mass of braids, jewels, dreadlocks, and odd bits of stuff that seemed to have collected there and never been removed.

The body was hidden by layer upon layer of ornate clothing, parts of it rotted away to reveal here a swath of gingham petticoat beneath a brocade topcoat, there a fur stole over an embroidered linen tunic. Overall, it gave the impression of having been added on to for centuries, not so much a human figure as an accretion of history.

Po took a deep breath and relaxed. Frightening as the figure was, it could do them no harm. It was dead. That much was obvious.

The rose—they were here to find the rose, and the sooner they did, the sooner they could leave. He opened *The Book of the Night* so that the light fell on the figure, and peered closely to discern from the myriad details of her costume something that might be the rose.

They searched her from head to toe and front to back, but found nothing. "If the rose is on her person, then it is beneath her clothing," said Ayma.

Po stared at her. He wanted to tell her not to look at him like it was up to him to do something. "Perhaps we should search the rest of the room," he suggested.

Ayma, clearly not eager to resort to the sacrilege of

removing the clothing from a dead body, nodded. She went to the harpsichord. It was very like ones he'd seen in the palace.

Po examined the desk. It was the same design as the harpsichord. A blotter and a dried-out bottle of ink sat on top of it beneath a thick layer of dust. Po ran a finger through the dust to reveal an ornate inlay of gold and mother of pearl.

The desk had five drawers, a shallow one in the middle and two deeper ones on each side. The side drawers were empty but the middle one rattled as he opened it. Inside, amid dust bunnies and cobwebs, were the remnants of a cloth sack, now rotted away around its contents—a handful of small metal objects. Each was composed of three metal rods that were perpendicular to one another, just like the sticks Hilloa had used in her demonstration about dimensions, except that some of these had tiny beads at their ends. Po had heard of these. They were an Old Earth toy called jacks. Amid them sat a small pile of pink-colored dust. That would be the remains of the rubber ball that had been used in the arcane game. But there was nothing that remotely approached a description of Endymion's rose or the Lion's Bloom.

"Nothing here," said Ayma, lowering the cover of the cabinet in the back that housed the harpsichord's strings. It would be a perfect hiding place. But she shook her head.

Po spent some time examining the carvings on the stairway. Any one of those flowers might be the bloom in disguise, affixed to the carving. He pried at a few, but with no results. He wandered back into the room again. Ayma was on her hands and knees, checking the corners and the edges of the floor.

Po knelt on the floor, too, running his fingers along the seam between the floor and the baseboard, when he heard that faint, rustling sound again. Was it mice? No—not mice. The sound grew words. "My pen. I dropped my pen." The voice, dry and faint, was nevertheless perfectly intelligible.

Po's heart was in his mouth. He stood up and turned around. The corpse had not moved. It still sat in the chair, but its eyes were open. Dark, fathomless, they gleamed in the dim light of the room. The lips, dyed deep red, twitched. Was it a smile? They parted. The teeth were black.

"Yammon," the thing whispered, and the smile grew.

Po stumbled backward, all the way until his back hit the wall. He struggled for breath. Ayma stood a few feet away, equally petrified. How was this possible? How could she still be alive after all this time? And what would she do to them now that they'd invaded her inner sanctum?

Ayma reached for him and pulled him toward the stairs. He understood now, the dread he'd felt on entering this place. It had felt wrong because it was. They should not be here. They ran up the steps to the little door.

Dry, dusty laughter issued from the corner of the room where the last Ancient sat. On this side, the door had no handle. And it had swung shut. Po scrabbled at the door, tried to pry it open with his fingernails, but it was no use.

"No!" Ayma cried. Tears streamed down her face and she, too, scratched and pried and pounded on the door. It was latched shut and there was no opening it.

She was panicking like a male. Again Po wished he were with someone who would know what to do. But they were both equally terrified and at a loss.

"We have to find the rose," he said.

She clutched his arm. "What if she already has it?"

Po was surprised when the answer came to his lips. "She must not, or she would not be down here all alone."

"Then that means the rose is not here, either, and we're trapped here for no reason forever, and . . ." Ayma stopped herself.

"Maybe she is too old to get out of her chair. Maybe the rose is here, but she cannot reach it."

"But we can."

Po nodded. It was the slimmest of hopes and everything they held dear, not least of all their lives, depended on it. But at least it was something. He had another idea. "Maybe she knows where it is."

"Probably," said Ayma. And then she caught her breath. She lowered her voice to the barest of whispers. "We can pretend we are going to fetch it for her, and get her to tell us where it is."

Po swallowed. He didn't like the idea of deceiving an Ancient. But Ayma was right. It was a good plan. "Do you want . . . ? That is, I can go and speak to her."

She studied him. Clearly she was tempted to let him take on the physical risk. But then she shook her head. "We'll both go."

21

The Last Ancient

They held hands. Po felt like the Barley King walking
to the scythe, but he felt something else, too; something strange and new. Ayma didn't expect him to defer to
her. She didn't want his flattery. It was almost as if she
didn't see him as a male at all, though of course, she did.
But it meant something different to her than it did to
him, and in the space between her expectations and his he
discovered what it meant to simply be Po.

He squeezed her hand and she looked at him. Just as he
was wondering if she felt the same way, she said, "We're
just two people."

Two very frightened people, possibly walking to their
deaths. His eyes scanned the floor, hoping against hope

to find the bloom before reaching the last Ancient and attempting to trick her.

As they came and stood before her, she smiled again. Those red lips parted and he saw that her teeth were not so much black as they were covered in all kinds of wires and beads. "Belrea and Yammon. Look at you. I never thought I'd see you again."

Po glanced at Ayma and she shook her head. She knew no more than he did what Endymion was talking about. Perhaps Iscarion was right—perhaps she was mad, or senile, or both. The question of how she was even still alive haunted the back of his mind, but there was no time for that now. Ayma looked at him, waited for him to do something. Po cleared his throat. "Mistress Endymion." He bowed, and Ayma gave a curtsey. "We are Ayma and Po, and we are here in search of the Lion's Bloom."

Her eyes glittered as she watched them. "The Lion's Bloom, my rose, you mean. How cute. Next you'll be asking me how to make Eggs. You're Yammon and Belrea, and if you're not, you will be. You are here to do my pleasure. Now hand me my pen!" She pointed at the floor a few feet from where she sat. A shadow, cast by her form, lay across the dusty carpet. Po knelt there and saw a darker shape.

He reached out and picked it up. It was a rod about the length of his forearm, with an oval bulb at one end, and it was made of the same coppery substance that entwined Eggs.

It was not as heavy as it seemed it should be. Ayma came to his side and they examined it closely. Po noted the striations in the long neck and the scalloped flourishes around the oval at the end.

"My pen . . . ," said Endymion, her hand, with its long, clawlike fingernails outstretched toward the object. "Yammon, give me my pen. It is not for puppets."

It did look rather like a long, elaborate pen. He looked at her. This was an Ancient. Her very existence was a miracle. Po stepped closer, holding the pen out to her.

"What are you doing?" said Ayma. "That's the rose!"

In an instant striations resolved into leaves and oval flourishes into petals. Po stepped back, but even as he did, Endymion's hand telescoped out of her sleeve on the end of a metal armature. He was so distracted by the apparatus emerging from the ragged cuff of her gown that he didn't even react until she'd already grasped the stem of the rose with her hand.

Ayma grabbed the rose as well. They pulled, but the last Ancient's grip was terrifyingly strong. She let out a high-pitched, keening wail and screamed, "Give it to me!"

"We musn't!" said Ayma, panting with effort. "Remember what we saw upstairs, on the stage? The blood? They used the rose to do that."

Po pulled with both hands and all his might.

There was a crack, and Po and Ayma fell on their backs clutching the pen. Endymion's hand was still attached to it. It looked like a weather-beaten glove stuck on the end of a long metal rod. The sleeve of Endymion's gown now hung empty and loose. Her other hand shook and a grinding, whining noise could be heard, but the appendage stayed where it was.

Shaking, Ayma yanked the pen from Endymion's disembodied hand and threw the appendage across the room. "Yammon's tonsils," she swore under her breath.

Endymion emitted a creaking sound and an orange

droplet appeared at the corner of one eye and rolled down her crenellated cheek. "Look what you've done, you wicked meat puppets. I can't repair myself anymore. But I could, if you would just give me my pen. It's not meant for you. You don't even know what it is."

Po had to resist the impulse to do exactly what the oldest woman in existence told him to do. He let go of the thing, and let Ayma hold it.

"It's the rose," she said.

"Wrong!" shouted Endymion. "Yammon, you don't love Belrea. You love me. Kill her. Give me my pen back."

Po didn't look at Endymion. He kept his eyes on Ayma. "Ancient one, forgive me. I cannot give it back to you. My people are starving, and it's my fault. I let the queen of Ilysies trick me and she ruined our crop. Now our only hope is to make the Plain of Ayor green again. This object—it can make the land green again, so we may live. I cannot give it to you. I must take it, and return to my people before they all die."

"That's not your story, Yammon."

"My name is Po, Ancient one."

"You look like him. He was my favorite, you know."

Her favorite what, Po wondered, but instead he said, "Everyone thinks you are dead, Ancient one."

"Theselaides told them so, did he?"

"Yes. In *The Book of the Night* he wrote that you died. It's been many centuries since then."

"That long?" She said it as if she'd overslept and missed breakfast, not as if she'd somehow survived for generations with no food or water. "I slept. I dreamed of my friends, back when they were still my friends."

"Your friends? The other Ancients?" asked Po.

Ayma plucked at his sleeve. "Please," she said. "Let's just go. We have the rose now."

She was right. "Use it, Ayma. Use it to make the Plain of Ayor green. Use it to open the door so we can leave."

"Okay. What do I do?"

"What?"

"How does it work?"

Endymion laughed. "You don't even know what it is, or how to use it. Yammon . . . Po."

Po turned. His mouth was dry and his heart beat very hard, high in his chest.

"I'll show you. I'll show you how to use the pen. Give it to me and I'll show you."

A voice in the back of his head warned him against soothing promises from women of power. Ayma, still clutching the pen, backed away from them both.

"You would like to go back to your friends, wouldn't you?" Endymion said.

Slowly, fearing a trap, he nodded.

She sighed. "Me too. Look at me. This isn't being alive, is it? You can't leave me like this. Just . . . give me the pen so I can fix myself, so I can join my friends. I'll give it to you when I'm done."

"She's lying," said Ayma. "She'll use it to torture us, Po. Just like she and her friends did in the old days."

Po thought of something. "I am an adept of kinesiology," he said. Would his abilities work on an Ancient? She wasn't a creature of flesh and blood—at least, not entirely. Could he heal her? "Maybe I can help you."

"Ah, kinesiology. Yes. I wonder what would happen if you tried to use it on me?"

Po knelt at her feet. The hem of her robe was edged in

gray paper with thousands and thousands of tiny words on it. Newspaper? Was that newspaper? "May I try?"

She stared at him. "If you can release me from this prison, you may keep the pen with my blessing, though you'd be better off without it. I'll even show you how Eggs are made."

Po placed his hands on the outsides of what he hoped were her knees. They felt hard, sharp, and cold. He closed his eyes and tried to breathe with her. Did she even breathe? Po felt nothing beneath his hands, not a glimmer of energy, not a spark of life. Still, he persisted.

Kinesiology was based upon attuning oneself to the life energy of another being, and whatever Endymion was, she was most certainly alive.

When integration came it came all at once, and it was unlike anything Po had ever experienced before. It completely and utterly consumed all of his awareness. There was nothing but this feeling. He couldn't put words to it. It wasn't a burning feeling or a freezing feeling. It wasn't the sting of an insect or the sharp agony of a cut. It wasn't the dull throb of a bruise or the bright pain of a headache. If anything, it was all of these at once and more. It was as if sensations were being forced upon him which were, in some way, too large for him. It was overwhelming more than anything else.

All the thoughts he'd ever had in his entire life rushed to the forefront of his awareness at once. He felt caught in a stampede. His own thoughts crushed him and all he could do was writhe in the all-consuming grip of whatever it was that was happening to him.

Po must have lost consciousness. When he came to awareness once more, he was still deep in the kinesthetic trance, in a space unlike any he'd ever experienced. It was the reddish black color he saw when his eyes were closed, and somehow it seemed more empty than the blackness of space.

This was not like any kinesthetic trance he'd ever experienced. "I'm not interfacing with your energy field," he said.

"Not yet. I'm using your kinesthetic sense to give you a vision," she said. "To show you this place."

"Where are we?"

"This is where universes are born. Look, listen."

There was a flash of light in the distance and a deafening explosion. Then the light mellowed and a sound could be heard. Po had heard this sound before. It was the Song.

Endymion reached out with all the hands of all her selves of all the times she'd been, and she wrapped them around that light, a glowing amber light. She held it and wound it with cords from her hair, cords of will and desire. It was a universe just beginning to form, and she stopped it. "You want to know how Eggs are made?" she said, holding a glowing amber ovoid. "This is how."

"You made the Eggs?"

"Not me. But Pierce's grandmother was one of the original seven who discovered the key to transcendence. He was always very proud of that."

"Pierce?"

"One of my friends. An Ancient, you would call him." She laughed. "And now, it's time for you to do something for me."

Everything shifted and Po found himself lying on his side. All around him stretched a vast desert of sand. He sat up, wiping the encrusted grains from the side of his face.

The grains stuck to his hand. Looking at them, he realized they were not grains of sand at all—they were whirling capsules of light. Eggs—each one a universe captured in the moment of formation.

In the distance stood a large sphere of gleaming metal. That, his sense informed him, was the center of Endymion's awareness. He walked toward it, and as he did something strange happened. The closer he got, the smaller it became. At last he knelt and picked it up. The sphere fit in the palm of his hand.

He examined the sphere more closely. What had appeared to be flawless from a distance was in fact pitted with numerous tiny cracks. He tried to seal those cracks. Since usually the surroundings he encountered while in a trance provided the stuff with which to help the diseased or wounded body heal, he lifted a handful of universes in his palm and tried using them to fill the cracks in the sphere. But the universes simply turned black and fell away.

The ball wobbled, as if it resented his attempt at healing it. And then Po's fingers lengthened, narrowed, and multiplied. They became fuzzy. His hands transformed into wings and detached from the rest of him and became a bird. It gave a caw and flapped away with the wounded orb in its beak.

Po shattered into a thousand a thousand pieces, fragments of himself. He found himself sitting on the floor of Endymion's tomb, staring at her empty chair.

Both of his hands were still attached to the ends of his arms as they should be. For a moment he just sat there, grateful to be back in his own mind with his whole body. He was exhausted.

"Where did she go?" Ayma stood over him, staring between him and the empty chair.

"I don't know." Ayma helped him stand and he leaned against her for a moment. "I'll tell you . . . ," he began, but trailed off because it all seemed too big for words. "I'll tell you about it later."

They went back up the stairs to the locked door. Ayma held the pen out to him. "Do you think maybe it's just a pen?" she said. "You write with it, and what you write comes true?"

"Maybe," he said. He really didn't want to be the one to try it and find out. But Ayma couldn't write. She handed the pen to him and he examined the thing. It did look a bit like a large, elaborate pen. Po examined the end that looked like the nib, if it were a pen. It was just a solid point. There was no opening for ink to come out.

Nevertheless, he held the pen as he would any other pen and found that despite its size, it felt balanced and secure in his grip. He looked at the door and imagined it opening. He composed a sentence in his mind: "The door in front of me opens."

As he wrote the words in midair, they appeared, glowing with golden light, and the end of the pen opened up like a flower blooming. Particles of light rose up from the blossom like pollen and dispersed. As the words faded, they heard a click and the door opened before them.

Po and Ayma looked at each other in wonder. A second later, Ayma took his hand. Po put the pen in his satchel. They would have to make the Plain of Ayor green next, but first it seemed like a good idea to get out of there right away. They left the old theater and sat down on the steps outside.

He took the pen and wrote, "The Plain of Ayor is a green and fertile land."

Haly stood in line with the others, waiting for her morning ration of food. She had never been so hungry for so long in her entire life. Her legs shook, and though she had just awoken, exhaustion threatened to overwhelm her. Increasingly she was sensitive to light, and had difficulty seeing in the dark. She recognized the signs of malnutrition, and she was far from the only one suffering. In front of her stood Arche. Arche's beautiful hair had lost its shine, and as she stepped forward she stumbled. Lack of coordination. Haly reached out to steady her but barely had the strength to clutch at her robe. Muscle weakness.

Haly held out her bowl to Burke, whose once robust plumpness had dwindled to slack. Worst of all was the dull look in her eyes. It was a crime against nature for Burke, one of the most prized minds of the Libyrinth, to be reduced to drudgery and endurance. No more were the book discussions, the lively conversations around the console in the main hall, the exploration of concepts as diverse as nanotechnology and rule of law. From sunup to long after dark they all worked the fields, and then they fell exhausted in their beds and got up the next morning and did it all again.

Burke put a spoonful of barley and a quarter of a carrot in Haly's bowl. They looked at each other, the truth so obvious it did not need to be said. This hardship, this sacrifice, was not enough. This meager ration of food would run out in the next week or so, and despite their best efforts, they were still two months away from the first harvest.

It was old news. Haly, Gyneth, and Peliac had taken inventory over a week ago and made the calculations. Those who had family in the nearby villages had already left. But people were struggling there, too. For those who remained at the Libyrinth, there was no place else to go.

They'd had no news of either Clauda or the Chorus of the Word. Haly hoped that wherever they were, they fared better than those they'd left behind. The shameful truth was that getting through each day took just about all the energy she had, and there was little left with which to worry about her absent friends.

Haly ate her food slowly, chewing each mouthful thoroughly to get every bit of nutritive value from it. She had just finished when Gyneth came running into the dining hall. "Come quick! Something's happening outside!"

He might have caused a stampede if everyone were not as exhausted as she was. People filed out into the Great Hall. The doors of the main entrance stood open, and for a moment Haly thought her vision was getting worse. Green light flooded in from outside.

Shouts of fear, despair, and bewilderment rose up from the collected population of the Libyrinth. Haly hastened outside and stopped dead in her tracks, unable to make sense of what she saw.

The sand was green. Haly knelt and scooped up a handful, expecting to dislodge a layer of some sort of freak snow or rainfall the color of newly sprouted barley shoots, but no. The grains themselves were green, as if they were always meant to be. She ran to the fields. Here the tilled earth had taken on a deeper, richer hue of green—more like mature bean plants.

"What is it?" said Ock, his voice laced with panic.

Haly felt the same way. She shook her head. Was this some kind of dream? She tried to wake up. It wasn't a dream.

The ground rumbled.

"Look at the barley!" Ock cried.

The barley shoots looked greener and more robust than she remembered. Was it just the light reflected from the green soil?

The ground trembled. "What's that now?" yelled Peliac, dropping the handful of dirt she'd been examining.

"I don't know," said Haly, but a moment later they had their answer as up from the ground shot silverleaf bushes— thousands of them. Everyone was jumping out of the way as the things erupted up from the ground right beneath their feet. It was a macabre dance, too bizarre to be truly funny. The barley fields, which did in fact look increasingly robust, were suddenly overrun by the silverleaf bushes, which were quickly passing the bush stage and becoming trees. They were growing right up through the barley shoots, uprooting them. In moments the entire new planting of barley was decimated.

22

The Lit King

C hange it back, change it back!" cried Ayma as she and Po watched what they had wrought. The ground everywhere was green, even the paving stones which were being torn up right and left as silverleaf trees erupted from the ground.

Po picked up the pen again. What could he write that would undo the damage that had been done?

"Hurry!"

"What Po just wrote about the Plain of Ayor being a green and fertile land never happened," he wrote.

In an instant, everything was as it had been. It had worked. Ayma hugged him.

"I think we'd better leave making the land rich up to Selene," he said.

"Or Censor Siblea," said Ayma. "He'll know what to do."

Po let go of her. "Will he? You put a lot of faith in him."

Ayma tilted her head and looked up at him. "Well, you put a lot of faith in her. I don't care how many books she's read—"

"But Siblea is just an old man."

"—she's still just a woman."

For a moment they stared at each other. And then they both laughed.

"Let's just get them away from the Lit King, okay?" said Ayma.

Po nodded and looked at the pen. "But how? I'm afraid if I write the wrong thing . . ."

"Well, it worked with the door. The problem with the second thing you wrote was—" Ayma broke off.

"No, go on. It's okay. You don't have to worry about criticizing me. Just say it."

"It wasn't specific enough. It was open to interpretation."

"So we'd better not say anything like, 'The Lit King sets the chorus free.' "

"Because that could mean that he just kills them all."

Po nodded. "How about, 'Selene, Hilloa, Jan, and Baris are alive and well and standing in front of Po and Ayma on the walkway to the old theater.' "

"You forgot Censor Siblea."

No he hadn't. "Okay, him too."

Ayma thought about it. "There could be other people with those names."

"Then how about, 'Those known to Po and Ayma by the names—' "

Shouts interrupted him. From the alley across the
street poured a crowd of people wearing brown robes. They
had mind lancets. Po gathered up the pen and grabbed
Ayma's hand. They ran to the side of the old theater.
Between the old building and a high wall was a narrow
alley choked with weeds and trash. He ushered Ayma in
ahead of him. Halfway down the length of the building, he
heard the mob behind them, crashing through the under-
brush. Po took off his satchel and held it out to Ayma.
"Take this and run. I'll slow them down and you can get
away."

"No," she said.

"Please. If they catch you and harm you, what do you
think will happen then?"

Understanding dawned in her eyes. Po would fight
them and be killed, and then she'd be alone with them.
She took the satchel and ran.

Ten paces later, the Lit King's people caught up with
him.

They drove him to the main avenue of the citadel,
where they proceeded to march him toward the
temple. They passed through the doors of the mammoth
building. The entrance looked like a huge mouth, gaping
open. It swallowed him. They came into a courtyard. Robed
figures hung from gibbets driven into the ground, their
lifeless bodies slowly twisting around and around. Po
stared at them as he passed, trying to see if any of them
were members of the chorus, but he couldn't tell.

They left the courtyard and ushered him across a large,
marble-floored entrance hall and down a set of stairs to a
dank place beneath the temple. They walked down a long,

dreary hallway lined with doors. The old woman who'd been among the group at the theater opened a door at the very end. "Your accommodations," she said, and giggled. The guards shoved him inside and slammed the door shut.

Selene, Hilloa, Jan, Baris, and Siblea sat blinking up at him. They were in a stone cell that was just barely large enough to hold them all. Dirty straw covered the floor. It looked like it hadn't been changed since the prisoners rebelled and a foul, stale funk hung in the air.

"Seven Hells," swore Selene. "They got you, too."

In the dim light it was difficult to make out details. "Has anyone been harmed?" asked Po.

"Not really," said Hilloa.

What did she mean by that?

"Not yet," said Baris.

Po's gaze landed on Siblea. He sat a bit apart from the others, his back against the wall. He'd barely even glanced up when Po arrived. "How were you taken?" Po asked him.

Siblea lifted his head and stared at Po. "The barley merchant betrayed us." He had a bruise around his eye, and blood crusted at one corner of his mouth.

"What about Ayma?" asked Hilloa.

"She got away." He wanted to say that she got away with the rose, which was really a pen, and he was dying to ask Selene about everything that had happened with Endymion, but if they were overheard . . .

"Where were you two?" asked Baris. "Did you find anything?"

"Don't answer him," said Selene. "If we don't know anything then we can't talk when we're questioned."

"Questioned?" Po had heard rumors about Singer interrogation techniques, how ruthless and effective they were. Would the Lit King, having been a prisoner of the Singers and likely subjected to such tactics, reject them? Or would he relish the opportunity to turn them on others?

"Did you experience something strange, maybe half an hour ago?" Jan asked him. Selene gave him a look.

A half hour—was that all it had been? The truth about the Lion's Bloom and his many questions about Endymion hammered inside his head, but all he said was, "Yes."

"We've got to get out of here," said Hilloa.

As if in answer to her words, the sound of a key in the lock broke through their muttered conversation like a thunderclap. The door opened and eight big guards with mind lancets entered, followed by the old woman and two other women who carried chains and manacles. The big guards stood around the chorus in a circle, mind lancets at the ready. If they resisted, they'd be subdued and chained anyway. Po's stomach turned as Selene and Hilloa each were manacled in turn. Both stared at him. Hilloa shook her head, but it was the expression of warning on Selene's face that stopped him from attacking the guards.

They were taken back up the stairs and into a great assembly hall, with tier upon tier of balconies and an enormous statue that had been defaced. The statue man's nose was gone, his face was painted with spirals, and the words "illiterate pig" were painted on the front of him.

At the statue's feet, in a chair made more ornate with apparently whatever was at hand, sat a man, one leg draped negligently over an arm of the chair. His face was covered with scars.

The man wore a robe with an intricate black-and-white

pattern all over the fabric. And he had a crown made of silver and gold wires, braided and looped together. He held a book in his hands and he read it to a group of young women. They wore very little and they sat at his feet, looking up at him in rapt and reverent attention.

"You know I am not used to such ceremonies, and there was something ominous in the atmosphere," he said, reading from it. His smooth tenor carried well across the amphitheater. He looked up and saw the chorus, and he set the book aside.

He smiled. It was an odd effect with all the scars.

Po watched Siblea. He was pale, trembling. "Thescarion."

"Yes. How flattering that you remember me. But of course you and I did quite a bit of work together, attempting to purify my soul. It didn't work, as you see; or rather, I was already too pure for you and your false religion. But now I may commence attempting to purify you. I confess, I did not think we would encounter each other again in this world. What good fortune—for me, anyway, and for all of those whom you tortured."

Siblea swallowed. "Thescarion. I . . ."

The other man laughed. "Speechless for once, eh? You won't be for long. It will be interesting to see how you respond to your own methods."

"We were in error, Thescarion," said Siblea. "I freely admit that. But we've been Redeemed and we've discovered the power of the Word. It was much as you said it would be. Take me, punish me if you must, but these others are your brothers and sisters in the Word. Do not harm them."

Thescarion gave a wry smile. "If they are with you, I do

not doubt that they are clever. We have had word of what occurred at the Libyrinth. This so-called Redemption. It's heresy. No true Redemption could occur when its most ardent supporters moldered in prison, underground, neglected and forgotten, even by their tormentors. No. They are at the least false prophets, and if they are with you, they are surely much more than that. Let us give them a demonstration of what they can expect if they give my people trouble. Shall we, Siblea?"

He nodded to three of the guards. Two of them seized Siblea by the arms while the third unlocked his shackles. Baris attempted to defend him but another guard struck him with a mind lancet and he fell to the floor, gasping.

The guards brought Siblea forward. The Lit King snapped his fingers at the women sitting at his feet. "Fetch the chair!"

The women scattered only to return moments later carrying a chair that was equipped with straps to hold the occupant immobile. "No," muttered Siblea, his voice a low moan, hopeless. Po strained against his own chains, desperate to stop whatever was about to happen.

Siblea was placed in the chair, and then the Lit King stood up. He snapped his fingers and another attendant appeared carrying a box with a handle. The Lit King opened it and drew out a knife and a small stone jar.

Po saw Siblea's larynx bob at the sight, and a faint sheen of sweat appeared upon his skin. The Lit King stood before Siblea and looked him up and down appraisingly. "Hmm. Where shall we begin?" He put on a show of giving it great thought, pacing back and forth, placing one finger to his chin. Suddenly he whirled to face Siblea once more. "I know! How about where you began with me?"

And with that he closed on Siblea, took the knife, and placed it on Siblea's cheek.

Po watched in horror as the Lit King carved a long, curving spiral on Siblea's face, starting at his cheekbone just below the eye and curving up to his temple and then across his forehead. During this, Siblea bit his lips and trembled, but he did not cry out. At last there was a great, bloody cut from Siblea's right cheek, across his forehead and around to his other cheek. His face was covered in blood. Po found he was shaking. At least it was over now.

But it wasn't. The Lit King wiped the blood away from the cut, which continued to ooze, stood back and surveyed his work, smiled, and then took the jar from his attendant's hand. He removed the lid and with a small spoon, lifted out a powder.

"It's lye," Selene whispered.

Very delicately, he put a little of the powder on the cut on Siblea's face.

Siblea screamed.

Little vapor trails of acrid fumes drifted up from where the caustic chemical ate into Siblea's wound. Po shut his eyes as the Lit King scooped up more of the powder and repeated the process on the next section of Siblea's wound. "These lines are to remind us of our inseparable connection with the Song that runs through all things," said the Lit King between Siblea's screams. "And so you might ask why I, a lit, would place them upon you, a Singer. But the answer is simple." He paused as he applied more lye and Siblea's cry became weaker. "Because I can."

23

492

Ayma took the satchel from Po and ran for all she was worth. She came to the end of the alley. Behind her, she heard the zap of a mind lancet and Po's yell. She wanted to turn back, but she knew what would happen if she did. Both of them would be captured, and worse, the pen would fall into the hands of the Lit King.

She turned to the right, pelting down a small side street. Fortunately it was empty, so there was no one to take notice of her. But where was she going to go? Her first thought was to take cover in her father's tavern like a mouse hiding in its burrow, but immediately she realized that was the worst place she could go. If Censor Siblea's activities had been discovered, they would be watching the place.

She turned another corner and slowed to a walk. Huddled close against the wall, head down, there was no reason now for anyone to take notice of her, and running would only attract attention. Besides, walking gave her a chance to think.

She didn't know that many people in the citadel anymore. Most of them had left on pilgrimage. Those remaining, mainly the wives and daughters of her father's friends and business associates, might also now be under the scrutiny of the Lit King's mob, because Siblea had held a resistance meeting in her father's establishment. At the very least, they did not need to borrow her trouble.

In the end, there was only one place she could think of to go.

The guards carrying Siblea led the way as Po and the others were herded back to their cells and thrust inside. No one bothered removing their chains. The chorus sat in a circle, staring at one another. "What do we do now?" asked Jan.

No one had an answer. Siblea sat very still, his back to the wall, his face a blank mask. Po had never seen anything like that in his life. From the looks on the others' faces and the covert, worried glances they shot Siblea, neither had the others. Hilloa nudged Po in the ribs. "See if there's anything you can do for him."

"Me?" said Po, surprised.

"Yes, you. You're a healer, stupid; act like one."

Her words galvanized him. Po crouched beside Siblea and awkwardly placed a hand on the man's shoulder.

He opened his eyes. "There is little you can do, Po. My injuries are painful, but not life-threatening. That is by design, of course. I administered such torture to hundreds of prisoners in my time, and not one died from it. Just hope that they do not put us to work at the forges. That is another story."

"Will they feed us?" said Baris.

"Let's not wait around to find out," said Hilloa. "Let's get out of here."

"That is easier said than done," said Siblea. "As you see, the door is locked tight. But I have an idea. The Lit King will doubtless wish to work with me further—"

"What?"

"Yes. It is no more than turnabout, Selene. I did it to him; I must accept it from him."

"No."

"Selene . . . do you know how many people died in this place while I was in charge of it? Four hundred and ninety-two. Redemption or no, can you honestly say I do not deserve this?"

Four hundred ninety-two. Po tried to get his head around that number and its meaning, but he was too exhausted to hate Siblea right now. He hadn't slept or eaten in over a day. This place stank and he didn't want to think about what might be in the straw they were all sitting in. He squirmed around to Hilloa's side.

"Are you okay?"

She nodded. "So far." They leaned against each other. In a little while, they heard the sound of the key in the lock again. Po tensed as two guards entered. One of them stood by the door with a mind lancet while the other ladled out cups of water and bowls of gruel.

They left again. Everyone ate the thin, sour-tasting gruel in silence, and drank some water. Hilloa fell asleep against him, and soon Po himself succumbed to exhaustion.

P o was awakened by the sound of their prison door opening again. Two large guards came in while one stood by the door. They took Hilloa by the arms and began dragging her toward the door. Po sprang at them. One of them struck him across the chest with a mind lancet. Agony ripped through his body and he fell back. When he tried to get to his feet again, the other guard hit him in the solar plexus with his mind lancet. Red fire consumed his vision and the edges of the world burned.

H e awoke in the straw, his head cradled in somebody's lap. His body felt like it was filled with shards of glass. When he tried to move, they sliced him. He lay still, but opened his eyes. It took a moment for his vision to clear. He was still in the cell. Hilloa's face looked above. She pushed a lock of hair from his forehead and smiled. It was a sad smile. "How do you feel?"

"Bad. But what about you? They took you."

"And now I'm back."

"What did they do to you?"

"Nothing. They took me to a room where the Lit King sat and they asked me a lot of questions about who we are and why we're here. Since you've been out, Selene and Jan have also been interviewed. Baris is with them now. It'll likely be your turn next. If you cooperate with them they won't hurt you much. I think the Lit King is saving the torture for Siblea."

Po turned his head and gasped at the sudden pain that rocketed through him. But he could see Siblea sitting just where he'd been before, silent with his eyes closed. He was either meditating or sleeping or desperately trying to maintain control—it was impossible to tell.

The guards returned with Baris, who bore a bruise under his eye and held his arm as if it pained him. They shoved the Singer boy into the straw and turned to Siblea. Baris sat up and threw himself at them. "Lit filth! Leave him alone!"

One of the guards kicked Baris in the neck, almost casually, then bent and took one of Siblea's arms. Another two guards came in and approached Po. "You. Get up. You're coming with him."

Po's insides squirmed like he'd swallowed a live eel. He looked from Hilloa to Selene. But neither of them had any instructions or advice for him. They just looked frightened. He got up. His head swam but he managed to stay upright and then he didn't need to worry too much about walking because the guards each took one of his arms and dragged him after Siblea.

They took them up several flights of stairs to a room that had once been richly appointed. Beautiful wood paneling on the walls, with words carved into every available surface, now stood defaced. The red carpeting bore burn marks and stains. A large desk stood in the middle of the room, the Lit King behind it. He smiled as they entered.

In front of the desk sat two chairs that were identical to the one into which they'd strapped Siblea earlier. "Restrain him," said the Lit King.

Po wasn't sure who he meant at first, but the guards apparently did. They put Siblea in one of the chairs and restrained him. Siblea betrayed nothing. His face was a stone mask.

The Lit King waved to Po's guards and they brought him closer to the desk. The Lit King looked him up and down. "I understand you're Ilysian."

Po said nothing.

"You put up quite a fight earlier when my men came for Hilloa. I thought you Ilysian men were like women. I didn't expect you to fight, but it's been explained to me. You'll never hit a woman, but you'll fight a man at the drop of a hat. You don't think much of men, do you?"

Po didn't know how to answer that, so again he said nothing.

"I asked you a question!" He nodded to one of the guards, who hit him with the mind lancet. It was just a tap on the shoulder this time, but that was enough to send Po to his knees. The Lit King stood and leaned over his desk so he could maintain eye contact with Po. "Answer!"

Po let his hate shine from his eyes. "I guess not."

The Lit King laughed. "You are going to be so much fun to break. By the time I'm through with you, you'll be doing things you never dreamed possible. You'll hit a woman and comfort a man. But first the easier of the two. Strap him in."

They pulled him up by the arms and shoved him into the chair. "Fight us and I'll zap you again," said one of the guards. Po was tempted to fight anyway but he could endure the torture with or without another mind-lancet attack; without was just marginally better. The guards strapped his arms and legs to the chair.

The Lit King came around his desk and leaned over Po. "There's a limit to how much pain a person can endure before shock sets in and the true severity of the agony is no longer felt." He nodded at Siblea. "We know, don't we, Censor?"

He reached up and untied one of the ties of his robe. The cloth fell, baring one shoulder. It was covered in swirling scars. He watched Siblea while he did it, and while he reached up and undid the other tie. But when the garment fell from his body and lay pooled at his feet, it was Po to whom the Lit King turned. "It took Siblea and me fifteen years to do this."

Every inch of his body was covered in scars. Po's mouth immediately went dry and he looked to Siblea. Siblea looked at the marks with familiarity and resignation. Po tasted bile. The next second he was fighting the urge to throw up. He searched the Lit King's face. The man was mad, but there was a light of intelligence in his eyes.

"He could only do so much at a time, you see, or it would be wasted. Every spiral and turn must be felt, must be experienced as it is embedded in the body, for the instruction to be effective. I quite agree. He did an admirable job, wouldn't you say?"

Po swallowed bile and searched his eyes. But he didn't see anything in there but fire.

"I would happily spend ten years to make you as I am, Siblea. But I don't have to." He turned to Po. "When he faints, you will revive him."

At dawn, Ayma lifted her head from the satchel, which had served her as a pillow, and crept from the little cubbyhole she'd found between a pillar and the thick stone wall of the dairy market in the market square. Already anybody with anything to sell was filtering into the area. It was nothing like it had been before the pilgrimage, but nevertheless the people who came had at least some resources, and some of them might need an honest pair of hands to help out in exchange for something to eat. She had done this before from time to time, and when she'd been able to find work, it had gone well.

Before venturing out to try her luck, however, Ayma tucked the satchel with the pen through the neck of her dress and smoothed it down. The wide band of the satchel simply looked as if she wore a scarf around her neck, and no one would take much notice of the bulge of the book and the pen at her midsection. She was far from being the only one who carried their last remaining possessions on their person at all times.

A man and a woman with a small child were busy shucking corn. They already had a line at their stall. The child kept wandering away and its mother had to fetch it, which meant they were falling behind the demand and the line was growing.

Ayma had learned not to ask if she could help or try to negotiate any kind of payment in advance. Instead, she simply stepped up to the overflowing cart and began pulling the ears free from their green wrappers. The harried parents glanced at each other and then nodded at her. When business slacked off at midmorning, they presented her with ten ears of corn, enough for her to eat and maybe even trade some with someone else.

That afternoon, gorged on corn and the peanuts she traded with a ten-year-old boy for her surplus, Ayma wandered the citadel, aimless. She had the strangest feeling, which had been creeping up on her ever since she realized that she could not go back to the tavern. She couldn't fathom why, but somehow the realization had taken her fear from her. It didn't make any sense at all, because losing her father's tavern, her only place of shelter from the horrors of the Lit King's citadel, should have been the worst possible thing that could have happened to her. But here she was, with a full belly, tired from good work and walking about the citadel as if she were on some sort of holiday. If it weren't for her anxiety over what was happening to Po and Siblea at the hands of the Lit King, she might describe her state of mind as happy. As it was, she felt as if she had emerged from a long confinement and could now look about her and breathe fresh air.

Her meandering path took her across Yammon Street. She paused in the shadow of a music shop and gazed at the Temple of Yammon at the far end of the boulevard. If there was anything she could do for Po and Siblea, she had to try.

For the first time she truly regretted not paying more attention when that man from the Lit King's mob had tried to teach her to write. At the time she'd been too focused on finding a way to wheedle food from him, but now . . . If she could write, she could use the pen. But she only knew two words, "the" and "and." That wouldn't get her very far.

Perhaps she could find someone else who could write and get him to use the pen to free the chorus or even kill the Lit King. But she didn't know anyone who could write who was not also a follower of the Lit King.

That night she slept in her cubbyhole again, and the next morning there was a pumpkin farmer to help. She tried not to think about what she would do when her baby came, but most of all she tried not to think about Po.

24

Siblea's Bloom

The room seemed much smaller than it had six hours ago. Siblea's screams had long since torn a ragged hole in Po's mind. He stayed inside that hole and only came out when the Lit King made him.

Now he kneeled at Siblea's feet. He did not look up into the man's ravaged face. He tried to ignore the blood dripping from the edge of his robe. It stank in here. He closed his eyes and he placed his hands on Siblea's feet, cupping the arch, fingers feeling for his meridians. The first time he'd done this for the Lit King, he hadn't thought he'd be able to achieve the concentration necessary for the trance. But he'd dropped into the attuned state as easily as falling out of a tree. His kinesthetic sense seemed to grow stronger all the time. Was there a connection between this and the many mind-lancet attacks he had sustained? When he'd assisted Adept Ykobos in treating Clauda, he'd often wondered if the weapon did something to its victims that heightened the body's sensitivity to energies.

Of course, there was no telling what treating an Ancient might have done to him. He wondered what state his own energy pathways must be in, but he did not bother to find out. He concentrated on Siblea. Three breaths and Siblea's pain became his own. He felt a constant burning throb in his face and arm. The worst were his hand and foot, where the nerves were so sensitive. They felt as if they roasted in a fire he was powerless to flinch from. This was the sixth time Po had revived Siblea. In his mind he saw the now-familiar flower that represented Siblea and the state of his body's energy pathways. It had been a beautiful flower once: orange and red petals and a yellow center with a vibrant green stem and broad leaves. Now it was crawling with ants. They did not destroy the flower or prevent it from absorbing sunlight or drawing nutrients from the soil—they simply marched up and down the plant with their needle feet and sank their needle jaws into it.

Po was a gust of wind and he pushed the ants off the flower with his breath. The blossom was covered with welts and discolorations. Though alive, it had drawn its petals closed, cutting itself off from its environment.

While the ants waited in a circle around the bloom, Po used his ability as wind to coalesce a cloud and bring soft rain down upon the flower. The rainwater had an agent in it to bring pleasure where pain had been. He watched as the plant gradually revived and opened itself once more.

He tried to believe that what he was doing was helping Siblea. He knew it was only making it possible for the Lit

King to hurt him more. But Hilloa, Selene, and the others were in the cell downstairs and the Lit King had made it clear what would happen to them if Po did not obey.

To his shame, he wished Siblea would simply die, so it could be over, but that was not about to happen, either. The torture was well thought out, excruciating, and non-fatal. Regardless, it was taking its toll. It had only been an hour this last time before Siblea had fallen into a stupor. And though the art of kinesiology was focused on the physical body and its energies, those could never be truly separate from the mind, which was Po's real concern. Po lingered in his trance as long as he dared, to give Siblea more time to rest. He forced himself to look at the man's face as he awoke. Siblea blinked. Po mouthed the words, "I'm sorry."

Siblea did not answer. The guards forced Po back into his chair. Po wondered if he could have made it without their help. He was trembling and exhausted from his work. Nevertheless, they strapped him in, though the Lit King never touched him. He was simply another member of the madman's audience.

The old woman came in and stood at the back of the room, watching. Po kept finding himself looking at her, hoping that she would intervene. But she merely smiled appreciatively as the Lit King carried on with his torture. He talked as he carved lines into Siblea's body. He compared what he did to what Siblea had done to him. Po found it difficult to sympathize with the Lit King.

"All those years, Siblea, all those questions. Should I ask you questions? Do you know how much I never told you?"

As far gone as he was, Siblea's eyes glittered at that.

The Lit King appeared delighted at the reaction. "You thought I told you everything, didn't you?"

Siblea nodded; perhaps he hoped it would placate him.

"You don't even know who I really am."

"You're the Lit King." Siblea's voice was a hoarse croak. Po was surprised he could speak at all.

"I am the direct descendent of Iscarion himself."

Po had an idea. Perhaps he could distract the Lit King from Siblea. "All of Iscarion's family and followers left after the folly," he said.

The Lit King turned and pointed at Po with the dripping knife. "That is what everyone was supposed to believe." He turned back to Siblea and made a cut along the length of his right index finger. His voice grew removed as he concentrated on his work. "But his wife stayed behind to guard his secrets, and she gave birth to a son and taught the Iscarion family secrets to him, and they have been kept, in trust, in an unbroken line to myself, the great-great-great-great-grandson of the Literate Iscarion."

"You're delusional," said Po.

The Lit King only smiled, and laughed a little under his breath as he reached for the jar. This was the worst part. Po permitted himself to close his eyes, but he could not shut his ears.

"All those years you thought you'd won, you Singers," the Lit King went on after Siblea's screams had ebbed. "But we have never left, and we have never given up our faith. We hid books, a whole library full of them, in the midst of your precious citadel, in the place you would never dare to look. Can you guess where we hid them? Can you guess, Siblea?"

Siblea did not answer.

"You hid them beneath the stage in the old theater," said Po. "Just above Endymion's tomb."

That seemed to surprise him. He exchanged a glance with the old woman, who went to the back of the room and pressed on a section of paneling. It opened to reveal a door and she went through it.

"Indeed," said the Lit King. "It seems you did a little exploring while your fellows were imprisoned. What else did you find, I wonder."

"You'll have to torture me to find out," said Po, while part of him quailed at what he was doing.

"Ha! You think I don't know what you are doing? Trying to distract me so I'll stop working with Siblea here, and switch to you. Such compassion, for this, a Singer priest. He tortured women, too, you know."

Po swallowed.

The old woman returned through the same doorway and whispered something in his ear. "Later, Mab," he told her. "Right now, I'm having too much fun with him." He nodded at Siblea. She whispered something else and he rolled his eyes. "Then let her do it." For a moment he and Mab just looked at each other, and then he shrugged. "Very well." He turned to Siblea once more. "Tell me, why did you and your people come back here?" It was the first question of any practical use he had put to Siblea.

Siblea's voice was barely a whisper, but he told the Lit King all about the crop fire, and the rumors of a terraforming device known as the Lion's Bloom. Po concentrated on the sweat trickling down his sides. He tried not to even think about Endymion's rose.

The next time he was released to revive Siblea, he went into a trance only to find that the flower was gone. In its place a seed pod lay on the ground. Po withdrew from the trance and turned to the Lit King. "His system is in severe shock. If I revive him now, he'll die."

The Lit King sighed. "Very well. Tomorrow is another day and my hand is cramping." He nodded to the guards. "Take them back to their cell."

Ayma was helping a woman fill sacks with dried corn when a group of dark-robed figures rode into the marketplace on horses, a wagon in tow. Ayma's boss for the day, a middle-aged woman named Loren, looked up and cursed. "The Lit King's mob. They'll steal everything if they can. Come on—help me get all of this back into the cart."

Ayma started heaving sacks into the woman's cart. Shouts filled the air as the Lit King's mob started seizing goods and throwing them into their wagon. A man fought one of them for a sack of carrots and took a blow across the temple from a mind lancet for his trouble. Ayma heard his shout cut off abruptly and he fell down and lay still. His wife knelt at his side, wailing. Everywhere people were running, pushing, screaming. Those that fought were soon subdued by mind lancets.

Being near the north end of the market, Ayma and Loren managed to get the cart loaded and were beginning to haul it away by the time a man rode up brandishing a mind lancet. "You there! Stop! That is property of the Lit King! You must relinquish it immediately or be guilty of treason!"

They tried to run faster but he spurred his horse on and got in front of them. The cart was unwieldy. Ayma tried to turn it but that required backing it up, and now another mounted follower of the Lit King had arrived. Loren pleaded, "I have children at home, sir. Please! I must feed them somehow! If you won't let me sell my corn, at least let me—"

The man swung his mind lancet in an arc aimed to connect with Loren's head. Time seemed to slow down, and Ayma felt as though she stood outside of herself as she reached up and grasped the haft of the lancet and wrenched it from the man's hand. She reversed its direction and caught him in the neck with the glowing blue ball at the end.

He screamed and toppled from his horse. Ayma turned and charged at the other two mounted men. In the corner of her eye she saw Loren's openmouthed stare. It was madness, yes, but all the frustration, fear, and rage she'd felt ever since the mob killed her father had come to a head with that one attack on a helpless woman. They had taken Po and Censor Siblea away from her. She didn't care what happened next, as long as she could hurt as many of them as possible.

She jabbed the end of the mind lancet into the midsection of the rider on the left. He convulsed, but grasped at the haft of the lancet, attempting to pull it from her grip even as he shook. Her hands slipped on the polished wood.

Suddenly a brick sailed past her and connected with her opponent's head. With a short, sharp shout, he fell backward and released the lancet. Ayma didn't dare turn to see where the brick had come from, but she had a good idea. Instead she turned and faced the third rider.

In moments others had caught on to what was happening and joined her and Loren. A brick-maker snatched the mind lancet from the second rider's saddle and went after a group of the Lit King's men who had surrounded a poultry merchant.

The guards shoved Po and Siblea through the door of the cell, slammed it shut, and locked it again. Siblea lay in the straw, unmoving. Baris crouched at his side. Selene and Jan looked at Po. Hilloa embraced him. "Are you all right?"

He nodded.

"You were gone for nearly a day," said Selene. "What happened?"

Po explained in as few words as possible. In the corner, Baris chafed Siblea's wrist. "Censor! Wake up!"

"No, let him sleep, Baris. He needs sleep, and water when he wakes." Until he looked back at Selene and Jan, he did not realize what he'd done. He'd corrected Baris—not to prove himself superior, but for the sake of another male.

Hours went by. Siblea slept and Po examined him.

"How is he?" asked Selene.

"He's strong. His body is in no real danger as long as he gets the rest he needs," said Po.

Neither Selene nor anyone else inquired after his mind and Po did not volunteer the information.

Ayma stood in the middle of the marketplace, one of about fifty women, all looking as stunned as she probably did. Her arms trembled with exhaustion and her breath came in ragged gasps, but she was alive and, apart from a cut to her hand from a lit's dagger that would probably scar, unharmed.

The same could not be said for many others. The market square was littered with bodies. The lits who had come to take their food were dead, except for the ones who had managed to get away. Many of the market people were also slain, especially the men. But most of those who had risen up in arms this morning had lived to tell the tale. Many of them tended to the wounded. Others stood around with their newly claimed weapons—mind lancets, bricks, awls, and pitchforks—slowly turning in place, looking about them at what they had wrought.

Ayma felt a deep terror, for retribution could not be long in coming. Several of the lits had escaped and they would surely go to the Lit King, who would send more people here to punish them. But she also felt a bloody exaltation, a bitter satisfaction that she had taken lives on behalf of her father and Censor Siblea, and Po.

Thinking of Po reminded her of the pen in the satchel that she still wore around her neck. "Can anyone here read?" she asked.

This got her glares. "I have Endymion's rose," she explained. "And it is a pen, after all—a pen for rewriting reality. If someone here can write, we can destroy the Lit King right now, without further bloodshed."

"We are led by a madwoman," muttered an herb seller.

Led? She was leading? She spotted Loren, bending over one of the few men who were still living. He was bleeding from a wound in his belly and she was trying to stop it. Several other women either stood or knelt at his side. Ayma looked over Loren's shoulder and saw the blood running from beneath her hands. The man looked up at Ayma. "I know you," he said. "You were with Censor Siblea."

She nodded. She recognized him now. He'd been at the tavern that day with Censor Siblea, discussing rebellion.

"Can you write, sir? Did the mob teach you?"

The man nodded.

Ayma scrambled to get the pen out of her satchel. At the sight of it, the man's eyes widened, and everyone else around took a step back, and eyed her with new speculation. "Please," she said. "Use this. Write—I don't know. Write something to make the Lit King dead, to release Censor Siblea and the Chorus of the Word."

Loren glared at her. "Please, Carl, don't try to move, don't talk. Your wound."

He shook his head. "I'm dying. It matters not." He lifted his hand and Ayma tried to hand him the pen but he waved it away and pointed at her. "This girl. She was with Censor Siblea. And she struck the first blow today. She carries on his work." He stared at Loren, and then the others, his strength faltering. "You must help her continue the censor's work. He came to liberate us. Now, you women, you must free him so he can overthrow the Lit Ki—" His eyes closed and he slumped backward.

Ayma looked at the pen in her hand. "Is there no one else?" she asked, but they paid her no mind. They were grieving and raging for their losses. She looked at them, at the rage that had so long been bottled, and which now spilled. The pen was of no use to them but, she wondered, what of their grief? Was it enough to drive them to storm the temple and free the chorus?

It seemed like a mad dream, but then twenty minutes ago she would not have believed what she had just seen. Perhaps if they could survive the next twelve hours, if they could get more people on their side . . .

But first things first. They had claimed the marketplace for their own, and they must not lose it.

The wails of the women rose into the sky like dark birds, and in flight, altered. The market square echoed with a new sound never before heard—a war cry.

25

Ayma's Army

Stack more hay behind that wagon," Ayma told a girl who was about a year or two older than her. The girl nodded and began piling another layer of hay bales behind the wagon they had turned onto its side in the middle of the street on the northwest side of the market. Flanking it were stacks of empty barrels, forming a barricade and blocking access to the square. They had had to work quickly, but now every road into the market had some sort of barrier from which they could attempt to defend it. Piles of bricks and broken chunks of paving stone sat near at hand, and every fallen lit had been ransacked for weapons. They had twenty mind lancets and two rifles. Five women, the widow and orphans of an olive merchant, stuffed rags into bottles of oil and passed them out.

When the barricades were as strong as they could make them under the circumstances, there was a pause, and Ayma saw many of the women looking at her. "This is madness," said a woman with long, dirty white hair. "We can't do this. We'll all be killed."

Ayma nodded. "Likely we will be. But so what? They've taken everything else from us, even our men. If there is even a chance of punishing them for that, then I do not think my life is so important. And if we can liberate the censor and bring back the priests, then that is worth many hundreds of our lives."

Many around them nodded at this, but some seemed uncertain. Ayma hoped they would not have much longer to wait before the attack. And then she heard it—the clatter and clash of the Lit King's mob on the move. It seemed to come from everywhere around them and she realized that they were converging on the square from all sides. They would not have the option of concentrating their defense in one place. For a moment Ayma looked at the faces of the women around her and wondered if their courage would fail them—if hers would fail her. But then Loren threw her head back and uttered that unearthly wail again. The others joined her and the sound of widows flew up to meet the cacophony of the mob.

F ar too soon, the door of the cell opened again and the guards came in. The old woman, Mab, was with them.

Siblea could barely stand up. "It's too soon," Po entreated her. "He needs more time."

To all appearances, she was insane. She cracked that grin of hers and said, "Not him—you." She turned, look-

ing over the rest of them. Suddenly she thrust her bony
finger toward Hilloa. "And her."

From what you've said, it sounds like up until now, the
Lit King's just been getting his jollies tormenting
Siblea. There was no purpose to it," said Hilloa as she and
Po were hustled down the hallway by the guards.

"Until the very end of the session, after I mentioned
Endymion's tomb. I shouldn't have, but I wanted to distract him from Siblea. After that he started asking real
questions."

"And now he's switched victims." Hilloa nodded as they
started up the staircase. "Listen, Po, I think he's going to
question you about what you and Ayma found in the old
theater," she whispered. "I think he's going to try to get
you to talk by mistreating me. We've been relatively
lucky so far, but . . ." She glanced at their guards and said
nothing more. They reached the same room Po and Siblea
had been in the day before. The rank odor of blood and
fear still hung in the room, but it was otherwise unoccu-
pied.

"You believe this?" said one of the guards to the other.

"I know. What are we supposed to do, just wait here
while he's off screwing around with that foreign whore of
his?"

"Yeah," said the other one. "I've got a keg of ale downstairs and if I don't get back there, Mason's going to drink
it all."

"That's a shame."

"Screw it, let's just leave them here."

"What, unattended?"

"Yeah. They're chained; we'll lock the door. What are they going to do? Come on—I'll share."

The other man nodded. "Fine."

They shoved Po and Hilloa into the room and shut and locked the door behind them.

"There's a secret door back here," said Po. They went to where he'd seen Mab press the paneling. One section of the paneling did in fact give in at Po's pressure, and there was a muffled click, but no door appeared. Po pulled and pried at the seam of the door, but it didn't budge.

"It's locked," said Hilloa. They tried the door they'd come in through, but that one was locked, too. "Before the Lit King comes, I have to tell you something. I've seen how he acts toward the women who follow him. And I know how the Singers are about sex. They think the worst thing that can happen to a woman is to be forced into it. I think . . . Po, I think he's going to rape me to get you to talk. But don't talk!"

"What?! Force you? I'll kill him."

Hilloa shook her head. "You might not be able to. He'll keep you locked up, and he'll demand that you talk. I don't know what you and Ayma found, but if he gets the Lion's Bloom, all is lost. Just . . . don't talk. Let him do that to me. I'm not going to die from it, you know? I'll survive. Whatever he does to me, don't talk."

Po shook his head.

"I mean it. Anything he does is not going to be any worse than what he's already done to Siblea. I'm strong. I'll be okay."

Po felt as if every cell in his body were vibrating at a frequency higher than anything in this plane of existence. Was this how the People Who Walk Sideways in Time transcended to a higher dimension? Was he going to become like Endymion? If so, it might make a lot of things much simpler, though he'd be very afraid for himself.

Hilloa took one look at him and sighed. "Po, I'm ordering you, as a woman—don't let him goad you into talking."

Her voice brought him back to the present moment. He swallowed. "As a man I have to tell you that tolerating such a thing is beyond me."

Her mouth set, firm and flat. "If you were my consort, you'd have to do as I say, wouldn't you?"

"Yes," he said reluctantly. "But I didn't get initiated, so . . ."

Hilloa shook her head and pulled him to her. "Forget that for now. How do I make you my consort?"

"You . . . you want me to be your consort?" He felt torn in so many different directions he wondered that he didn't split apart. He had been so attracted to Hilloa at one time, but it hadn't worked out, and since then he'd been Queen Thela's toy, and then he'd met Ayma . . . If they ever reunited with Ayma again, would the two women share him? Hilloa might be fine with that, but what would Ayma make of it? "Uh . . . you don't mean it," he said.

"Yes, I do. Be my consort, Po." She pulled herself up on her toes and kissed him.

Her lips were so soft and warm. Her mouth was sweet. He fell into the kiss as if diving into the ocean. Their chains clinked together as he lifted his hands to stroke the sides of her face. She wrapped her arms around his waist and pulled him close, so that he pressed against her.

Hilloa. Already he felt himself falling for her all over
again. Her kindness, her intelligence . . . he broke the kiss.
"You're only doing this so that I'll obey your wishes when
the Lit King comes."

She blinked up at him, her face flushed. "Not just for
that," she said, and kissed him again, hard. She was trembling, and her cheeks, when they brushed against his,
were wet. He held her tight and made his mind up for
himself.

A yma had known the streets of the citadel her entire
life, so why, now, should they look so different? She
ran at the head of the howling mob, with a mind lancet in
one hand and a brick in the other. The Lit King's people,
who had been on the attack moments ago, now fell back
before her. Perhaps the wild exhilaration made her see her
city in a new way. All she knew was that they had surprised everyone, most especially themselves, when the Lit
King's reinforcements came.

The very most she had hoped for was to defend the
square. Instead they were overrunning the whole citadel,
their ranks swelling by the minute as ordinary people saw
them fighting and joined in.

Ahead was the Temple of Yammon. Ayma's mob and
many others converged upon it. "We must free the censor!" she cried, and the call went up behind her, but it soon
became incoherent as the surging tide of people burst forth
with an inarticulate roar.

Taken by surprise, the Lit King's people scrambled to
the gates of the temple, struggling to push the great iron
doors closed. If they succeeded, there was little hope of
getting inside to rescue the Chorus of the Word. Ayma

and the others dashed toward the narrowing archway. A scarred man in a brown robe grappled with her, and she just managed to twist her mind lancet from his grasp and strike him across the back of the head with it. He screamed and fell, and she ran on. Shots rang out, but she did not know if they came from her own people, firing at the lits who were amassing on the walls above, or vice versa. A blur of motion on her right resolved into the butt of a rifle a second too late, and pain exploded across her face as it connected with her jaw. She staggered, but the press of bodies carried her forward, and she managed not to fall and be trampled underfoot.

The lit who had struck her was borne along also. He raised his rifle again and she thrust her mind lancet into his midsection. With an abbreviated scream, he went down beneath the pounding feet of the mob.

When they reached the gates there was no more than a five-foot gap remaining. Ayma was terrified that the press of the mob would push them closed and crush them all against the wall. A tall man leaned past her and grasped the edge of one of the gates, then pulled it back.

"Back up! Back up!" Ayma cried, and the people around them pushed back against the oncoming rush, providing a momentary gap in the crowd. Ayma scrambled around the edge of the door, pushing on it while the man pulled, and others around her flowed though and past her and took on the members of the Lit King's mob who were struggling to pull the doors closed.

Others did the same with the other gate, and soon both doors were pressed flush against the walls and the mob poured through the gate, overwhelming the Lit King's people, who now fled before them.

"To the dungeons!" Ayma cried, pelting across the cobblestones toward the central tower. People scattered before them.

Ahead she saw one of the lits who had given her food. He tried to hide in the space between a pillar and a wall, and the rest of them might have run right past without seeing him, but she had spotted a ring with keys at his waist. She spun around the pillar and seized the keys. She tore them from the cord that attached them to his sash. He stared at her, pale and sweating. She knew he did not know her. Did not remember. She jabbed him in the solar plexus with the butt end of the mind lancet, and as he doubled over, she ran on.

26

Mab

When the Lit King entered the room by the secret door, Po launched himself at him. He wasn't about to wait to see what he planned to do to Hilloa or to him. He'd done plenty already. Clutching the chain that bound his wrists in both hands, Po swung it across the man's face. It connected with a dull thud and the man's breath left him in a soft gasp.

Behind the Lit King, Mab stood framed in the doorway. Their eyes met and she smiled, stepped back, and shut the door on them all.

The Lit King grabbed Po by the hair, dragged him forward, and kneed him in the groin. Po doubled over, retching. A sharp pain to the back of his head made dark spots swim before his eyes. By the time he managed to straighten up again, the Lit King was on Hilloa, pushing her back against the wall, one hand around her throat. Her eyes glittered and sweat gleamed on her face.

Po took the rage that filled him and tamped it down into a solid ball in his midsection, glowing with purpose. He picked up the chain between his feet so that it would not clink as he crept forward.

"She wants to know about the rose," the Lit King said to Hilloa, his face very close to hers. "But I know that's just an old woman's tale." He chuckled. "Still, it will be fun, convincing him to talk." His hand on Hilloa's throat flexed and she gasped for air. Po knew she'd seen him, but she didn't glance at him, not even now, as he rose up behind the Lit King and lifted the chain that bound his wrists.

In one smooth movement he swung the chain up and over the other man's head, pulling back hard.

The Lit King gurgled, then threw his head back. Po dodged the attempted head butt and used the opportunity of the man's head being thrown back to loop another pass of the chain around his neck. He jerked the ends tight. The Lit King scrabbled at the chain, attempting to pry it loose, but it was too late. Po had him now.

"Po!" cried Hilloa. "Stop this! You're killing him."

Po shook his head and kept his grip firm on the chain, bearing the frantic kicks against his legs. The Lit King made a sound like a loose-sprung wagon on a cobblestone road.

"Po!" shouted Hilloa. "Let him go! We're redeemed people. We don't kill."

So this was what it was like to disobey a woman. It seemed funny to him that Hilloa was upset about his defiance of an entirely different principle from the one that truly presented a challenge to him. But the look that she gave him made him go cold inside. He had to do this, though, didn't he?

As the Lit King's struggles became more feeble, Hilloa took one step toward them, then halted, her hand in midair. What would he do if she tried to free the man? If she opposed him physically? How far was he willing to go with this newfound independence? He tightened his hands on the chain and pulled them even tighter, feeling the muscles in his arms and back strain and tear.

The Lit King shuddered and went limp. Hilloa looked at him with a funny expression on her face, some mix of horror and relief. He wanted to ask her if he was really her consort, but he knew it was the wrong question.

She went to the door. "Come on," she said, not meeting his eyes now.

He dropped the Lit King, who sprawled lifeless on the floor, and followed her through the hidden passageway.

W hen they got to the dungeon, Ayma stuck the oversized key ring in the crack of the door and slammed it shut, breaking the ring. She pried apart the jagged ends and started handing out keys to people as they passed through the doorway. "Open all the cells," she said. The hallway between the cells quickly filled with milling, confused people as the citizens searched the doors for the lock that matched their key, and the inmates who had already been liberated wandered out looking dazed.

There was one key left on the ring. Ayma worked her way down the rows of cells, trying each unopened lock in turn. At last she felt the click of tumblers turning and the heavy iron padlock on the door to a cell at the far end of the dungeon sprang open. She heaved the heavy bar off its brackets and pushed the door open.

Inside were Censor Siblea, Baris, Jan, and Selene. No Po. She unlocked their shackles. The censor struggled to get to his feet. Baris supported him by one hand. Ayma took his other hand, which was hot and crusty with scars. He hissed as her fingers grazed the wounds. She moved her grip to his upper arm, helping Baris hoist him up. He trembled. Ayma exchanged glances with Baris behind the censor's back. He shook his head. Not good.

For the first time since she'd grabbed a mind lancet in midswing this morning, she wondered what to do next. She hadn't thought beyond getting the chorus out of prison. "Where's Po?" she asked the censor.

He didn't answer. His head bowed, he seemed to be concentrating very hard on remaining upright.

"They took him and Hilloa away just before all hell broke loose. To interrogate them, we think," said Selene.

Ayma's stomach clenched.

"We have to get him out of here," said Baris, meaning the censor. "Someplace safe, where he can rest."

She stared at him wide-eyed. He spoke to her as if he expected her to know what to do.

"We have to find Po and Hilloa," said Selene. "If . . . what's going on, an uprising?"

Ayma nodded. "They're attacking and killing the Lit King's people. It's a good thing you still have on the clothes I gave you. You don't want to be caught in a robe right now."

Outside in the hallway, the crowd thinned out as the other cells emptied and people headed upstairs.

"The third tower," whispered Censor Siblea.

Ayma and Baris leaned closer. "What?"

"If the Lit King is questioning them, they'll be in the third tower. I know the way."

"But—"

He shook his head. "With your help, I can manage."

The little group surrounded Siblea and they made their way out of the cell and down the hallway. It was slow going. At the stairs, they could hear the sounds of fighting above.

"Maybe we should stay here until things quiet down," said Baris.

Siblea, Selene, and Jan all shook their heads. "No," said Siblea. "Carry me."

"But your wounds," said Ayma. She'd seen enough to know he'd been cut on his back, his chest . . .

"What's more pain now? We'll move faster and we'll all be safer."

Baris, solidly built beneath his layer of fat, hoisted Siblea into his arms. They hurried up the steps. Jan cracked open the door at the top and peered out.

"We want the doorway directly opposite this one," said Siblea, his voice faint and tense.

Jan nodded. There was a pause during which they heard a roar of voices and several screams. Jan's face went pale. "Seven Tales, they're slaughtering one another," he said. "We have to stop this."

"After we find Po and Hilloa," said Selene.

A moment later, Jan said, "Now!" and pushed the door open.

The once pristine marble floor of the rotunda was awash with blood. Several bodies lay around the place. The doors to the courtyard stood open and people were still fighting out there. The smell of smoke billowed in at them as the wind changed direction.

"What set this off?" Baris wondered aloud.

"The Lit King's mob came to the marketplace. I . . . We fought them and things just kind of kept going from there," said Ayma.

Censor Siblea gave her a piercing look. She was shocked to see a small smile curve his lips.

"They'll destroy the whole citadel if they keep it up," said Baris.

"No," said Siblea. "Just the Lit King's mob."

"Hurry!" said Selene, and they ran the rest of the way to the third tower.

But just as they were about to open it, a panel opened in the wall behind one of the pillars. She hadn't even known there was a door there. Ayma tensed and reached out to Baris to warn him, but then Po and Hilloa stepped out of the dark opening.

Yammon's tonsils, what had they done to him? Though she couldn't see a mark on him, Po had the same haunted, pain-ridden air about him as the censor did. He appeared thinner, but that could just have been the dark circles under his eyes, the haggard set of his mouth. She remembered how her father had looked, those last days of his life when the fight against the Lit King was going badly and they were closing in on him. Po had that look now, as if everything were closing in on him from all directions, but when he saw her that all went away and he smiled. "You're okay."

There was a loud explosion from the courtyard and a

wave of people, lits and citizens alike, came rushing into the rotunda. "In there!" said Selene, and she pointed to the secret door. They piled inside, finding themselves in a landing at the bottom of a staircase, lit softly by skylights far above them in the gloom.

Po and Hilloa were both in chains. Ayma still had the key she'd used to free the chorus. She found that it unlocked their shackles as well. Meanwhile, the others surrounded them with greetings and questions.

"Po! Hilloa!" said Selene, embracing them each in turn. "Are you all right?"

"What happened to you?" asked Jan, his brow creased. "Did the Lit King—"

"The Lit King is dead," said Po in a flat voice. A look passed between him and Hilloa.

"You killed him," said Ayma, grinning, certain it was true.

Po blinked at her, seemingly lost between her expression and the bleak look Hilloa wore. He nodded.

A sigh went through the others. There seemed to be a variety of reactions to this news, from Selene's thoughtful sadness to Jan's discomfort to Siblea's exhausted relief and Baris's grim satisfaction.

"How did you get out of the cell?" asked Hilloa, and then glanced at Ayma. "When did you get here?"

"Ayma started a revolution," Siblea said with a note of pride that warmed her through and through, though what he said was not strictly true.

"I beg your pardon, Censor," she said, "but it was you, not me. You got the people thinking of all we've lost. I just happened to be in the right place at the right time."

Hilloa seemed to throw off some of her preoccupation and gave Ayma a wry smile. "Much the same can be said for many a pivotal figure of history."

That gave Ayma a strange feeling that only became stronger when she noticed the way Jan, Baris, and Censor Siblea were looking at her. Uncertain how to react, she looked to Po, who gave her an encouraging smile and then swayed on his feet. She and Hilloa steadied him. His arm was warm across her shoulders, and she could feel him trembling. "He tortured you, too, somehow," she said.

The others exchanged glances. They knew something about that and she would have it from them, but—

"Forget about that now," said Po. "The important thing is we're all okay. Do you . . ." He hesitated, as if he wasn't sure he could bear the answer. "Do you still have the pen?"

"Yes!" she said. "I almost forgot, with everything that's happened. She pulled the satchel from its hiding place in her dress and hung the strap around his neck. "I kept it safe for you."

They smiled at each other and for a moment she felt as if it were just the two of them, like that night in the kitchen of her father's tavern.

"The pen?" said Selene.

Po nodded and fumbled in the satchel and withdrew the pen. "Endymion's rose," he said, handing it to Selene. "It's not a terra-forming device. It's a pen. A pen for rewriting reality."

Selene turned it over in her hands. The dim light in the stairwell gleamed off its long, graceful lines. "How does it work?"

"You write what you want in the air, and it comes true."

"But you have to be careful," said Ayma. "We tried it once and it didn't work so well."

"Was that what happened, when all the vines broke through the floor and then disappeared again?" said Jan. "We thought we were going to be able to escape, but . . ."

At a glance from Siblea, Jan subsided, but not before they all saw the look on Po's face.

"Sorry," said Jan. "You couldn't have known."

"So be careful what you wish for, huh?" said Selene. "Well . . ."

"What do we do now?" said Baris.

"We need to find the food the Lit King has been hoarding, and start redistributing it," said Siblea.

Selene nodded at this, and looked speculatively at the device in her hand. "What if we write, 'The location of the food the Lit King has hoarded is written on the wall in front of us'?"

"I can show you where the food is," said a voice.

P o turned to see Mab, the old woman who had attended the Lit King's interrogations, standing a few steps above them in the gloom. His heart sank. He was so tired, and he hurt, and he'd thought, when he and Hilloa found the others just now, that he might be done with things he didn't know how to cope with.

"Why would you help us?" demanded Selene.

"Our leader is dead. The people of the citadel are overrunning us. You're right—the best way to put an end to all this fighting is to give the food back."

The rest of them all looked at one another, uncertain.

"As you may recall, Selene, under circumstances such as these, pragmatists can make good allies," said Siblea.

Po knew he was referring to the role he played prior to the Redemption. Still, Selene looked uncertain. "It could be a trap. She knows about the ro—the pen."

"I'm an old woman, and I've been in prison a long time. When the Lit King overthrew the guards, what was I to do? I'm glad he's been overthrown in turn."

The others seemed mollified but Selene still frowned. "I don't know," she said. "I have a funny feeling about this."

"Then we had best keep an eye on her," said Siblea. "We'll keep her with us and pursue our own course."

Selene held the pen between her thumb and forefinger and spoke as she traced the words "The location of the unconsumed food stolen by the Lit King will appear written on the wall in front of me, in Old Earth English, right now."

Those who had not seen it before gasped as the bud at the end of the pen opened and the little golden lights drifted into the air. Po looked at their faces, lit by the glow, alight with wonder.

When the lights faded and disappeared, Ayma raised her mind lancet. In its ghostly blue light, they saw words on the wall. "The unconsumed food the Lit King stole is in the storehouse above the main kitchen of the temple," the words read.

"Okay then, let's go," said Hilloa.

"What about her?" said Selene. "She knows about the pen."

Mab held up her hands. "Please don't hurt me. I only wanted to help you."

"We won't hurt you," said Hilloa.

"Stay with us," said Jan, moving to her side. "We'll keep you safe."

Hilloa took the old woman's other arm. Baris picked up Siblea again. Selene opened the door and looked out. "All clear," she said, and took the lead.

They made a funny-looking group, walking out across the rotunda: Siblea in Baris's arms and Hilloa and Jan escorting Mab, each with a hand on her shoulder, not so much compelling as guiding and watching. Po looked at Ayma. She held out her hand. He took it, and they followed the others.

The courtyard between the main temple and the out-buildings, including the kitchen and storehouse, was awash with chaos. Those of the Lit King's people who were still alive fled in the direction of the main gate, chased by angry citizens waving weapons that ranged from mind lancets to pitchforks. More bodies lay fallen, and the wounded attempted to crawl.

A loud crack came from the far end of the courtyard. "The stables," said Siblea. Someone had broken the lock on the doors, opened the stalls, and let loose all the animals. Frightened by the noise and the smell of blood, elephants, horses, cows, sheep, and goats all stampeded toward the gates. A number of enterprising citizens pursued them, attempting to corral a few for themselves.

When the wave of animal and human bodies cleared and the courtyard was passable once more, they found a crowd of people with torches surrounding the kitchen outbuilding.

"No!" shouted Siblea. Selene ran across the courtyard and the others followed, with Baris, still carrying Siblea, lagging far behind.

"Stop!" cried Selene. "No! The food is in there!" This caused them to hesitate, but the man who seemed to be in charge of the group—at least, people were coming up to him to ignite their makeshift torches—looked her up and down dismissively. "And who are you and how do you know that?"

The woman beside him spotted Mab between Hilloa and Jan. "Look! They have a lit with them. They must be—"

"Loren!" shouted Ayma, releasing Po's hand and running forward. "She's our prisoner! Look! That's the censor! We know because he knows. We're with him. Loren, you know me."

The woman Ayma called Loren hesitated. She looked at the man and nodded. But the crowd around them rumbled with uncertainty.

"Listen to me, everyone!" shouted Ayma. "You've won! The Lit King is dead! His people flee for their lives. Now please, put down your weapons! Any further destruction only devastates your own home. The citadel is ours!"

"Listen to her!" Loren yelled. "It's her! The one who started the rebellion!"

A cheer went up among the crowd and people started putting out their torches.

"Thank the Tales," sighed Selene. She stood a little back from the others, as if still uncertain about the crowd. Selene was always wary, Po thought, and she was often right to be. He stayed by her side, for mutual comfort and to enjoy the spectacle of Ayma being proud of herself. Selene smiled and put a hand on his shoulder. "You did good, too, Po."

He swallowed the gasp that this glittering moment, full of wonders, elicited. "I killed," he admitted, not wanting to say that going against Hilloa's command bothered him most.

She nodded. "But you saved Siblea's life. You found the pen and kept its secret, and you helped Ayma. Because of all of that, we can give people back the food and seed grain the Lit King stole. With luck, there will be enough left over to feed the Libyrinth until the new crop comes. This is your victory, too. Because you could see past your own preconceptions."

Po's aches and pains seemed to fade away in the warm glow that filled him.

"I was wrong about you," said Selene. "And I want you to know I'm sorry."

The words stunned him so that for a moment he did not notice what was happening before his very eyes. As Jan and Hilloa turned to say something to the man at the door of the outbuilding, Mab darted straight for Selene. She snatched the pen from Selene's hand and shoved her. Selene stumbled and fell. Po turned to block Mab's way but she swerved around him and dashed across the courtyard, back in the direction of the temple proper.

Po ran after her, chasing her up the steps and back into the rotunda. She went behind a pillar and never came out the other side. Po searched the wall for another one of the secret panels and at last found it. He pushed it and it swung open to reveal another staircase like the one they'd been in before. He heard footsteps echoing above.

He followed.

In the dark and the silence, in the absence of Siblea's suffering and Hilloa's peril, Po suddenly realized how much pain he was in. His hands and feet were numb from the many mind-lancet attacks he'd sustained in the previous two days. His head ached and he was exhausted and hungry—but he forced himself onward. The staircase spiraled up and up. He thought he saw a light, warmer than what came through the skylights, far above. He strained for the sound of Mab's footsteps, but heard nothing now.

Another couple of turns and a new sound came to his ears. A faint melody. He tried to think about why Mab would come this way. Was that her singing? No.

The light grew brighter. Warm, golden light. He hastened toward it. He heard voices now, talking, though he could not make out the words. But he recognized Mab's voice and . . . was that Selene? He'd left her behind in the courtyard. Mab had pushed her to the ground. How could she have gotten up here so quickly?

At last he reached the last curve of the staircase and he could see the open door above. Something nagged at the corner of his mind but he was so tired, and in such pain, and warm light and soft singing were very like the things he craved most of all.

He tried to creep up silently and hide behind the door to get a good look at what lay on the other side, but his foot scraped on the stone, and he could not get behind the door without first crossing its opening. Po stood in the door frame, looking into a sumptuous round room decorated in the manner of an Ilysian lady's bower. On one side of the room was a gauze-draped bed; on the other, a writing desk, lounging chairs, and a low table for refreshments. And in the middle of the room sat an ornate brass tub filled with steaming water. As he came up to the doorway, Mab turned from the woman in the tub, who stood with her back to him. The familiar, graceful form made his breath hitch and his groin tighten. Long, dark, curly hair cascaded down her alabaster back. His mind reached for the wrong name at first, before realization denied him of all breath.

She held the pen in her hand, turning it this way and that as it caught the light reflected from her bath. As she turned to face him, he saw the satisfaction in her smile.

"Hello, Po," said Queen Thela.

27

The Queen's Consort

Thela stepped out of the tub and walked toward him, naked and glorious. Po couldn't stop staring, at her smile, her body. His heart hammered. What was she doing here? How long had she been here? But most of all, what would she do with the pen?

She held it in her hands like a long-stemmed rose, its graceful curve accentuating the elegant lines of her hands and arms, the languid beauty of her movements. She followed his gaze and lifted the pen, tilting it this way and that. Its burnished amber surface caught the light and sent sparkles dancing up and down its length. She tapped the bulb at the end against her palm. She turned it to examine the opposite end, which was angled like the nib of a quill pen. "This is a most interesting device. The pen, I believe it's called, or sometimes Endymion's rose or the Lion's Bloom. It does rather look like a flower," she noted. "But pen is by far the most accurate term, isn't it?" Not waiting for an answer, she lifted the pen as if to write with it.

Po found his voice at last. "Please, Your Majesty, don't use it. We tried, when we first found it, and the results were . . . Everything turned green!"

"Ah, is that what that was all about? But you undid it, didn't you?"

"Yes, but . . ."

She nodded. "Your point is well taken, Po. Wishes are perilous. One never knows how they will be fulfilled. A device like this must be handled with precision. Mab told me a little about it, but I think you could teach me more."

He nodded. "Yes. I'll show you how it works." He held his hand out. Mother, let his face not show what was in his mind.

She tilted her head and smiled at him. "Oh, Po. That's so cute. You're trying to trick me."

His stomach twisted. "No! No, I'd never—"

She crossed to the other side of the room and waved her finger at him. "Oh yes, you are." Her tone remained playful but the look in her eyes was anything but. And then the lilt went out of her voice as she said, "And I can't have that. Now let's see, where to begin?" Her tongue poked out of the corner of her mouth as she contemplated. "I know," she said, and she lifted the pen and began to write in midair. Glowing words appeared. "The door behind Po . . ."

Po turned. What about the door? Would she seal it? Should he leap through now, while he still could? But if he did, he'd be leaving the pen with her. He couldn't do that. The next instant, it was too late. The door was gone, replaced by a solid wall of stone.

"There," said Thela. "If anyone comes after you, or Mab, they will not find us. Of course, I can't trust you to help me understand the pen now; you'll lie."

He put his hands on the wall and pushed, but it was useless. In panic, he pounded at it.

"Now that's just silly," said Thela.

Po watched as she strode to the window. Mab came to her side and they conferred.

"They've found the food," said the old woman. "If they return it to the villages, the Libyrinth will have many friends in the plain."

"But I can stop them. I can make it so this day has never happened. I can erase the Redemption from existence. I can turn the food to dust or make every rock in the plain bloom with life. I can do anything I want."

Feeling as if he were outside of his body, Po walked toward her. He had to keep her from using the pen. He had to take it away from her, and she would resist. He'd disobeyed a woman this very afternoon, but that paled in comparison to what was demanded of him now.

Thela turned to look at him, a speculative gleam in her eye. Mab stood between them. They watched him, waiting, he realized, to see just how far he'd fallen from the ideal of Ilysian manhood. If he did get the pen away from Thela, what would he do? He couldn't get out of the room unless he used the pen to do it, and he knew her. Thela and Mab both, they wouldn't give him time to write anything. They'd fight him and they wouldn't stop unless he . . . he . . . The room swayed around him at the thought of what he might have to do.

Po gripped the wall for support as everything that had happened since the Libyrinth's crop burned suddenly seemed to crowd into his head at once. It was her fault. All of it. And now, he was contemplating the unthinkable, and that was her fault, too. "You burned the crops and you set me up to take the blame for it. How could you do that to me?"

Never letting go of the pen, Thela slipped into the robe Mab held out for her. She looked at him and shrugged. "It was necessary. I'm sorry if you were hurt, but there are larger issues at stake."

She spoke with such dispassionate conviction that for a moment, he nearly accepted her explanation. He actually found himself thinking, *Of course, she knows what she's doing,* and with that thought came a flood of relief. The notion that no matter how bad things seemed, someone wise and benevolent was in charge was like a narcotic to his overtaxed spirit. It would be so easy just to accept her words.

But if he did, he'd be handing the whole world over to her, along with everyone he loved, without ever even trying to save them. "What of the Lit King?" he said.

She raised an eyebrow. "My, haven't we become the noisy rooster?"

Po ignored the insult. "You were working with him— a male supremecist."

She shook her head. "A male supremecist, *Your Majesty.* His agenda here suited my purposes. Using him to turn the villages of Ayor against the Libyrinth made good sense. And you—" She pointed the pen at him. "You've forgotten who you are."

If he didn't act now, he never would. Po rushed her and

grabbed the pen. They grappled for it. "The Libyrinth has ruined you," she said.

"No. I don't think so."

"That's even worse."

He yanked the pen away from her. Mab lunged for it and he turned again. This time, when Thela dodged in front of him, he put his free hand out to ward her off. The impact was harder than he'd thought it would be. She stumbled. "Give it to me, you abomination!" she shouted.

Po backed up, stunned at what he had done. "You'll have to be branded now," he said. Out of the corner of his eye he saw Mab, trying to sneak up on him. Would he hit her, too, if he had to? He inched away from both of them.

Thela stood. "The chorus is your family. The males will die, Selene and Hilloa will be branded."

"By whom?"

Thela did not answer. Po lifted the pen. *The pen does not exist*, he thought, and he started to write.

"Stop him!" shouted Thela.

Mab charged him. Po tried to dodge her while he was still writing, but it was no good. She corrected and struck him full in the chest, pushing him backward. She brought her knee up sharply and pain rocketed through Po's groin and abdomen. She wrenched the pen away from him as he fell and handed it back to Thela.

Po's half-finished sentence, "The pen does . . . ," evaporated into thin air with no effect.

Po lay on the ground, lost to himself, to everything he'd ever known. He looked at Thela. Her cheeks were red from exertion, her hair tangled. She clutched the pen. She would not risk getting it near him again. He'd lost his chance.

Thela stared down at him. What was she waiting for? Why didn't she kill him?

"Your Majesty, would you prefer me to execute him?" Thela shook her head. "No. He won't die. Not yet."

There was a pause. Po's breathing sounded harsh in the silence. Then Mab said, "With respect, Your Majesty, there is a great deal to be said for not leaving toys around to trip over later."

Thela sighed. "Wise counsel. But he is an adept. A *male* adept. That is a rather unique and useful thing. Besides, I like him. And I do need practice with the pen. Let's try this." She raised the pen and wrote in the air. "Po is incapable of doing me harm."

Po had no arms or legs. He rolled on the floor, nothing but a trunk and a head. He would have screamed, but his mouth was gone, too.

"Oh dear," said Thela.

Mab giggled.

Po's heart hammered so hard, it made his lungs work like a bellows. He wanted to open his mouth for more air but he couldn't. He still had a tongue and teeth and a throat, a whole mouth, inside, but it wouldn't open. His stomach turned and he fought the rising bilge of panic. He couldn't throw up. He'd choke.

Thela frowned and shook her head. "No. I don't like that. Let's see . . . how about this . . ." She wrote, "In all but one respect, Po is as he was before I last wielded the pen. The only difference is that now, he will only do what makes me happy."

One moment, Po lay on the floor with no arms, legs, or mouth, and the next, he was just as he'd been before. He lifted a hand to his mouth and bit his finger to stifle a whimper.

Thela tilted her head to one side and smiled with genuine affection. "It will be all right, Po. A lot of foolish people have put foolish ideas in your head and you're confused now, but you'll see. With the pen, I can make the whole of the land fertile, for everybody, and there need be no division between Ilysies and the Libyrinth. I can become redeemed, like you. No one need suffer ever again."

Their eyes met. She looked so sincere. Po wanted to believe her. He was tired and hungry and he hurt, and all that he loved in the world was in the hands of the one person he was least equipped to deal with. "Please," he said. "Your Majesty . . . don't hurt them."

Thela handed the pen to Mab, and went to him. He got to his knees and prostrated himself before her, though his tortured muscles screamed in protest. She clicked her tongue and lifted him up by the shoulders. "It's all right now, Po," she said, and kissed him. "Don't worry. Anything I do with the pen will be for the good of everyone. Just as my alliance with the Lit King was. You don't know how it would have been if I had not tempered his madness. But I'm sorry all of this has been so hard on you. And I'm sorry about that little mistake with the pen." She ran her hands down along the sides of his face. "But don't worry, I don't think I'll need to use it on you again."

Po thought he'd have to make an effort to relax at her touch, but it came naturally. What she'd done to him with the pen . . .

He stroked her neck. "I missed you so much," he said.

That's not how he felt at all, but the words just popped out of his mouth.

She smiled and ruffled his hair. "I didn't want to leave you, my calf, but a queen has duties. What's important is that we're together now."

He closed his eyes, and he didn't have to pretend to be lost in the feel of her hand in his hair. He lifted his face and kissed her, and she drew him close. All of this was what the pen had wrought, but his thoughts were still his own, and he was beginnning to get an idea. "Now? And tomorrow?"

"Mmmm," she said. "I have missed you, too, Po. Yes, I think you will make a fine consort now."

At one time, he had dreamed of this. Now, with an inward lurch he realized that even if she were the kindest, most just monarch in history, the luxury and security of being a queen's consort no longer appealed to him. He wanted the confusion and excitement of being with Hilloa. He wanted the complex joys of Ayma's friendship. He wanted to joke with Jan and shock Baris. Most of all, he wanted the difficult puzzle of just being himself. "Oh Thela, I'm so happy!"

"You see? Didn't I tell you everything would be all right?"

He nodded, holding her close. Suddenly, he sat back, holding her shoulders at arm's length. "Remember the first time we met, when I rubbed your feet?"

Her eyes widened a little and he knew that he had genuinely surprised her and made her happy. "Yes."

He nodded. "Back then, I wanted to give you a kinesthetic massage. But I couldn't, and later, I don't know . . . there just wasn't much time and I never did. But now . . . Please, Thela, let me give you a foot rub."

Thela got a lopsided grin and then turned to look at Mab. "You see, it's working."

"Please." He pulled away from her and went to one knee. The lies came so easily now. "You have made my dream come true, Thela. Please let me make you feel as I do."

Mab rolled her eyes and Thela laughed. She went to the couch and sat down. "Mab, start packing, please. Very well then, Po," she said, indulging him. "But don't take forever about it. We have things to do."

Moving slowly to conceal his weariness, Po knelt at her feet and placed his hands on the meridians at the sides of her arches. Silently he implored the Mother to give him the strength he needed for what he was about to do. He closed his eyes and breathed with Thela.

He dropped into a trance and before him lay the landscape of Ilysies. The high, snow-capped mountains, the river winding down through the foothills to the lush green lowlands and the shining city beside the sea.

But the vision was not a perfect mirror of the land that was entrusted to Thela's care. There were differences. At the peak of the tallest mountain, a location which corresponded to the crown of Thela's head, stood a shining golden temple. It stood out among all the organic imagery, and Po recognized it as a construct of thought. It was exquisitely beautiful, simple in its design, pristine. In other words, perfect, and therefore utterly unreal. Though not to Thela.

The real trouble began at the start of the lowlands, where the land leveled out and became most fertile. But not here. Ruins choked the riverway, turning what should have been perfect farmland into a swamp. Po examined the ruins more closely and found countless versions of the same structure, each resembling the temple at the top of the mountain, but flawed in some way. They were all slowly sinking into the mud of the swamp, but some had been built more recently than others. One was so recent that it still stood tall and proud, nearly perfect but for one crooked pillar. This gave Po an idea.

He focused his attention on Thela's perception center, which corresponded to the foothills of Ilysies. There on a promontory he found a glittering golden object—an axe with a heavy flat head that could also be used for hammering. On the other end of its handle was a knife blade, the surface on one side hashed for sanding. This tool could do almost anything, and it was made of the same shining gold as the temple. This was how Thela perceived the pen, as the perfect tool that would finally enable her to create perfection in the real world.

Unless he managed to alter that perception. Could he do that? She had written that he would only do what made her happy. She would not choose to think of the pen in a different way, but the change could make her happy. There was one sure way to find out. If the act violated what she'd written, he'd simply be unable to do it.

But he might not be able to do it for another reason. This was an entirely new application of kinesiology. If he did this, he'd be willfully altering one of Thela's thought-forms. He was pretty sure that was a misuse of his ability, if it was even possible.

At the same time, if he did nothing . . . He thought of the chorus down in the courtyard right now, of everyone back at the Libyrinth, and of the people in the villages of the plain. All of them would be at Queen Thela's mercy, and as far as he could tell, she didn't have any.

He was beyond exhausted. He wasn't entirely sure he'd even survive attempting this, but he couldn't think of anything else to do. Po breathed deeply and concentrated all of his kinesthetic awareness. He became a hawk soaring high above the land. He swooped and snatched the tool from its resting place and flew with it to the swamp, where he sought out Thela's most recent effort at replicating the golden temple of perfection.

When he was directly over it, Po dropped the tool. He waited, forcing himself to keep breathing as the tool tumbled, end over end, through the air. At last, it struck the roof of the newly built temple and shattered it with a sound like breaking glass.

The sound broke him out of his trance and he slumped to the ground.

"Po!" exclaimed Thela, staring down at him. "What did you do?"

Terrified, all he could do was stare up at her and shake his head.

"I don't feel any different, and look at you."

Thank the Mother. "I'm sorry. I tried really hard, but I couldn't get anything to work. I must be tired." That was an understatement—he could barely move.

She shook her head. "I never should have let you work on me in your depleted condition." She climbed down off the couch and sat by him, lifting his head to pillow it in her lap. "You can kill yourself, you know, pushing too hard in a kinesthetic trance."

He knew that, but he said, "I can?"

She nodded.

Even speech was an effort, but he forced himself. "I'm sorry, Thela. I tried, but I am not very good."

"You're better than you think, but Ymin herself would be hard-pressed to heal a hangnail in the condition you're in. I see that now."

"I wanted to . . ."

"I know, and that's why I let you try. But enough—it's time we went home, Po. I need time to study the pen, consider what is to be done with it, and strategize my next move. I've been away from Ilysies for too long. It does not do to conquer the world but lose your home." She looked up to where Mab stood looking out the window. "The pen," she said.

Po stiffened, then realized he probably should have stifled that response. But Thela only smiled at him. "I know. The pen is dangerous, very dangerous. And it is fortunate that I have it, and not someone who would wield it irresponsibly. Can you imagine what Selene would have done with it? We'd all be running around with three heads or something. To be honest, I'm not even entirely sure it should be used at all. Certainly not before it is fully understood. And yet, at the moment it is our only way home. And I want to go home, don't you?"

All Po wanted to do was get back to his friends in the courtyard, but that could not be. Even if he wasn't incapacitated, even if there was a door to this room, the change he had wrought in Thela's mind and body was not of a permanent nature. It would need regular reinforcing. "Of course," he said.

Mab handed Thela the pen and she wrote, "Thela, Po, and Mab are instantaneously transported to Thela's bower in the Palace of Ilysies."

The words glowed in midair. As they dissipated, Po had the strangest sensation, as if he were stretching in several impossible directions at once, and then the walls surrounding them were white, not gray. Tapestries of songlines became gauzy draperies over sun-drenched windows. There was a bed shrouded by veils, a pool for bathing, and couches and low tables for eating. He tried to stand, but found he could not.

Thela drew him close. "There now," she said. "Rest easy. Didn't I tell you I'd make you my consort one day? And now here we are. Welcome home, Po."

28

Harvest

Distributing the food among the citizens and preparing the rest to be transported to the villages took the rest of the day and most of the night, and all of Ayma's concentration and effort. "Roger, will you take these and add them to the cart that you just loaded?" she asked, handing a man nearly twice her size two sacks of seed barley. "And do you know when Loren is returning with more wagons? We can't do much more until she does."

It struck her that this time she did not hesitate to give an order or ask a direct question. She'd done both so many times this night, she supposed she had to get used to it some time. She thought of how she'd been when the chorus had first come to town, of how her life had consisted of wiping down the bar and furtive scavenging for food. How small she'd been, how afraid.

She'd never before experienced anything like this past day, this ceaseless stretching of her abilities and sense of who she was. It was as if she walked on the periphery of her former life and beyond it, until she was shocked to still find ground beneath her feet.

The sky was turning gray and most of the people had either gone home or departed with the wagons destined for the villages of the plain. It just remained now to pack up the rest for the people of the Libyrinth.

She climbed up on a barrel of dried beets and sat down, feeling for the first time the full ache of her tired feet. Siblea, who seemed to have gotten stronger as the night wore on, finished tying off a rope and sat down beside her. He handed her a flask of water, and she drank.

She surveyed the courtyard, dread seeping up through her newfound confidence like a muddy river overflowing its banks. In spite of every effort, Po, Mab, and the pen had not been found. "They're still searching?" she asked Siblea.

He nodded. "But we went through the whole place, with people stationed at the exits, before nightfall. If we didn't find them then . . ."

As if summoned, Selene, Baris, Jan, and Hilloa came out of the temple and crossed the courtyard, exhaustion and grief drawn in every frown, every slumped shoulder.

"Nothing," said Selene.

"It's as if they vanished into thin air," said Jan.

"Do you think Mab used the pen to spirit them both away somewhere?" asked Ayma.

"What?" said Selene, her tired eyes sharpening their focus.

"I said do you think she used the pen?" She could be more patient with Selene now, she found.

"No. The name. You said—"

"Mab? Oh yes. She was notorious. An Ilysian by birth, I believe, she taught twenty-five people to read before they—"

Selene slapped her forehead. "I'm an idiot! Mab! Of course that was Mab!"

Ayma was relieved to see the others also looking at Selene as if she'd lost her mind. So it wasn't just her.

Selene saw their looks. "My mother's spy. I heard her mention the name once. Mab is my mother's woman."

"The queen of Ilysies," said Hilloa.

Selene was a princess? Ayma pushed that revelation aside and tried to focus her tired brain. "So she's been working for Ilysies, all this time."

"And she took the pen," said Jan, "which means . . ."

Selene looked ill. "That the pen is now, or very soon will be, in my mother's hands."

Silence fell over the little group. "And what about Po?" They all shrugged.

"We'll search again," said Jan. "Maybe somehow, we missed—"

"We missed nothing, Jan," said Siblea. "They're gone."

"We'll still take you back with us," said Baris. "We'll honor Po's promise."

She shook her head. "No, thank you. I'm going to stay here and help rebuild things."

"As am I," Siblea announced.

"You're going to rebuild the Singer priesthood?" asked Selene with some suspicion.

"No," he said. "The temple will become a university.

We have the Lit King's library and I'm hoping we can borrow some books from the Libyrinth." He looked to Hilloa. "And some scholars."

Hilloa raised her brows. "I don't know." She looked back at the temple, as if hoping to see Po come walking out the door. "I don't . . . I'll think about it. After we get this food home."

Haly couldn't put it off another day. They wouldn't make it until tomorrow without some protein. Of course, with no elephant they could not cultivate as much land, but it didn't matter how much acreage they could plow if they were too dead to do it. She went into the kitchen and fetched Hepsebah's largest knife.

"You're—" said the former hearthmistress, breaking broom bristles into a pot of boiling water to make straw soup.

Haly nodded.

"Want me to do it?"

"No," said Haly. "It should be me."

There had been much heated debate over Zam. At least, as heated as they had energy for anymore. Many had called for her slaughter weeks ago, while others pointed out that it would cripple their long-term efforts at agriculture. Others, and she knew she was one of them, argued against it because they liked Zam.

Entering the now near-empty stable, Haly thought of Po. He'd been Zam's favorite. She was glad he wasn't here for this.

Poor Zam. She raised her trunk feebly. They turned her out daily to forage for silverleaf, but it was barely enough to sustain her. Her skin hung in loose flaps on her skeletal form. This was a kindness, when all was said and done.

Gyneth and Hepsebah followed her with a large brass bowl to catch the blood. They positioned it beneath Zam's neck. Nothing must be wasted. Haly raised the knife. She locked eyes with the elephant. That great dark eye regarded her gently and blinked. She knew.

Haly tightened her grip on the blade.

"Wait!" It was Peliac, running down the central aisle of the stables. "Stop! They're coming!"

Haly dropped the knife and it fell into the brass bowl with a loud clang. "I saw them, they're almost here," said Peliac, panting.

They all hurried out of the stableyard and through the settlement to the first of the low hills surrounding the Libyrinth. From there, a procession of wagons was clearly visible, making its way toward them. Her heart soared, up and up. Haly forgot about everything else, and started to run.

She only made it as far as the foot of the hill before her legs collapsed beneath her and she fell. The others stumbled to a halt as well. Behind them, she heard voices as more and more people came out to see what was happening.

When it arrived, the wagon train, led by the Chorus of the Word, was more abundant that she ever could have hoped for. It contained cartloads and cartloads of grain, dried fruits, and vegetables. There were also goats and cows and chickens, and her heart lurched when she saw the great gray beast bringing up the rear. It was an elephant—a bull elephant. The people at the head of the wagon train ran toward them, their faces impossibly bright. Haly searched them. Some were unknown to her. And then Selene leaned over her, the strangest expression on her face. "Seven Tales," she muttered, lifting Haly up into her arms as if she weighed no more than a child.

"We almost slaughtered Zam," said Haly. She must be out of her mind. Why was she going on about that now? "The bull . . ."

"Yes," said Selene, carrying her to one of the wagons and placing her on top of a bale of hay.

The person driving the wagon turned. It was Hilloa, looking older and more beautiful than Haly remembered. "Redeemer, everyone has been so generous. Every village we passed through on the way home showered gifts upon us. They're going to help us."

The wagon listed to one side and there was Baris, climbing up, and Jan after him. Each hugged her in turn. They were all so strong and full of life. "Because of what Po and Ayma did," said Baris. "You won't believe it all when we tell you what happened."

"Ayma?"

"We'll tell you all about her, and everything," said Selene, hoisting Gyneth up beside Haly. "When we get everyone fed."

ABOUT THE AUTHOR

The Boy from Ilysies is Pearl North's second young adult novel. She has published various works for adults under another name. She makes her home outside Detroit, Michigan, and is currently working on the final book of the Libyrinth trilogy.